My Friend My Father

My Friend My Father

Jane Duncan

Macmillan London

ISBN 0 333 06411 9

First published 1966 by
MACMILLAN LONDON LIMITED
London and Basingstoke
Associated companies in Auckland, Dallas, Delhi,
Dublin, Hong Kong, Johannesburg, Lagos, Manzini, Melbourne,
Nairobi, New York, Singapore, Tokyo,
Washington and Zaria

Reprinted 1967, 1970, 1978, 1983

Printed in Hong Kong

985649

*To the memory of
my father*

PROLOGUE

I N the pale dawn light, away on the far horizon of my memory, I see that, at Christmas of 1912, before I was three years old, I wrote with the help of my friends George and Tom a letter to Santa Claus in which I asked him to bring me a book. On Christmas morning, the book lay on the steel fender before the kitchen fire and, beside it, lay a letter from Santa Claus which said in very big, queer curly handwriting: 'Dear Janet, Here is your book. I was very pleased to get a letter from Reachfar. Love from Santa Claus.'

I showed the letter to everybody who came to the house and kept it inside my book and quite often, I would take it out and look at it. Everybody said it was very kind of Santa Claus to write me a letter when he had so much to do and, although they all seemed to think that Santa was some mysterious person whom they had never seen, although they were certain he existed, like God whom they had never seen either, I treasured in my mind the secret of knowing with certainty something that none of these grown-up people knew. There was, for me, a strange familiarity about that big curly handwriting. I had discovered that if you put your fingertip over the big curly bit of the S the remainder of the letter was the exact capital S which my father made when he signed his name D. Sandison, an S with a light forward upstroke and an authoritative firm downstroke that formed two loops and immediately the knowledge came to me that Santa Claus was no other than my father. This was no surprise to me for, unlike the grown-up people, I had always known that my father was all the great and mysterious people who were known about but never seen. I had known this ever since I began to say my prayers at night, repeating after my mother: 'Our Father which art in heaven—'

Part One

1914

'Our Father which art in heaven—'
                    ST. MATTHEW vi. 9

IT was early April of 1914 and it was my mother's birthday. My mother was tremendously old. This was her twenty-ninth birthday. About a month ago, I myself had had a birthday when I had become four years old and next year, I would have a birthday again and be five years old and then I would be big enough to go to school. When I went to school, I knew, I would learn all sorts of things and very soon become grown-up like all the other people in our house but even now, while I was waiting to be big enough to go to school, I was learning new things every day, it seemed. This day of my mother's birthday had been a great day of learning things and it was extraordinary how many things I knew now that I had not known only yesterday although, yesterday, I was only one day younger.

Today, for instance, I had learned a great deal about birthdays. Of course, I had always known—by 'always' I meant ever since the time I knew anything at all—about birthdays for, in our house, somebody's birthday was always coming along and a dumpling would be made and put to boil and bubble in the big black pot beside the fire, just as my mother's birthday dumpling was hubble-bubbling in there now. Aunt Kate had mixed it in the big basin just after mid-day dinner and I had helped to cut the suet down into little bits and nip the stalks off the raisins and measure the brown spice in a teaspoon. Then Aunt Kate had taken down from the top shelf of the dresser the little glass dish with the lid that held the 'dumpling things'—the tiny silver thimble which, if you found it in your helping of dumpling, meant that you would be an old maid who would never get married and the pearl bachelor's button and the silver three-penny piece which I was often very lucky about getting in my helping as if the sweet-smelling delicious-tasting dumpling had a secret knowledge that I needed all the money I could get to put away in my bank to help to pay for my 'higher eddication' when I was big enough. Then, when Aunt Kate and I had put the things in and had stirred them round until they were all lost in a mystery of flour, suet, spice and raisins, Aunt Kate said: 'Well, Granny, we are ready for you!'

Smiling, my grandmother came from the scullery, drying her newly-washed hands, her old worn wedding ring sparkling on her finger. Laying the towel aside, she plunged both hands deep into the mixture in the basin and after a moment took them out again but her wedding ring had gone. Somebody would find it in a helping of dumpling that evening at supper, probably Aunt Kate, for she had a way of getting the ring that meant that you were to be married soon, just as I had a way of getting the three-penny bit and the ring would return to my grandmother's finger.

Yes. I had known about birthdays and dumplings for a long time now but it was only today, somehow, that I had discovered what birthdays really meant. It was very strange how you could know about a thing, thinking that you knew all there was to know about it and how you could then discover that there was far more to know about it than you had ever dreamed of. It was only today that I had discovered that people went on having birthdays every year for ever and ever. Hitherto, I had thought that only children like me had them until they were five and big enough to go to school and then I had thought that maybe you had them until you were grown-up and thus grown out of them. I had thought that all the dumplings that were made in our house were milestones on my way to being five and going to school. But I saw now that all these ideas were very silly for, just before Christmas, we had had a dumpling for Tom's birthday and I knew that Tom was grown-up and away from school long

4

ago and, besides, the dumpling did not make *me* one bit older or nearer to going to school. It just showed that I had not thought this thing out properly until today.

Of course, there was not a more difficult thing in the world than to think something out properly and, with me, the process always ended in trouble. My way of finding out things that I did not know or of thinking things out was to ask people who did know by being grown-up and having thought things out already but the members of my family, it seemed to me, had little understanding of the need to get to the bottom of things. Of course, they were busy but, still, I was busy too with this birthday business. How did they suppose I was ever going to get grown-up and clever at school if they would not help with thinking things out?

When, at breakfast, Aunt Kate had told me that she and I had a busy day ahead with Mother's birthday dumpling, I naturally began to think about birthdays. On my own birthday, I had been four years old and had another year to wait to be five and go to school. If my mother was having a birthday today, she must have a years old too.

'Mother, how many years old have you today?'

'Twenty-nine, Janet.'

'On the very doorstep of the wintry thirties,' my father said and my mother looked across at him and then she laughed for he was only pretending.

'It is very ill-mannered to be asking questions about the ages of leddies,' Tom said.

'Leddies doesn't *have* ages,' said George.

'That's a pack of lies!' I told them. '*I* have an age and the Minister is everlasting asking me how old I am and the *Minister* can't be ill-mannered! Dad, have you got a years old?'

'Och, surely,' he told me. 'I am thirty-five. I was born in 1878.'

'What is 1878?'

'The year I was born, surely! Tell me your own birthday, the

5

way you will have to tell it to the Dominie when you go to school.'

'Tenth of March 1910,' I said promptly but this is what I meant about not having thought a thing out. It was only now that I discovered that years had names just as months did and that 1910 was my year.

'Mother, what is the name of your year?'

'My year? Oh, 1885.'

'Tom, have you got a year? George, have you?'

'Be quiet, Janet, with your ask-ask-asking,' said my grandmother, 'and let people get on with their breakfast. It is nearly half-past six of the clock!'

And all day it went on like that. I had not nearly got this business of birthdays thought out before my grandmother had chased me out of the kitchen. I then went to my mother and Aunt Kate who were making the beds upstairs and in a very short time my aunt said I was deaving her so I went out to Tom who was cleaning the stable, while my grandfather yoked the horses out in the yard. 'Tom, has Granda got a year?' I asked, looking out at the tall spare figure whose long white beard was lifting a little in the morning wind.

'Aye, but it was away back before I was born and I am not knowing it. Get out o' my road now till I get at the barrow.'

A new thought struck me as I looked out at Betsy, the Clydesdale mare, who was standing in the yard outside. Only that morning, before he left for Poyntdale where he worked, my father had said that he hoped to get the young mare's foal before he came home that evening. If the foal got born today, today would be its birthday so our Betsy, too, must have a birthday.

'Tom, has Betsy got a year?'

This time, Tom did not tell me to get out of his way. Instead, he leaned on the stable brush for a moment and said: 'Aye, she has that. And that is something that is very interesting—her year is 1910.'

6

'That's *my* year!' I protested.

'Aye and what's more, Betsy's birthday is the tenth of March.'

'It is *not*! That's *my* birthday!'

'Aye but it is Betsy's too. You came at four o' the morning and Betsy chust before dinner-time. Mercy, that's the way her name is Betsy! We called you Janet Elizabeth and we called the foalie Elizabeth Janet and Betsy for short.'

I was stunned, so stunned that Tom wheeled the barrow of dung away to the midden and then disappeared with my grandfather and the horses before I came out of my trance to find myself all alone beside the stable corn kist. I then went back into the house. 'Granny, has the roan cow got a year?'

My grandmother was pouring the cream into the churn to make the butter and she bent a stern eye upon me. 'Janet Sandison, go outside this minute and fill the hens' pot with tatties and stop deaving people with your continual ask-ask-asking.'

How they expected me to think things out and get big enough to go to school while they all took up this unco-operative attitude most of the time, I did not know but, after having had my nose bitten off at mid-day dinner, I kept my cogitations about years to myself and then the mixing of the dumpling provided a new interest. Then, just as we were ready to empty the big basin of dough on to the floured cloth and put the dumpling in the big pot, another new bit of learning took place. Aunt Kate, putting the currants and raisins away in the cupboard, came out with a brown paper bag.

'Goodness, there's a few big blue raisins here,' she said. 'Isn't that grand? Miss Tulloch had none at the shop last week. Quick now Janet and help me to take the stones out of them.'

It was a nice sticky job, taking the pips out of the big raisins and Aunt Kate said regretfully: 'It's not a dozen that's in it altogether.'

'You can't have a dozen raisins,' I said. 'Dozens is eggs.'

She looked at me with her bright dark eyes. 'You can have a

7

dozen of anything, foolish,' she said. 'Twelve of anything is a dozen.'

I barely believed her. 'Twelve people?'

'Of course!'

'Twelve horses?'

'Surely.'

I was silent and forgot to help her with the rest of the raisins but with her quick fingers she soon had them done, had the dough in the cloth and had it all gathered up and tied tightly round the neck with the string.

'There we go!' she said and dropped the round bundle into the bubbling boiling water.

'Kate, twelve dumplings?'

'Och, yes. Now, be off, Janet. I want to get the kitchen tidied up.'

I called Fly, my collie, and we went off up to sit in our cave in the sunny side of the haystack where I gave my attention to dozens, twelve and figures in general.

Until now, this thing called counting had not had, for me, much interest or much sense. At school, I knew, one learned three things called reading, writing and counting and I had learned a bit about the first two already. I did not know when or how I had learned to read and write. They were things I had known 'always' and so easy to do that it seemed foolish to walk all the way to Achcraggan School to learn them. Counting was different. I could do what was called 'counting up to a hundred' and I could recite 'Two Times' and 'Four Times' but it seemed to me that these two were rather dull poems that did not make a great deal of sense. Poems like:

'A laird, a lord, a lily, a leaf,
A rich man, a poor man, a beggar, a thief'

had a more melodious sound than the poem called 'Two Times Table' and were much more rhythmic for dancing to across the

8

cobbles of the yard. 'A laird, a lord' however was a special poem with a particular function in the way that the poem that began: 'Oh worship the King all glorious above' was special in that it could never be spoken or sung except in church. 'A laird, a lord' was a telling poem for, when you counted the pips out of your damson jam to it, it told you what you would be in the future and it was a comic thing, somehow, that it always told that Tom would be a beggar and George a thief. In one way, you knew that George and Tom would never be either of those things because no Reachfar people could ever possibly be either beggars or thieves, but it was comical and satisfying that, time after time, when they were certain that the poem and the pips would tell them that they would be a lily and a leaf, which meant an earl and a duke, the result was invariably a prophecy that they would be a beggar and a thief.

George, Tom and I were accomplished poets and orators at this time and we were also experts in poetic criticism but I shall tell of this a little later perhaps. We had agreed a long time ago that, in the words of Tom: 'A lot o' things would be danged tedious if it wasna for a bittie poetry to keep one going' for there was no doubt that, by some conspiracy, the most tedious jobs around Reachfar tended to fall to the lot of us three. We were also very fond of music and, although the Almighty had not seen fit to endow any of us with a singing voice, that did not prevent us from singing, although we did this only when out-of-doors on our own. We preferred tunes with a good lively lilt to them, to cheer us on our tedious way of clipping turnips or mucking out the pigs and the tune of 'Onward Christian soldiers' was a favourite, to which we had various lyrics of our own but we always began with our 'song of working in general' which went:

> When we're grooming horses,
> Janet, hold that tail!
> When we're filling oat bags,

> Janet, hand that pail!
> When we're clipping turnips,
> In the frost and snow,
> Janet get that bot——tle
> From the whin-bush down below!

Naturally, songs such as these were never heard by the rest of the family for my grandmother would have regarded them as sacrilegious, but we could afford to be quite public about our poetry for the more sonorous, solemn and even lugubrious it was, the better we liked it. At this time, our main source of poetry was in the works of Sir Walter Scott and on wet Sunday afternoons the house would be haunted by our three voices, chanting in dreary unison from Tom's attic bedroom:

> 'There are twenty of Roslin's barons bold
> Lie buried within that proud chapelle
> Each one the holy vault doth hold—
> But the sea holds lovely Rosabelle!
>
> And each St. Clair was buried there,
> With candle, with book and with knell;
> But the sea-caves rung and the wild winds sung
> The dirge of lovely Rosabelle.'

Everything in my limited life at this time could be transmuted into word-sounds and rhythms which are, after all, the basis of poetry. The black kettle by the fire sang a song to me and all the house sounds had been translated into words in my mind so that 'Yaw-aw-took!' was my version of the shutting of the door of the kitchen cupboard which dragged along the floor before closing with the sharp 'took!' But counting, the monotonous rhythm of 'Two times one are two' did not belong to the world of poetry. In fact, it seemed to belong to the tedious turnip by turnip, forkful by forkful of dung routine world that George, Tom and I used our poetry to counteract but the discovery that the number twelve could also mean a dozen lifted counting on to a more mysterious and more satisfying plane. However, that twelve and a dozen came into the pleasing category of 'being the same only different' was a serious matter that had to be checked and proved to my own satisfaction.

In our sheltered cave at the bottom of the stack, while Fly closed her golden eyes to have her afternoon sleep with her head in my lap, I considered this affair of twelve of anything being a dozen. Until this time, a dozen had been, for me, the Song of the Eggs. Every Friday forenoon, my grandmother and I packed the baskets of eggs and butter which went to Miss Tulloch's shop in Achcraggan and which were paid for her by her in sugar, flour and boot polish and other commodities which did not grow on Reachfar. The big crocks of eggs which had been collected during the week were brought in from the milk-house and placed on the kitchen table, along with the big baskets which were lined with large clean huckaback towels. The Reachfar hens were individualists to a woman who would not lay in the nest-boxes provided for them unless, as Tom said: 'They were fair beat or taken real short' and so, because they laid in stable mangers, under the garden hedge or in the coal shed, their eggs had to be washed by my grandmother in a big bowl of water and dried carefully by me with a kitchen towel. This part of Friday morning was tedious but the prospect of the Song of the Eggs made it bearable.

When all the eggs had been washed and dried, my grandmother placed her left hand on the handle of the basket and, with her right, picked up a clover leaf made of eggs and placed it inside on the white towel. As she did this, the song would begin in my head:

> Eggs are going to market,
> To Miss Tulloch's shop.
> Eggs are very breakable,
> So do not let them drop—a dozen!

And, at this point, my grandmother would pick out from the crock a single egg that was too small or mis-shapen or faulty in some way and place it on a plate. I do not know when I learned that this meant that one dozen eggs had been placed in the basket nor did I appreciate for a very long time that this placing of a faulty egg on a plate was a facet of time and motion study in a clear-thinking woman who had never heard of such a science, a busy woman who knew that she might be interrupted in her counting task and had thought of this insurance against having to begin her count all over again. For me, the hand going to the plate was a little coda at the end of a verse, like 'Hallelujah' at the ends of the verses of a certain hymn in church and so, inside my head the song went:

> Eggs are going to market,
> To Miss Tulloch's shop.
> Eggs are very breakable,
> So do not let them drop—a dozen!

At the end of the operation, I was allowed to count the discarded eggs on the plate—'Mother, seventeen dozen this week!'—which had the effect of convincing my family that I could count a little, but I could not. To count from one to seventeen was merely a rigmarole and what pleased me was that I had heard the rhythmic Song of the Eggs in my mind, while I watched the rhythmic movements of my grandmother's hand, a lot of times. I did not, at this stage, think of it, even, as seventeen times.

My family was further deceived in that, the Friday after I had pleased them by counting the eggs on the plate, my grandmother said to me when the last basket was nearly full: 'All right, Janet. Let me see *you* put in a dozen now.'

I could not pick up a clover leaf of eggs at a time with one hand as she could but had to take them from crock to basket one by one, but I knew that there should be a clover leaf in the basket at the end of the first line of the song in my head:

12

went the song and, standing on my stool looking down into the basket, I saw the clover leaf take the satisfactory form and, listening to the song in my head, I went on to the second trefoil. 'A dozen!' I said when the fourth pattern was complete, speaking the coda aloud and moving a small egg from crock to tally plate. 'I told you she could count, Elizabeth!' my grandmother said triumphantly.

'And she doesn't even have to do it aloud,' said my aunt.

'I am still not convinced that she is an infant prodigy,' smiled my mother.

I got down from my stool. I did not like the sound of this infant 'porridge-y' which my grandmother and my aunt were making me out to be. I felt insulted as I retired from the kitchen and resolved that I would not tell any of them, not even George and Tom, about the Song of the Eggs.

Now, I reached out from the haystack cave and picked a clover leaf from the grass of the stackyard. I pretended to be my grandmother packing an egg basket and went 'Eggs are going to market—' with clover leaves. A dozen. Twelve. I counted the leaves. One, two, three four. Aunt Kate was all wrong. Four was a dozen. No, wait. There was more than one egg to a clover leaf. Three to a leaf. I counted round all the leaves of the four trefoils and came up to twelve. Twelve *was* a dozen. And wait—four clover leaves of three eggs each made twelve, a dozen. 'Four times three are twelve—' I recited out loud and in a flash discovered that counting was not merely a poor form of poetry at all but a quite separate and interesting thing by itself. For the remainder of the afternoon, I counted everything in sight, from the hens around the stackyard to the spokes in the wheels of the hay-rake but, interesting as counting was, there was a reservation in my mind that reading was more interesting still. I would prefer to be a 'great reader' like my father, when I grew up, rather than a great counter. I had never heard of anybody who was a great counter, now that I thought of it.

I did not know, as I have said, when or how I learned to read but last Christmas, before my fourth birthday, I had been given two books of my very own. I had a third book, called my 'A,B,C book' which was the one that had arrived on the fender after I wrote to Santa Claus but I did not look at it very often nowadays because I preferred my new book that had come on to the fender last Christmas and which was called *Pilgrim's Progress*. My other book, which Lady Lydia Daviot at Poyntdale had given me as a Christmas present, was more beautiful to look at than *Pilgrim's Progress* for it was full of coloured pictures but George, Tom and I had come to the conclusion that the poetry in it was pretty poor and did not make a great deal of sense.

In the winter time, on Sundays, George, Tom and I spent a large part of the day in Tom's bed because, if we stayed in the kitchen, we got in the way or disturbed people with our tongues 'that clapped everlasting like kirk bells' and this was our main time for dealing with educational matters, reciting poetry and reading. On the first Sunday that we retired to Tom's bed with my new books, we naturally embarked on Lady Lydia's one first because of its gay colourful pictures. It was called *Nursery Rhymes* and this led to trouble straight away. Mr. Macdonald at Achcraggan was a nurseryman who had a nursery where we bought the young cabbages for the garden in spring but I had always known what a rhyme was and I knew it was not a thing that grew in a nursery. A rhyme was made of words and was not a plant with leaves that grew in the ground like a nursery cabbage.

'It means a *young* rhyme like a little cabbage plant,' said George.

'Don't talk capers!' I told him. 'Rhymes aren't young or old or big or little—they're just for ever and ever and always the same.'

'No, no, that's not what George means at all,' said Tom in a peace-making voice. 'It's rhymes for young *people* that's in it—people that's in the nursery.'

'What nursery? There's nobody in Achcraggan Nursery except Mr. Macdonald and he's got a long white whisker!'

Everything became quite involved and I was more than a little bad-tempered before George and Tom had got around to explaining about the room at Poyntdale House where Master Anthony, Master Torquil, Miss Laura and Miss Grace had lived when they were small being called a nursery. So the book got away to a bad start but, even so, it was found to be full of faults when subjected to further cool examination.

While Tom and George lay back in the bed with their pipes going well, I, comfortable and warm between them, read out to them the first page which had a picture of a little girl wearing a long dress and a lot of ribbons and carrying a long stick also bedecked with ribbons.

> 'Little Bo-peep has lost her sheep and doesn't know where to find them.
> Leave them alone and they'll come home bringing their tails behind them.'

This finished the page and I turned to the next one but only to discover that it had a new picture of another little girl with a lot of ribbons, running away from a spider.

'That's all of that story,' I announced.

'D'ye tell me that now?' said Tom, astonished. 'It's a poor kind of a bittie that's of it and this lassie with a-all the ribbons about her is not much of a shepherd to my way of thinking.'

'Indeed no,' George concurred. 'What d'ye think Herself would say if we was to lose all the sheep, Tom?'

'Herself' was their private name for my grandmother.

'Wheesht, man, before ye bring a judgment on us!' said Tom. 'Janet, chust read that story to me again till I see can I make any sense off it.' I read the story again whereupon he said: 'No, dang

15

it, it has me fair bamboozled. Are you understanding it, George?'

'Not me. Tom, if their tails wasn't behind them, where the deevil would they be? Hanging from their noses?'

With this, we all had a good laugh and decided that the book had some points after all.

'Let's have the next one, Janet,' said George when we had finished laughing.

So, on we went through the book but, although kindly disposed to Lady Lydia and all her works, the people in this book of hers seemed to us to be incredibly silly. Miss Muffet was afraid of spiders, Jack and Jill could not even carry a pail of water without falling and Tom became very angry at the very name of 'Mary, Mary, quite contrary'.

'It's my belief she will be worse nor any of them,' he forecast. 'I never could abide people that's contrary.' And, sure enough, her garden made him furiously indignant and especially her picture for she was wearing a long pink dress with a lot of ribbons and was watering a row of cockle shells with a little red can.

'She is as bad as poor wee dighted Rory west at the Mill o' Gruanach that went out and stood up to his knees in the dung midden to see would it make him grow,' he said. 'There is chust no sense in putting sea-beach shells in a garden!'

But the book worked up to a fearful climax for on the last page was a picture of a goose with a big flower-trimmed hat on and a ribbon round its neck and the following story:

'Goosey-goosey-gander, where do you wander?
Upstairs and downstairs and in my lady's chamber.'

I went no further but raised the first protest: 'A goose could never get *into* a chamber!'

When it had been explained to me that 'chamber' in this case did not refer to a receptacle like the one in the cupboard beside my grandmother's bed, George took his pipe from his mouth

16

and made a final shattering pronouncement. 'If a goose went up a stair,' he said, 'there'd be a fine ould mess. You might as well have a cattle-beast with the spring skitter in the house as a goose —or a gander either, the dirty clarty brutes!'

And so we laid aside the prettily-coloured nursery rhyme book and began to read instead about the trials and tribulations of 'that poor devil Christian' as he was always to be known to us in *Pilgrim's Progress*. However, although the nursery rhymes did not make much sense, I remembered them for their pleasant jingling rhythm and it was to the beat of one of them that I hopped and skipped into the house as it came near to supper-time, a time that I recognised by a series of unconsciously-known symbols which were the mark of things that I had 'always' known. From the stackyard, I had seen Tom water the horses and lead them into the stable; I had seen the smoke eddy from the chimney as the supper fire was built up; I had seen the hens gathering in from the grass fields and the moor towards the steading and in my own stomach I had the 'supper feeling'. I did not know that these symbols sent me hopping and skipping in the direction of the house but in I went to the warm spicey smell of the birthday dumpling.

The bigger of the two hands of the clock was crawling near to the black mark at the top of the dial while the smaller hand hung straight down from the screw in the middle, pointing to the black mark at the bottom. Soon now, my father would come, his feet treading a firm but springy tramp-tramp along the cobbles of the yard towards the door and then the family circle would be complete, and we would have supper, for George was already home from work at Dinchory Farm. This was one of the finest moments of my day, although all my moments were fine and my life was one long succession of fine new wonderful things. I sat now watching the hand of the clock, trying to see it move, but it took a long long time to progress from one little black mark to the next so that my attention would wander from it to the panel of painted roses below the dial or to the carved oak of the clockcase and when I looked back at the hand, I found that it had eluded me and had crept on to the next mark while my attention had been distracted.

I sat on my stool of scrubbed white wood in the middle of the big rag rug that lay before the hearth and, on one side of the fire, to my left, my grandfather, with his eagle's eyes, proud eagle's beak of a nose and long white beard, sat in in his high-backed chair, smoking his pipe. At the other side of the fire, to my right, in the warmest corner of the big kitchen, sat my mother, her knitting needles clicking and glittering in the light from the fire. Behind me, my grandmother and my aunt were putting the final touches to the big white-scrubbed supper-table and in the scullery off the kitchen George and Tom were washing their hands to be ready for the meal.

I had discovered that when it was necessary to have patience, like now while I waited for my father to come home, it helped to think of something pleasant and George and Tom being my special friends, I began to think about them now. George was really something called an uncle, because both he and my father were the sons of my grandmother and grandfather, but I was in something of a muddle about this uncle business. It was very confusing because George was an uncle only to me. He was not Aunt Kate's uncle. To her, he was a brother. And he was not my mother's uncle. To my mother, he was something called a 'brother-and-law' which seemed impossible in a way because you could not think of George having any connection with the law. The law was a commanding thing and everybody knew that the commanding person around Reachfar was my grandmother— even people down in Achcraggan nearly four miles away would tell you that my grandmother's 'word was law'.

But there was nothing suggestive of the law about George. He was just a person very much like Tom or me, who had to do what he was told around Reachfar and never said a word about being an uncle except when I managed to creep up behind him and tickle his neck and make him jump. Then he would say: 'Ye wee limmer, to be so disrespeckful of your uncle!' and then he would laugh his big laugh, as if to be an uncle was the funniest thing in the world. Of course, for George, the world was full of funny things and he seemed to be laughing all the time and nobody could be with him for long without laughing too. He could make even my grandmother laugh quite often and, once or twice, he had made even my silent grandfather smile and shake a little so that his long white beard jumped up and down.

Tom was something the same as George, only different. Tom could easily be a brother to George or an uncle to me but he was neither. My mother said that Tom was 'a friend of the family who helps us with the work around Reachfar' and not a brother or an uncle because his name was not Tom Sandison but Tom Forbes. Brothers and uncles, I gathered, had to have the same name as you had, just like mothers, fathers, aunts, grandmothers and grandfathers and the people with other names like Forbes were called 'friends'. We were all, except Tom, called Sandison. My mother was Elizabeth Sandison, my grandmother was Catherine Sandison and Aunt Kate was Catherine Sandison too. George was George Sandison, I was Janet Elizabeth Sandison and my father was Duncan Sandison. My grandfather, who sat very still, moved about very quietly and seldom spoke except to give a final ruling on some point of family policy, was John Sandison, a very grand remote personage who, for me, was invested with a mysterious and awful power for I had recently learned, although I could not quite yet believe it, that he was the father of my father. So far, I had not been able to discuss this with Tom and George even, because it was a thing so overpowering and awe-inspiring that I could not find words for it. I had never thought that my father could have a father. I thought that my father had 'always' been there, like God. In fact, he *was* God for I could not separate the two and when, at bed-time, my mother sat beside my bed in my attic room, clasped her hands on her knee and said: 'Our Father which art in Heaven—' and I had to repeat the words after her, the picture in my mind was of my father as I had left him sitting beside my grandfather by the kitchen fire. You see, these words called 'my prayers' which made a beautiful poem that did not rhyme were all true. My father, by working as grieve for Sir Torquil Daviot at Poyntdale, the big estate to the north of Reachfar, gave me my daily bread. My father delivered me from evil like the time when I was very disobedient one day and climbed into the stud bull's pen at Poyntdale and my father got me out just as the bull was coming for me. And my father did not lead me into temptation but told me all the time to try to be a good girl. George and Tom were the ones who led me into temptation, for they would tease me sometimes to make me lose my temper which was a feeling that came over you and caused your head to buzz and your feet to stamp and my grandmother would say to them: 'Stop tempting the bairn, you two! You are not to tempt that craze that is in her!'

It was a bad thing, I knew, to 'have a craze in you' such as I had and I did not want to have it but, in spite of that, it rose in me, red and blazing, when Tom and George led me into temptation. Even my grandmother, who knew nearly everything, did not know how this craze had got into me for she often said: 'It is not from her father that she took it. Duncan was always quiet o' the temper but she puts me in mind of George as a bairn when she gets in a rage.'

It was difficult to believe that George had ever been a bairn and small like me for he was terribly big now, nearly as big as my father who was the biggest man in my whole world, taller and broader than Sir Torquil at Poyntdale, taller and broader even than my eagle-nosed grandfather. When my father and George came through from the passage into the kitchen, they had to lay their heads to one side to avoid bumping them on the top of the doorway and it was the same when they went from the kitchen to the scullery and it had become a habit, so that even when they went into the barn, which had a great high door that went right up to the roof, they ducked their heads to one side.

While I had been thinking, the hands of the clock had crept on. My father must soon come now for the clock was about to make its supper-time song, winding itself up a little first—there it was: 'Ip-it—' and then with one hand straight up and the other straight down it said: 'Tee-tee-tee-tee-tee-tee!' and then hurried ticking on to put the big hand right round the dial once again. But tonight, watching the clock anent my father's home-coming, I made a sudden discovery as it played its silvery little tune 'Tee-tee-tee—' for I had been inspired to apply to it, quietly inside my head, my newly developed interest in counting things. It stopped its tune when I had counted to six and in that second there came a click inside my head as I realised what my grandmother meant when she said: 'For pity's sake, Kate, are you going to be all day at that baking? It's past ten o' the clock!'

'Six of the clock!' I said in a loud voice.

There was a sudden silence over the kitchen, broken only by the crackle of the fire and the bubbling of the supper porridge in the big pot on one side of the fire and the bubbling of the dumpling on the other. I looked round at my family from my low stool, my mother with her knitting in her lap, my grandfather with his pipe in his hand, my grandmother and my aunt by the table, George and Tom in the scullery doorway. They were all staring at me and I wondered if I had done something wrong.

'Mercy, she can read the time!' my grandmother said and they all began to smile.

'Oh, I don't know,' my mother said doubtfully and, putting her knitting aside on the top of the big meal barrel beside her chair, she rose to her feet. 'Janet,' she said, looking down at me, 'look at the clock. If this hand was here and this one here, what time would it be?'

I looked at her pointing fingers. I tried very hard to think but no. There was no tune to count, just the silence of everybody waiting for me to speak.

'Look,' my mother said, 'suppose my finger is the little hand of the clock and count as I move it.'

I watched and counted: 'One, two, three—'

'And suppose the big hand is pointing up to the top?' she asked.

'*Three* of the clock!' I said.

'Three cheers, Tom, for a clever lass!' George shouted in his big voice that made the white-washed rafters ring and 'Hurray, hurray, hurray!' cheered Tom and added: 'My, there is somebody that is going to get a right fine surprise when he gets home from Poyntdale the-night!'

'I know the very thing,' George said next. 'Wait you till I get yon ould watch of mine that fell in the midden drain and was never no more good.'

He went away upstairs to his room and came back with a silver watch, very like my father's working-days watch except that this one of George's did not tick any more, but the hands of it could turn round to any position and my mother took it from him and began to teach George, Tom and me to tell the time. George and Tom, you must understand, were exactly like me and had to learn everything just as I did, whereas the rest of my family knew everything already and my father knew most of all. Tom and George did not have to learn about farm work, of course, because that was something that everybody knew. You 'always' knew how to plough and sow corn and plant potatoes and it was only a question of growing big enough to be able to reach up to put the harness on your horses and Tom and George, being big enough, naturally did farm work, George as grieve at Dinchory Farm to the west of us and Tom at home at Reachfar with my grandfather. But when it came to really clever things, like learning to read the clock or count, George and Tom had to be taught to do them just like me and did not know everything already like proper grown-up people such as my father. This made them very comfortable and close to me and even made me feel quite clever sometimes for George was inclined to be very 'thick in the head' and make a lot of mistakes when being taught anything so that the two of them did not fill me with awed admiration, as my father did. Yet, I liked that feeling of being so filled with awe and admiration that I vibrated inside.

George, this evening, was being very thick in the head about this business of learning to tell the time, for instance and when it came to his turn and my mother would show him the watch, he would start to count round the dial: 'One, two, three, six—'

'Och, och, George, you're all wrong again, man,' said Tom. 'Isn't he, Janet? What should it be, think you?'

'One, two, three, *four*, George,' I told him.

'Och, so it is! One, two, three, four, Mary at the cottage door!'

'Stop your nonsense, George Sandison,' said my mother sternly. 'You are not paying attention. I am going to give Janet your turn. Well, Janet?'

I looked and counted. 'Five of the watch!'

'And a-all's well!' said George and everybody laughed.

In spite of George's being very slow and backward, we soon learned about the half-pasts and the quarters and about these last George was very funny because he said that they made him think that the face of the watch was cut up like four scones on a girdle and he was very fond of a good scone and just after we had finished all the quarters, the clock on the mantel went: 'Ip-it-tee-tee!' and I looked up at it.

'Well, Janet?' my mother asked.

'Half-past six!'

'Hurray!' shouted Tom and George.

My mother put the watch on the mantel beside the clock. 'I am afraid they are still waiting for the young mare at Poyntdale,' she said to my grandmother. 'I hope Duncan isn't going to be very late.'

'Och, we are not that desperate hungry for our supper thenight,' Tom said. 'We can wait a whilie. In the meantime, Janet, we'd better get our boot-cleaning done.'

I fetched my going-to-bed boots from under the dresser. My going-to-bed boots were flat soles with white fluff inside which had red woollen tops made of crotchet by my mother and they tied round my ankles with woollen cords that had tassels at the ends. I took off my black, laced working boots and put them on. One-two pairs of boots. No. One-two-three pairs of boots because, upstairs in my attic bedroom, I had my highly-polished, buttoned Sunday boots. I then fetched the old sack and the box with the brushes and blacking from the scullery and spread the sack on the hearthrug at Tom's feet. Then, with the old knife, I scraped all the sticky bits from Tom's, George's and my own boots, Tom put the blacking on and George polished until we had a row of clean boots ready to put under the dresser for the morning.

'What's a pair?' I asked suddenly.

'A pair o' horses,' said George.

'What's a pair of *boots*, stupid?' I shouted at him.

'Janet!' said my mother, remonstrating.

'Well then, what *is* a pair of boots?'

'Lord, she's at it again,' my aunt said. 'It was dozens at dinnertime.'

At the word dozens, that great light broke with a click in my mind again and I picked up George's boots, one in each hand. 'A pair is one-two boots!' I announced and dropped the heavy boots one-two at his feet.

'Ech, ech, mind your poor old uncle's toes, you wee limmer!'

'Aye, that's right though. There's two boots in a pair,' Tom said.

'And two horses?'

'Surely. Here, put the boots bye under the dresser.'

I did as I was told, putting my own in the middle of the row, one-two-three pairs of boots, three twos of boots, three twos are six! Anxiously, I counted along the row. Yes. There were six boots.

I sat down on my stool again as the clock struck seven, looked up at the mantel and noticed George's watch which my mother had put there after our clock lesson, George's watch which he had dropped in the midden drain and which did not tick any more. Now here, I thought, is another thing that I never knew before—that George had ever had a watch. Having a watch—one-two watches, indeed—had been one of the things that made my father different from most of the other men I knew, for my father had a big white working-days watch and a yellow watch with a lid over its face which he wore to church on Sundays and the lid flew open in a magic way when he held it before you and you blew on it. In the bedroom where my mother and father slept, there hung on the wall beside the bed a black velvet pad with two hooks on it and every day, except Sunday, the yellow watch hung there, very beautiful against the black velvet and, on Sundays, the big white watch hung there, having its day of rest although it went on ticking just the same. I had never seen the two watches hanging there at the same time but now I supposed that they did when my father went to bed, so that they could have their night's sleep just like the rest of us.

It was necessary for my father to have a watch when people like George, Tom and me had no need of them, because my father was a very important person, grieve at Poyntdale as he was. Poyntdale was what people called 'a big undertaking', with its hundreds of acres of good arable land, its mansion house, its big home farm and its ten pairs of working Clydesdale horses which were quite apart from the riding horses and the pair of beautiful greys who drew the wagonette to church on Sundays.

At Poyntdale, in the 'farm street', there were quite twenty houses where the ploughmen and cattlemen lived, making a little village all by itself and then, scattered round the estate, were all the houses of the foresters, game-keepers and shepherds. All the ploughmen, the cattlemen and the shepherds came under my father's charge, as did all the working horses, the cattle and all the broad acres of arable land. Naturally, a man with so much to see to had to have a watch—one, two watches—a working-days watch and a Sunday watch.

It astonished me that George had once also had a watch but it was less astonishing, somehow, to know that he had let it fall into the midden drain which merely went to prove in a satisfactory sort of way that he was not really the right sort of person to own a watch at all. My father would never drop a watch into the midden drain. I do not mean to convey that I disapproved of George in any way—far from it. I was, indeed, relieved that George's watch had come to a sad end in the midden drain for, if I had discovered George to be a valid watch-owner, I should have been forced to recast my whole estimate of him and to change his position in relation to myself. For me, watch-owners were people of a quite different status from George, Tom and me. They were people who had about them an aura of greatness and distance and awe, like Sir Torquil, the Reverend Roderick Mackenzie the minister and my father. The first two of these were great but the greatest of all was my father. Surely, very soon now, he would come home.

'I think Janet will have to have her supper and go to bed,' my mother said. 'It's well after seven o'clock. Go and get washed, Janet.'

I could hardly believe my ears. In my mind there occurred the very opposite of that click and the white light breaking as you suddenly discovered that you knew something. There was a sudden black darkness and a rushing buzzing sound, a whirling chaos but, when I looked round at the assembled members of my family, all their faces were as calm as my mother's voice had been when she made that shattering pronouncement. I felt that the whole world had suddenly disintegrated and was tumbling about our ears although none of these people around me seemed to know it. I sprang up from my stool between George and Tom.

'But Daddy's not home!' I screamed.

'Janet,' my gentle mother said sharply, 'don't scream like that. Go through and wash your hands and Granny will put your porridge out.'

I looked to either side of me, to George and Tom who usually helped me in every difficulty but no response came from them. They were calm and smiling, as if the world were perfectly normal, as if they could not see this appalling thing that threatened me, this hideous insecurity of going to bed when my father was not in the house, this horrible thing that had never happened before in all my life.

'No! Will *not*!' I shouted.

My mother, very tall, rose to her feet and looked down at me.

'Janet, go and wash your hands at once.'

I looked round again at them all and all their faces were solemn, distant, unsympathetic, disapproving of me, a bad girl who was disobedient and, with a terrible loneliness, I saw that they did not know that this was something that could not, must not happen, that I should go to bed without seeing my father come into the kitchen, his head leaning towards his left shoulder, his ruddy face smiling while his big hands reached out to me.

'Janet Sandison, do as you are told!' my grandmother thundered.

It was terrible. How was it that they did not know that I must see my father come home? Surely this was something that everybody must know without being told, for it was something that could not be told, a thing for which there were not any words, a thing that was part of 'always'.

'No! Will *not*!' I shouted, ran out of the circle round the fire and threw myself on the floor by the big white dresser.

'George,' my mother said, 'please pick her up for me and take her through to the scullery.'

My mother was not very strong and she knew that she herself could not carry my sturdy protesting weight. George rose from his chair, Tom following him and they both came to stand towering over me.

'Janet,' George said in a coaxing voice, 'get up and walk to the scullery like a proper person and not lie there like a drunken tinker wife.'

Oh, the insult of it! My friend George was calling me a drunken tinker wife, as if all the world were not too dangerously wrong already without that. I began to cry, drumming my heels on the floor.

'Janet,' came Tom's voice, 'we'll not eat all the dumpling. We'll keep a bittie for you to have tomorrow.'

Oh, the shame of it! They thought I was a baby making a fuss about a bit of birthday dumpling.

'Go away!' I yelled, scratching and kicking. 'Go away!'

But they did not go away. George's big hands went round me and he picked me up so that my feet in my going-to-bed boots were level with the high top of the dresser. I stiffened the whole of myself into an arch like the bridge over the moor burn and kicked harder than ever as I screamed above all the rest of their voices: 'Daddy! Daddy, come home! Daddy, I am *needing* you!'

'Just a wee minute there, George,' came the gentle voice of my granny as opposed to the law-giving voice of my grandmother and it arrested George, with me in his arms, in the doorway to the scullery.

'Janet?' she said on a questioning note, standing close beside me and looking at me narrowly and the breath that I had gathered for the next howl came out in a shuddering sob. 'Quiet, now, there's a good lass. Put her down, George.'

George stood me down on my own feet and my granny turned to my angry, white-faced mother. 'You should let her stay up for a whilie, *m'eudail*, to see will he come,' she said gently. 'Her wee heart just beats on him, you know.'

The black buzzing in my head stopped now although the tears still ran out of my eyes and the sobs made me shake all over. People outside mostly called my granny Mrs. Reachfar and she was so wise that some people thought she was a witch, but a witch was a wicked person and my granny was wise without being wicked. It was because people outside always saw her being Mrs. Reachfar, laying down the law, that made them think she was a witch for, quite often, when she was being MY GRAND-MOTHER in capital letters and laying down the law around the house, I felt myself that she was nearly a witch. But when she was being my granny like this, you knew that she was not a witch at all but a terribly wise, terribly grown-up person who knew more than my mother or Tom or George or anybody—she knew more about some things than even my father. Look how she knew this about me when I had never told her for I had no words for telling it. My granny had the words when she said: 'Her wee heart just beats on him.' I could feel my heart doing it now, beating: 'Daddy, daddy, daddy' against my ribs.

My mother was looking down at me, her face stern but not as white and cold as it had been before. 'I am black burning ashamed of you, Janet, for making such an exhibition of yourself,' she said. I looked up at her, shuddering and sobbing. It was a terrible thing that she should be black burning ashamed of me and I was bitterly sorry about the exhibition which, yet, seemed to have been forced upon me. 'I want Daddy to be home,' was all I could say.

'We all want him to be home,' she said, her face growing less stern, her voice growing warmer. 'Now, Tom is going to wash you and you will put on your nightgown—'

I stared up at her. I was being sent to bed in disgrace. Even my granny, the great power of Reachfar, had failed me. My heart seemed to beat 'Dad—' and then stop.

'—and then you will be ready to have supper with Daddy and go right off to bed,' she finished.

My heart began to beat again. I looked from my mother to my granny who had gone back to her chair near the fire and had turned into my grandmother again. She bent her straight blue glance upon me.

'And shut that scullery door, Tom, for pity's sake,' she said with her eyes on my face. 'The draught from through there is something terrible.'

Tom disappeared into the scullery. I fetched my nightgown from upstairs, crept quietly back through the kitchen to join him and quietly shut the scullery door again.

Tom and George helped me to wash at the scullery sink on alternate nights and took the opportunity of washing themselves at the same time, but it usually happened after supper and not before it, like this.

'I am chust like Sir Torquil, dressing for his dinner the-night,' said Tom, drying his ears, 'and not chust washing my hands before my supper like the usual. Ye know, I think I'll chust give my feet a dip while I am about it.'

This was such a departure from the norm that, tense as the atmosphere was, I simply had to stick my head into the kitchen and say: 'George, Tom is washing his feet for his supper!'

'Bless my soul,' said George, 'now that is a very good idea. A person can eat more dumpling with clean feet. I think I will chust do the same myself,' and, leaving the circle at the fire, he joined us in the scullery.

'So it is yourself, George,' Tom welcomed him. 'Chust hold on for a minute and I will be done of the basin. The three off us is chust as well out o' there—' he jerked his head at the kitchen '—for a whilie. It will let everybody get calmed down, like.'

'And be able to enchoy the dumpling,' said George.

I kept very quiet. I felt very ashamed. George and Tom never scolded me in a serious way but when I had behaved very badly they took my disgrace upon themselves like this, more in sorrow than in anger, as if they accepted their fate to be exiled to the scullery as I was and yet, at the same time, making it clear to me that the exile was my responsibility.

So, while George washed the upper part of himself and then filled the basin and set about his feet and Tom stood against the sink smoking his pipe, they discussed in an oblique way the undesirability in society of people who 'took tantrums and were not reasonable' until I burst out with: 'I just wanted Daddy to be home!'

Tom looked round at me as if he had newly discovered that I was present. 'And what for did you not chust *say* that?' he asked.

'Instead of lying on the floor and kicking your feet?' George added.

I looked from one of them to the other and gulped helplessly. 'There is nothing difficulter in the whole world than saying things,' I said.

Tom and George looked at one another and then: 'Dang it,' said Tom, 'it is myself that is not sure that that is not the God's truth, George.'

'That's so,' George agreed. 'Och, well, we'll say no more about it. Come on ben to the fire. They'll have got over things by now,' and, to the tune of the Barren Rocks of Aden, he began to sing:

'Blaw, blaw my kilt awa', my kilt awa', my kilt awa',
Blaw, blaw my kilt awa' but leave me wi' my trousers!'

and, all singing, we marched in Indian file back into the kitchen.

'I think we ought to have supper at eight o'clock, Granny, and not wait any longer,' my mother said. 'Duncan will have dinner at the Big House if he is still down there at eight, and Tom and George must be starving.'

'I hope they're not having bother with that young mare,' George said.

'Sir Torquil would have been up for Granny by now if it was anything like that,' Tom reminded him, for my grandmother was one of the best amateur veterinarians in the countryside.

I sat watching the clock, feeling a little frightened, for to have supper without my father at the table with us would be a thing too strange to come within the bounds of life as I knew it. Fearfully, I watched the big hand crawl on towards the top of the dial, and, when it was nearly there, my aunt rose and poured some boiling water into the teapot and still that firm springy step did not sound from outside. With all my might, I wished, holding my breath, for the hand of the clock to stand still. Earlier, before six o'clock, I had not been able to see that hand move in spite of all my efforts but now, in spite of all my efforts to stop it, I saw it creep on, sinister, inexorable, away beyond my control. 'Ip-it—' the clock sighed and began to strike the hour and I felt my spine go limp with fear and disappointment but just as the final 'tee!' sounded, Fly came out from her place under the table with the other dogs, came to my knee and gave a small pleased whimper.

'Shush, everybody!' I said.

For a moment, the clock ticked busily into the silence as if to stop us hearing anything other than the passing of time but then it came, that springy tramp-tramp along the front of the steading, past the window and into the passage of the house. I felt that I was going to burst and I could not speak or move but sat tight and still on my stool with my hand on Fly's head. Then the door opened and he stood there in the evening light, his head tilted towards his left shoulder, his ruddy face under his dark hair, his big white teeth gleaming as he smiled and said: 'Mercy, is that my lass still not in bed?'

My father was home. Everything in the world was secure and right again as I went to him. He put his big hands round my middle and put me up over his head so that my going-to-bed boots kicked the rafters and it was a strange and lovely thing to look down at this big smiling face which, at all other times, was so far up and above me.

'Did you get your foal?' my grandfather asked while my father held me up there.

'Aye,' he replied, still smiling up at me, 'a bonnie little filly just about an hour ago.' He gave me a shake from side to side and set me down on the floor. 'You shouldna have waited like this for me,' he said then, looking at the supper-table.

'We thought it best to wait,' my grandmother said in her law-giving voice and bending a stern eye on me.

'We had a little trouble here tonight,' my mother added.

I felt my face grow hot and I backed in between my friends Tom and George.

'Oh?' said my father, his eyes, solemn now, coming to rest on me.

'Not at a-all,' said Tom. 'There was no trouble o' the world.'

'It was chust that we didna care to go to our beds when you wasn't home,' said George, 'so we chust waited. We did a puckle lessons while we was waiting,' he added in an ingratiating way.

'I see,' my father said, still looking at me however and not at Tom or George.

'They was very special lessons,' said Tom in a way more ingratiating still.

'They was indeed,' said George. 'It's yourself that would be surprised.'

'Do ye tell me that?' my father asked but he was still looking at me and his face was still very solemn, almost stern.

'Janet,' George said, 'would you chust tell me the time now?'

I looked up at the clock. The queer black figures round the dial seemed to be jumping about. One hand was pointing to the side of the fire where my mother sat, the other was on the other side. It was not a half-past or a quarter-past anything—it was some unknown quantity—panic rose in me and the whole clock seemed to jump up and down before my eyes. But wait—it had struck eight just before he came home but the big hand had not yet quite made the 'scone' which would make it be quarter-past.

'It's *nearly* quarter-past eight!' my voice said shrill with strain and somehow the words sounded like a reproach as I looked up at my father, although I had not meant them to sound like that.

'Mercy, so it is!' he said. 'I had no idea it was so late.' Then all the dark solemnity was gone from his face as his delighted smile broke over it. 'My, what a clever lass that can read the clock!'

I felt shy now, overcome by this tremendous praise and stood picking at the knee of Tom's grey tweed trousers.

'But a clever person's brains gets tired at the end o' the day,' Tom said, 'so Janet is chust going off to her bed as soon as she has had her supper. Aren't you, Janet?'

'Yes,' I said, still looking at the knee of the trousers.

'Now, come on, you women, for pity's sake,' George said in a joking-angry voice. 'How much longer have we got to wait for that dumpling?'

I do not remember eating the dumpling. All I remember is that when my mother came to hear me say: 'Our Father which art in heaven—' that night, I saw before me as I said the words the face that laughed up at me while my going-to-bed boots kicked the rafters of the kitchen.

On the fourth of May of that year, Aunt Kate and I made another dumpling for, on that day, my father became thirty-six and, for that dumpling, we took the pips out of no less than thirty-six big blue raisins, one for each year of his life. It was another exciting day for he was late for supper again but I was allowed to stay up this time without any need for what George and Tom referred to in a shame-faced way as 'tantrums and unreasonableness'.

My tantrum and unreasonableness of the evening of my mother's birthday did not pass into oblivion until the next day when, after breakfast, my mother took me away to her own room.

'I quite understand, Janet,' she told me gravely, 'that you wanted to see Daddy before you went to bed last night but no matter what you want, screaming and kicking on the floor is not the way to get it. It is a disgrace to the name of Sandison to behave like that. Do you understand?'

'Yes, Mother.' I felt very humble. 'Mother, it was because I was frightened,' I tried to explain.

'Yes. I see. But even when you are frightened, you must try to control yourself. All proper persons have control of themselves.'

'Yes, Mother.'

'And there is no need to be frightened if Daddy is late in coming home. Up to now, he has always been here when you went to bed but quite often, after you are asleep, he goes away back to Poyntdale if a cow is calving or anything. You know that his work is to look after all the horses and cows for Sir Torquil?'

'After bed-time, too?'

'Yes. All the time, whenever he is needed. But if he goes out at night, he always comes home again. Daddy will always come home again.'

Up in the cave in the haystack, with Fly beside me, I thought of this remarkable fact that, while I slept, my father might be away at Poyntdale and not in his chair beside my grandfather's in the kitchen. It took a little time to get used to the idea but gradually I began to feel that it was not so strange after all. People had a habit of not staying where you left them, like the time I left my grandmother in the barn and went to steal sweets out of the jar in the kitchen press for George, Tom and me.

When I got down from the chair with the three sweets in my hand, there she was in the kitchen and not in the barn at all. It had been silly, I saw now, to think that my father never moved from the place where I left him when I went to bed. Someone as powerful as my father was, when I thought about it sensibly, capable of going to America and being back by morning.

However, although I now felt quite sure that my father would always come back, I still wanted to be present when he came and when, on his birthday morning, he came to breakfast in his second-best suit and told us that he had to go to Dingwall with Sir Torquil that day, I took serious thought.

'We may be a bittie late in getting back,' he said.

As soon as he had gone away down the hill, George to Dinchory and Tom and my grandfather to the stable, I set about arranging things.

'Granny, can I get to stay up for Daddy's birthday dumpling even if it is late?'

'You will have to ask your mother.'

'But Granny, don't *you* think that I could get to stay up?'

'Och, Janet, get out of my road with your ask-ask-asking!'

I went to the scullery. 'Aunt Kate, can I get staying up for—?'

I went to my mother's room. 'Mother, can I get staying—?'

I went out to the stable. 'Tom, will you help me to get staying up for Daddy's birthday dumpling even if it's late?'

By six o'clock in the evening without a single tantrum or any approach to unreasonableness, I had them worn down and was sitting on my stool in front of the fire when my father came home shortly after seven.

However, although I do not remember by what means a sense of something which George and Tom called 'fair play' had been induced in me, the fact was that when, shortly after his birthday, my father had not come home by six-thirty one evening and my mother said that I must have supper by myself and go off to bed, I went quite happily and willingly although, over my porridge, I said to Tom and George: 'I have never seen such a carry-on as this, with Daddy being late every other night, in all my born days.'

'It is always like this in the spring o' the year with the foaling and the calving and everything, you foolish little craitur,' said Tom.

I wished to contest this. For me, this was not part of 'always'. I tried to remember back to the year before when Betsy had foaled the red colt but I could remember only the new long-legged colt and no more.

'I am *not* foolish, Tom Reachfar, and it wasn't always like this!' I said angrily.

'It is chust that you canna mind on last year because you was too little,' said George.

'Do you mind on more as you get bigger then?'

'Surely. Your minder gets bigger and you can keep more in it,' he assured me, 'chust like I can hold a bigger plate of porridge than you can.'

'Has everybody got a minder?'

'Och, yes,' said Tom, 'only some people has much better ones than others. Now, take the minister. I would say he has about the biggest and best minder in this whole parish with all that Latin an' Greek an' Hebrew he keeps in it. Wouldn't you think that, George?'

'It is a surprise to *me*,' said George, 'that his minder doesna burst with all he keeps packed in it.'

'Poop to that old minister!' I said. 'Daddy is bigger than he is and Daddy's got more in his minder than any confootered old minister!'

'Janet,' came my mother's gentle protest from her chair beside the fire.

'It is this way,' Tom explained peaceably. 'Maybe your Dad's is bigger on the whole but he hasna packed it as full as the minister's.'

'That's right,' George agreed. 'That is chust the way of it. Now take the case of myself. I am sure I have a fair-sized minder but there is not a great deal in it at a-all.'

'You never spoke a truer word,' said my aunt. 'Move over till I pour out Janet's milk.'

For some time after that, I gave a fair amount of thought and did a fair amount of ask-ask-asking about 'minders' in general which caused my mother to explain to me that the correct word was memory and that although, in an everyday way at Reachfar, we used the phrase 'to mind on', the correct word for this was 'to remember'.

'Mother, I can't remember getting born.'

'No. Nobody can.'

'But I can mind—remember the red colt getting born.'

'Yes. The red colt is younger than you.'

I thought for a moment. 'Can you remember me getting born?'

'Oh, yes.'

'And Daddy can remember *you* getting born?'

'No. I wasn't born at Reachfar, you see.'

I stared at her. I thought that all Sandisons were born at Reachfar. 'Where then?' I asked.

'Near a town called Elgin, in Morayshire.'

'Where is that?'

'Away across the Firth from Fortavoch.'

I had more than ever to think about now. There were not only times that were other than my own and outside of my memory; there were places too that were away beyond my furthest horizon. In a way, I 'knew about' America but I had never thought of it as a place where somebody might be born. What a tremendous thing it was to be alive. There seemed to be no limit to the things you could come to know and pack into this big bag inside you that was called your memory.

It was very soon after this that, one hot afternoon, all of us except my father were having a fly cup of tea round the kitchen table, for George had come home from Dinchory at dinner-time, so that he and Tom and I could take the honey off the full bee-hives. This was the pale-coloured clover honey and when we had taken it from the hives, the bees would set about making the honey from the heather that bloomed in August and September and fill the hives again with a richer, darker, more fragrant stuff.

George and Tom were a little quieter than usual as we sat at tea, our three hats with the veils and our three pairs of gloves lying on the broad sunlit window-sill, for George and Tom loved honey but they did not like to work with the bees. As a rule, my friend Danny Maclean, who had the bee farm away west on Dinchory Moor, came to help us with this job, but there was so much honey this year and Danny was so busy with his own hives that we could not wait for him.

'Have you many more to do?' my mother asked.

'Chust four more hives,' Tom said. 'Ye know, it is a queer thing about bees. It gets kind of on my conscience like to take their honey from them and them working so busy to make it.'

'I have never noticed your conscience to the fore when it comes to eating it,' said my grandmother. 'I have never seen such two big soft lumps of men that was so frightened of a puckle bees. You and your conscience!'

'It is not *my* conscience,' said George. 'I chust plain don't like the stingin' wee booggers an' that's the truth.'

'That's enough of your bad language,' my grandmother told him as Fly came out from under the table and gave a little bark. 'Wheesht! I wonder who is coming?'

Fly stood with her head cocked, her nose pointing to the west and after a moment or two the long sinewy form of Danny the Bee Man with his lank black hair above his brown leathery face appeared in the kitchen doorway.

'Man, it is ourselves that is pleased to see you, Danny,' said

39

George, 'Come in and get a drop tea. Tom and me was chust thinking on putting fire to them hives up there.'

Danny smiled, showing his big white teeth, drew a chair to the table and sat down. He did not talk a great deal, except to bees and to them he spoke a language of their own, a humming tuneful language that had no human words in it but the bees liked it, for Danny could put his hand into a hive, take hold of a queen bee and the whole swarm would settle on his hand and forearm. Danny did not wear a hat, a veil or gloves for no bee ever thought of stinging him.

Fly went back under the table, lying at my feet but just as we finished tea she came out again, pointed her nose to the east this time and gave a pleased little whimper. Then I heard that firm, unmistakeable springy tramp-tramp along the yard.

'That's my Daddy!' I said.

All the eyes in the room turned to the clock which stood at a quarter past three. My mother rose to her feet. 'What in the world can be wrong?' she said.

'Sit down, *m'eudail*,' my granny said, laying a hand over the thin-fingered hand on the table-top. 'There is nothing wrong with *him* whatever—he is coming like a steam engine!'

My mother sank back into her chair as my father appeared in the doorway. 'Hello,' she said uncertainly. 'You are early today.' She attempted a shaky joke. 'Have you and Sir Torquil fallen out?'

'No,' he said but he did not smile. 'How are you, Danny? No. Sir Torquil stopped work for the day. Germany has invaded Belgium. War has broken out.'

'*War*, Duncan?'

There was, to me, something terrible in the fact that these two words came from my silent grandfather's place at the head of the table. My father merely nodded and threw his tweed hat on the window-sill on top of our bee veils and gloves. That was queer too for each of our men had a hat-peg in the passage and never brought their working hats into the kitchen. Bee-hats were different, being the symbol of a special activity. The kitchen seemed to be full of eyes, eyes all staring into one another, searching. What was war? What was this that had broken out? I knew that it was a nuisance when the sheep broke out into the turnip and once a sickness called 'the measles' which was little red spots all over you had broken out among the children at Achcraggan School but my family never looked like this about sheep or measles. What was war?

Suddenly, everybody began to talk at once, questioning my father, a babel of questions and, after some time, I heard my mother's voice speaking alone, puzzled, frightened. 'What in the world will happen?'

'God only knows,' my father said. 'I don't.'

For a horrified moment, I stared at his sad face which held the same puzzled look as the faces of all the others. My father did not know. This was the end of the world. If my father did not know, nobody in all the wide world could know. I was plunged into an abyss of blind darkness. 'Oh, Daddy!' my heart cried as I ran out of the silent frightening kitchen with all the staring eyes and, with Fly behind me, I fled away to hide in the moor.

The whole honey-smelling day was suddenly horrible for Fly and I were late in coming home and I had a scolding for worrying everybody. Danny was still with us, sitting in the circle round the fire when I was going to bed and George, having washed me, brought me out of the scullery in my going-to-bed boots.

'Janet is chust off to her bed everybody,' he said loudly and there was a chorus of goodnights but they were perfunctory, as if my departure upstairs were of little moment in this frightening new world. My mother showed no sign of rising to come with me to hear my prayers. As I went out of the door, I noticed that my grandfather was gazing away through the window towards the trees on the moor with a frown creasing his high forehead and, as the door closed, I heard my grandmother begin to speak: 'I

41

can mind on my grandfather telling of the time of Waterloo—'
Waterloo. It had a sinister sound. The day we saw the weasel in
the march wall, George had said: 'It is about time that brute
met his Waterloo. Go up to the house and get your gun, Tom.
Janet and I will sit here and give him enough confidence to get
right impudent and come right out.'

The weasel's Waterloo had been a matter of gratification to the
three of us for it is not easy to give a weasel a Waterloo with a
gun but, now, as I sat down quietly on the stairs outside the door,
too frightened to go upstairs all alone in this suddenly haunted
house, it occurred to me that the Waterloo had been an unhappy
affair for the weasel. Waterloo. The very word had a sinister,
strangely final sound.

Part Two

1922

'Where there is no vision, the people perish: but
he that keepeth the law, happy is he.'

PROVERBS xxix. 18

BY the time I was twelve years old, that click and flash of white light in my mind at the discovery of some new understanding, such as the understanding of the face of the clock, had become less frequent because, I think, in the eight years that had elapsed I had made so many discoveries that they had become a commonplace rather than the extraordinary for me, so that the first thrill of understanding did not now visit me so piercingly. I think it is true that, with use, the perceptions become less keen or more diffuse so that there is no longer the same cutting edge or the same blinding flash at the moment of comprehension.

In the eight years, too, many outward events had taken place, the most important of which, for my father and me, was the death of my mother in the spring of 1920, at the birth of my brother, John. When this happened, when I was ten years old, it caused in me a memory black-out, a merciful kind of anaesthesia, from which I did not recover completely until my father and I were in south Scotland in a completely new environment, on a dairy farm of which he had become the manager. I went to school from there to the little town of Cairnton about a mile away; a local woman kept house for us and an entirely new relationship developed between my father and me, a relationship based largely, I think, on our feeling that we were both strangers in a strange land.

By the time I was twelve, I knew beyond all doubt that my father was not omnipotent and omniscient as I had believed so firmly when I was four but this did not make me love him the less.

I was a slow-witted, slow-maturing child but, in a vague yet pervasive way—a way quite different from those blinding flashes that used to come to me—I understood that the death of my mother was something that had struck him a stunning blow from which a large part of his inner self would never recover and, in a more definite way, I understood that I had a better grasp than he had of the political and economic features which had led to the position, after the Great War, when Sir Torquil could no longer afford to keep at Poyntdale a grieve of my father's calibre. Sir Torquil was hard-pressed to keep Poyntdale itself and did so only by ruthless selling of timber and much of the outlying land and, in the mind of my father, as in that of my grandfather, this was blinding cataclysm. In a way, the death of my gentle young mother was easier for them to encompass than the disintegration of Poyntdale for, to peasant people who live close to the earth, death is an accepted part of life, its inevitable end.

My father and I, as far as Cairnton was concerned, were strangers and sojourners and content to be so for—although I knew this of myself at twelve years old, I had not realised its truth of my father—we both counted the days we spent there, from summer to summer, when we could get away on holiday to Reachfar. This may have been ungrateful to the southern countryside that harboured us and gave us our living but it was so. Our six years in Cairnton were six long slow climbs towards the summer summit of Reachfar, where we rejoined our family in the place where we belonged.

This annual visit to Reachfar brought a curious complexity into the relationship between my father and me. At Cairnton, the strange land where we clung together for mutual support, he placed me on a much more grown-up footing with regard to himself but when we came home to Reachfar, I reverted to my childhood position in the family, on the 'bairn's side' of the table between Tom and George while my father sat, as he had always done, on my grandfather's right hand. The cradle that contained my little brother John stood, at meals, on the right of my grandmother at the other end of the table, in the place where my mother used to sit, for John did not come to Cairnton but stayed with the family at Reachfar.

Every year, I travelled north at the beginning of July, to be met at Inverness by Tom and George. My father, who never had more than a fortnight or three weeks of holiday, came north about mid-August and then he and I travelled south again in time for my school re-opening early in September.

In 1921, when the summer holidays came and it was time for me to travel north, my father asked Mr. Hill, his employer, to release him from work for part of a day that he might go to Glasgow to put me on the Inverness train but I do not remember much of that first journey. I remember clearly, though, the evening in 1922 before my departure when my case was packed and all was ready for the morning. My father and I were working in the garden that surrounded our house.

This garden was something that our housekeeper, a Cairnton-born woman, could not understand for, when we had come to the house less than two years ago, it had been a thorny wilderness, four feet high in rank weeds, with broken walls and gates and a heap of bottles, old pails and a rusty iron bedstead overgrown with nettles lay about a yard from the back door. Before my father had been in the place for a week, in spite of working from six in the morning until six and often later at night at the dairy farm, the thorns, weeds, bottles, pails and bedstead were gone, the house was surrounded with freshly double-trenched earth and in every spare moment during that first winter, when it was daylight and there was no frost, my father was busy with cement, repairing the gaps in the wall.

'Whit work!' said Jean, our housekeeper. 'If Ah wis him, Ah widnae bother masel'. He'll get nae thanks.'

I had early come to the arrogant conclusion that Jean was not a highly intelligent woman and I became firmer still in this belief when she could not see that, just as she was so house-proud that she could not rest if our house had a speck of dust in it, my father could not bear to have around him land that was untended. But I was wrong—or, rather, incomplete—in this estimate of my father. The drive behind him was something far stronger and deeper than a dislike of bad husbandry. It was a drive that came from a need in the blood to tend the earth, to work in it, to turn it over and smell it, for on the dairy farm where he worked, there was no cultivation, no smell of earth or dung, only the sickly sweet smell of gallons of warm milk. And also in the drive within him was the longing for his own earth, the earth of Reachfar, for I think that when he dug his spade deep into the ground of Cairnton, he made an earth-blood contact with the ground on the hill of Reachfar but these things about my father I did not know until forty years later when I discovered the strange compulsion that made me, his daughter, labour and sweat to grow a few potatoes in the hard-baked earth under the merciless sun of a West Indian island.

On this evening before the holidays, when we worked together in that Cairnton garden, it really was a garden. Where all the herbaceous plants, the rambling roses that climbed up the walls of the house, the pansies that coloured the borders, the cabbage, the cauliflower and other plants had come from, I do not know, for in those days my father would never spend a penny that he could avoid spending. But gardeners are notable for great generosity with plants they themselves do not want and for hideous miserliness with plants that they treasure so, probably, my father who wanted any and every plant for his empty earth had become the receiver of all the throw-outs. And everything he planted grew and flourished. At any rate, the garden in less than a year had become a local sight, for Cairnton was a quarrying and mining town enveloped in dust where few people could make things grow and the respectable townspeople, since the summer had come, had formed a habit of taking their Sunday afternoon walk the mile out to Cairnshaws to look over our mended wall at my father's garden.

'It *is* a bonnie garden, Dad,' I said to him as we leaned on our hoes at the end of the turnip plot. 'What a difference from when we came!'

He puffed at his pipe and looked around him. 'It seems to me,' he said quietly, 'that one always tries to leave a place better than one found it if a person can manage it at all.'

This was one of the few times in my life since I was four years old that that click and flash happened in my mind and, in this moment, I felt that I had been vouchsafed a clear vision of some basic fibre in my father.

As he stood there in the light of the early July evening, the handle of the hoe upright from the ground to shoulder level at the end of his extended right arm, there was about him, for me, the aura of a crusader. The evening sun shone on his strong-growing dark hair which had, as yet, not thread of grey. It shone on the contentment in his hazel eyes and around the firm mouth under the short-lipped sandy moustache and as I looked up at his ruddy-coloured face with the marked high-bridged nose, I saw in him for the first time the strong blood and bone resemblance to my grandfather. And then I remembered my grandfather's hands, big hands that were in no way coarse but long of finger and blue-veined with age. I looked at my father's right hand that lightly held the hoe and saw there my grandfather's hand, the long fingers, the square thumb-nail with the big half-moon at the base.

'Dad,' I said on an impulse, 'you have hands just like Granda but your veins aren't blue.'

He smiled down at me. 'Maybe I haven't as much royal blood as Granda,' he said and we both laughed before he went on: 'It is natural that I would have hands like Granda, I suppose. I am his son. Blood tells in people, just as it does in animals. People

49

never get away from their blood. Talking of hands, look at your own.'

I looked at my own right hand which was holding my hoe just as he was holding his and saw for the first time that I too had 'hands like Granda' except that the veins were not blue. I felt a surge of tremendous pride, a pride tremendous yet humble, that I had inherited this from this father of mine.

'Am I like you, Dad?' I asked in a hushed voice, looking up at him.

He looked down at me. 'Aye, a bittie in some ways, maybe.' He paused, looked away over the fields beyond the garden wall and put his pipe in his pocket. 'But you took your eyes from your mother,' he said and, turning his back to me, he began to hoe along between the next rows of young turnips. It was the first time since we had arrived in Cairnton nearly two years before that he had spoken to me of my mother.

Between the months of March, when she died, and September, when he and I travelled to Cairnton, her name was mentioned frequently, in quiet voices, at Reachfar and at Inverness, in the course of our journey south, my father had spoken to me momentarily of her but, thereafter, when the train had hauled us southwards and across the barrier of the Grampians, it seemed that my mother had been left on the northward side, at Reachfar. And it seemed better this way for I felt that she would not have liked this grey, dusty little town with its constant grinding rumble of quarry machinery and its intermittent shattering explosions as another hill of rock was blasted down. Hers had been a still calm spirit and her big grey eyes had liked to look away to the far distances that lay about Reachfar, away to the east to the North Sea beyond the entrance to the Firth or west to the hump of Ben Wyvis or north to the hills of Sutherland. My mother did not belong in this little valley where the little Cairn Burn ran down to the little town which huddled in its dusty hollow.

On this evening, when my father spoke of her so unexpectedly, the words had an effect in my mind similar to the sudden moment of awareness which had come to me at four years old when my mother had told me that she had been born not at Reachfar, but near Elgin. Until that time, I had no real consciousness of place. I knew that there was, about four miles from Reachfar, a village called Achcraggan where the eggs and butter were exchanged for groceries each week—I had even been to Achcraggan on most Fridays and on a number of Sundays, to church—but in my mind the place had no actuality. It was something like counting, a vague abstraction. People did not get born there, or eat their porridge or go to bed but when I discovered that my mother had been born near Elgin, I saw that people would be born at Achcraggan too. These places were, as I put it in my mind: 'just the same as Reachfar in a way, only different', but they were no longer abstract, just as the abstraction, the irrelevance died out of counting when I discovered by the application of this science that I had six or one-two-three pairs of boots.

Now, when my father spoke of my mother to me, I think that I accepted for the first time that she was dead. Until this time, the knowledge of this thing had lain in my mind but it was a knowledge so terrible that I could not look at it, examine it or think of myself in relation to it or as its harbourer. I left it to one side, an abstraction, as irrelevant as Achcraggan had been when I was four years old. Yet, all the time, I had felt a nagging sense of loss because, no matter how I ignored that thing at the back of my mind, my mother had become strangely unreal and, although I did my best to believe it, I could not truly believe that she was still on the other side of the Grampians and that when I went home to Reachfar, I would find her there.

When my father looked down at me and said: 'But you took your eyes from your mother,' there was in his own eyes a dreaming light that glowed as if there was, reflected in it, the gold of some rich treasure that was stored at the back of his mind and the awareness suddenly came to me that there was in this life we live another dimension as well as those of place and time, the dimension of the 'minder', the memory in which time and place could be fused to become one, in which time and place were preserved for ever and in which being born and dying, the two dominant characteristics of outward life, did not exist. For me, I suddenly knew, my mother was not dead and, for me, she could never die. In my outward seeming, according to my father, I had her eyes but, in my memory, I had all of her that I had come to know in the ten years she had been with me and I could never lose this. And, even tonight in the Cairnton garden, I had come to know more of her from that light that had shown in my father's eyes when he spoke of her. My father had a memory too and he had known my mother for longer than I had and in a different way, I discovered. She had left with each of us something of herself, something which we could share and exchange, and dimly I became aware that sharing and exchange of this kind, the communication of something that lies deep and dear in the mind is a thing that pays compound interest. If we shared and exchanged what we each had of my mother, I knew, the coin of this thought would not become shabby or deteriorate but would multiply and increase in value. I did not, that evening, know this in these words, of course. I knew it only in a faint wavering way, as if a hesitant dawn were coming up over the furthest horizon of my mind but the urge was in me to talk to my father of my mother and not to flee from the thought of her as I had been doing for the past two years.

But, as I had told George and Tom long ago, there is nothing 'difficulter in the whole wide world' than saying things and the deeper and dearer the things are in the mind, the more difficult they are to say, for they have to be mined out of the treasured depths and on the way to the surface the debris of the mind's everyday clutter sticks to their brightness, sullying them, distorting their symmetry, bruising and damaging them. It is only genius that can dig out from the depths the pure unsullied gem and bring it to the surface in all its perfection of beauty in words or paint or sound, and I was no genius but a clumsy groping child.

As we hoed along between the turnips, I a step or two behind my father, I said to his broad back: 'But Dad, I am not nearly as bonnie as Mother was, am I?' These trifling words were all that I managed to bring out from the rich treasure house that is hidden in all of us but it has to be remembered that this was my first attempt at this sort of mining, that I had but newly discovered that the treasure was there to be mined.

'Well, now—' my father said thoughtfully and hoed on to the end of the row in silence.

I was bitterly disappointed with the words I had spoken, disappointed that the golden nugget of feeling for my mother which I had brought to the surface should have come to light encased in this dross of trivia of my own everyday life, for that is what this was. Jean, our own housekeeper, was a woman of conventional ideas. Along the road from us lived a little girl called Annie Black who was as conventionally pretty as the dolls of that time, with golden ringlets, blue eyes, pink cheeks and my days with Jean were one long comparison, to my detriment, of this prettiness with my own long-legged, pigtailed coltish plainness.

'Well, now,' my father said again as he turned at the end of the turnip row, 'you couldn't be as bonnie as your mother yet because you are only twelve years old. It takes time for a person or a thing like this garden here to get bonnie.'

'Annie Black is bonnie already and she is not much older than me.'

'Aye, that is so. Of course, a lot depends on what you call bonnie. Your mother was never anything like Annie Black. Your mother was dark o' the hair, like you.'

That every person had his or her own conception of beauty,

that beauty, indeed, lay in the eye of the beholder, was an idea new to me but a very acceptable one which I embraced at once.

'I would rather be like Mother than like Annie Black,' I said.

'If you will be like your mother, even if you don't grow so bonnie—if you are like her in other ways, you will do,' my father told me.

'But I might get bonnie like her too?'

'You might, but I doubt it. There is too much o' the Sandison blood in you. Look at your hands—they are nearly as big already, and you only twelve, as your mother's were when—as your mother's were.' He was silent for a moment, seemed to be searching in his mind for something and then: 'But don't you bother your head about being what people call bonnie. Being bonnie isn't everything. You have one thing that is better than your mother had—you have good health. Reachfar and the Sandisons gave you that if not much else. If you have good health—and good brains are important too—any living creature that has good health and good brains according to its kind, even if it is a horse, it is never ugly.'

I had never been sick in my life and every year since I went to school I had won the first prize in my class so it seemed that my brains were all right too. I was glad that I had those two things that my father seemed to think desirable and I wondered if he were aware that I had the brains as well as the health and was truly pleased with me. When you love someone as a god, as I loved this man, this love creates its own shrouding mystery so that you never know whether your god is pleased with you or not. To find out, you try to approach a little nearer to the throne in roundabout devious ways.

'Had my mother got good brains?' I asked.

'Surely!' he said on a note of astonishment. 'If not, where do you think your own bittie brains came from? From George or Tom?'

Brains or learning of any kind in juxtaposition to George or

Tom was an idea that wore the concealing straitjacket of the conventional family joke and, although I felt a stirring deep in my mind of the thought that George and Tom had queer subtle brains of their own kind, I could not put the vague thought into words for argument. I set aside for later consideration the brains of George and Tom and wallowed in the mental warmth of the knowledge that my father thought that I had a 'bittie brains' of my own.

'Your mother,' he went on, 'had more brains than all the rest of us at Reachfar put together. And your mother had education. That is why I want you to work hard at school and use the brains that you got from her. Your mother said, from the day you were born, that she wanted you to get the same chance of schooling as if you had been a boy.'

His voice suddenly sounded very happy, as if this time he had talked of had been a very happy one and, instead of starting to hoe down the next row of turnips, he laid his hoe against the wall, sat down on the garden seat he had built and began to fill his pipe. He chuckled before he began to speak and then he surprised me by saying: 'You never saw your granny knocked down and put in her place by anybody, did you?' This very idea was to me so fantastic that I could only stare at him bewildered and beyond speech. 'Myself saw it only the once,' he went on, 'and it was your mother that did it, three days after you were born. It was in the evening, when Granny was bathing you beside the fire and your mother was sitting up in bed and I was watching how granny handled you and you so small. The rest of them was all ben in the kitchen.'

I could see the ground-floor bedroom at Reachfar which my mother and father had occupied, with the big bed with its white counterpane and on the wall at one side the black velvet pad with the two hooks for the watches.

'Granny had you on her knee and was putting powder on your bottom and she sighed and said: Aye, a grand strong baby,

Elizabeth but it is a pity that you didna make a boy of her. Indeed, we had all thought that a bittie, you know,' my father added.

I felt hurt, hurt that through no fault of mine I had been a disappointment to my family. It had never occurred to me until this moment that, always, in our part of the country, the old tribal instinct made people still hope that all first children would be boys.

'Your mother herself,' my father was going on, 'just after you were born, said to me: "I am afraid she is a lady, Duncan." ' He paused, looking across the garden, musing with that happy smile about his mouth.

'You were—you and Mother too—you were disappointed?' I asked in a low voice.

'No, no! It is a funny thing but a body *canna* be disappointed with a baby. I could never even be disappointed with a calf or a foal, myself, as long as it was sound in wind and limb. No. We were not disappointed. It was more that your mother was frightened that *I* would be disappointed and at the same time I was frightened that *she* would be disappointed but we soon got over that. Indeed—' he chuckled aloud '—we were as pleased as if nobody in the wide world but ourselves had ever had a baby before. But with Granny it was a little bittie different. Granny belongs to the old old Highland people out o' the west, as you know, and she was thinking on Reachfar and a boy to farm it when I would be an old man and things like that. Anyway, that is what she said, that it was a pity your mother didna make a boy of you and we were sitting at the fire, looking at you and not thinking about a thing much when I heard your mother's voice: Granny Sandison, she said, if you ever even think a thing like that again, I will leave this house for good and take Duncan and my baby with me and you will never see us again as long as you live!' He paused and made a little gulping noise in his throat before he went on: 'I got a terrible fright. I thought something had come over her and had made her delirious, you know, because I had never seen her yon way before. She was sitting straight up in the bed, with the long plaits o' hair hanging down in front of her shoulders and yon big eyes of hers had flames in them. Boys! she said. If that little girl gets a proper chance in life she might be more use to the world than a hundred boys and anyone who looks down on her for being a girl will answer to me for it. Give me my baby! I will attend to her myself!—It took us a whilie to get her calmed down,' he continued thoughtfully, '—George and me, that is, for she had ordered Granny out of the room by now. You never saw your Granny ordered out o' anywhere, did you? No, nor me, ever again but then Granny never again said anything about you not being a boy. And it was a funny thing, that. As you got older, Granny was fonder of you than any of us, almost, and was always the one to take your part when there was serious trouble. And Granny got fonder than ever of your mother too. People like your Granny,' he said thoughtfully, frowning a little, 'thrawn-natured people like that are always fonder of people that stand off from them, people they can respect, people that can give them a good salting when they need it. People like your granny seem to enjoy a good fight, too. I canna understand it right, myself. I don't like fighting and people being at variance with one another. I think your granny would have domineered us all at Reachfar if she hadna been just that wee bittie frightened of your mother from that time when you were only three days old.'

My mother had now taken on another layer of character in my mind. What I had remembered was a gentle image, a person who moved quietly and spoke in a low voice even when she had scolded me but the picture of the virago with the long plaits of hair and the flames in her eyes who had defended me from the big white bed gave her a new character and increased her stature.

'The idea of putting a girl to a big school like Cairnton

c

Academy here is still new to your Granny,' my father continued. 'Although she doesn't raise any objections to it, I think it is still a very strange thing to her that she will never get used to for, when people get old, it gets harder for them to get used to new things.'

'But haven't girls always gone to school?' I asked.

'Och, no. Not girls like your granny, in the west, when she was young. Mind you, Granny can read and write but she just learned that much because the minister o' the parish took an interest in her. She would be a lively nipper of a bairn, I am thinking. The funny thing is that she believes in education but only for boys, when it comes to it.'

'But my *other* granny, Mother's mother, must have believed in education for girls because Mother had education, you said.'

'That was nothing to do with your other granny,' he told me. 'Your other granny died when your mother was born and your other granda died at sea when she was just eighteen months old and she was left a complete orphan without even a cousin that could be traced but she was brought up by the parish minister and his old housekeeper. Granda—she used to call him Granda —Granda Gordon—he was a drunken old bachelor but a great scholar and he must have been a very fine man too, to take in a bairn like that who would have had to go to an orphanage place but for him.'

My father was speaking as if all this were something that was familiar to both of us and that we were discussing in a friendly way, apparently unconscious that he was telling me something that was a new, dramatic and wonderful story to me. All that I had known before was that my mother had been Elizabeth Reid, that her father had been owner-captain of a small boat and that I could not see my granny and granda Reid because my granny had died and my granda had been lost at sea. I had a strange feeling, as my father spoke, that she had deliberately withheld from me the knowledge of her own early life because it must have been a strange, sad and insecure one, compared with my own lot in the heart of our family at Reachfar.

'Anyway, he was rewarded for what he did, for your mother minded on him with gratefulness all the days of her life. You know, sometimes I will be wondering if that is the everlasting life that the minister will be speaking about from the pulpit on Sundays.' He looked up at the evening sky. 'The scientific men tell us there is no Heaven up there but just countless miles of open space and stars and planets and I am thinking that the everlasting life and Heaven is to be minded on in a good way by your friends. Your mother minded on old Granda Gordon and she used to speak to me about him too so that *I* mind on him and I am always thankful to him too for what he did for her when she was a bairn. Maybe that is Granda Gordon's Heaven.'

'And now *you* are speaking about him to *me*,' I said, 'and I am thankful to him too for helping Mother so isn't that a little bit more of Heaven for him?'

My father looked down at me with something like wonder in his eyes.

'That is true,' he said quietly. 'That is true and it took brains to think of it.' He smiled at me. 'And later on, if you tell *your* bairns about him, they will mind on him and make a bittie more Heaven for him.'

We both began to laugh but it was tremulous laughter that shook on the brink of awe at the perpetuity of this Heaven that we had discovered.

'Tell me more about him,' I said after a moment.

'In a way, I don't seem to know very much when it comes to telling it. He was a minister, as I said, and fond of his dram—it was a wine called claret that he drank and he was a great scholar and the more claret he drank, the more he talked and the cleverer he seemed to get. Your mother used to say that she wished she had written down a lot of the things he said. He was

59

so clever that a lot of the simpler people round about thought he was a kind of lunatic but ignorant people will often be thinking that about those that are cleverer than themselves. Very clever people are always a bittie ahead of their time, as you might say, like the people who invented the aeroplanes. I was born just about the same time as they were but I was never clever enough to get the idea that men could fly like birds and most men who were born when I was are very much like me, a little cleverer and better schooled, maybe, but nothing startling. And then, as well as being more than naturally clever, Granda Gordon had the schooling as well—he was chockful o' Latin and Greek and Hebrew and had the Bible nearly by heart, not to mention educating your mother better than many school-teachers are educated at college.' Here was something else I had never known, largely, I saw now, because I had never noticed it, but I was remembering that, although my mother never helped me with my lessons, she could always correct my pronunciation of the names in the Greek mythology when George, Tom and I were doing a bit of reading on that subject and this was something that nobody else at Reachfar could do. 'Your mother used to imitate him,' my father was going on, 'laying off the Bible with the bottle of claret beside him and I can aye mind on the thing he used to say at the end o' the evening, as she used to tell. He would empty the last of the bottle into his glass, hold it up and look through it at the light o' the lamp and say: Vision, Elizabeth! Where there is no vision, the people perish! That bittie comes out o' the Bible and it is true. I think it is the truest and best bit that is in the whole Bible nearly. I always mind on the time that George, Tom and I carpentered the new scullery table in the barn one winter. When we carried it into the kitchen, your mother was sitting at the fire and she looked at it and said: Vision, Duncan! Where there is no vision, the people perish! in the voice o' Granda Gordon. I couldna think what she meant until, dang it, the table wouldna go through the door from the

60

kitchen to the scullery although the three of us nearly perished, trying to make it go. That is why yon table sits up on blocks. We had to cut six inches off the legs to get it in.'

We laughed again at his story and then my father went on soberly: 'But Granda Gordon had more vision than about things like the legs o' tables. One of the things that made people say he was a lunatic was that he wanted to put your mother to the university at Aberdeen and make a minister of her.'

'A minister?' I asked. I was aware of living in a later century than Granda Gordon but I had never thought of and had never heard anyone else think of turning a girl into a minister.

My father looked down at me. 'Aye. A minister and why not, if you think of it?'

I thought of it and could not think why not so I was silent.

'There are no leddy ministers as yet but they will come. In Granda Gordon's early days, there were no leddies at universities at all but by the time your mother was fifteen—that was in 1900 —a few leddies were at the universities, especially down south in England where they are always in front of us up here in these ways, so Granda Gordon had the vision to see that your mother could learn to be a minister just as well as a boy could.'

'But Mother wasn't a minister!'

'No. Granda Gordon died when she was eighteen. She was left all alone. The old housekeeper had died two years before that. And the queer thing is that Granda Gordon's vision failed him in a way that wouldna happen to stupider men. He forgot to make a will. Your mother used to say that maybe he thought he would live for ever. He used to tell her that he wouldna leave her much money because he had spent it all on books and claret but that she would get the books and the furniture. But he didna put it in writing in a will and when he died an old second-cousin of his arrived and sold the lot and went off with the money.'

'And only Mother was with him when he died?'

'Nobody was with him. She found him dead in bed one morning. He was over ninety. I have often thought to myself that when a man has to die, that is the way to do it—just do it quietly in your sleep and not be a nuisance to yourself or anybody else. He had had his claret and his talk the night before and he was just lying there, as if he was sleeping. She spoke to him two or three times before she knew he was dead.'

It may have been that the evening was growing chill but I gave a little shiver as I thought of the young girl in some big room in some old manse, realising that her Granda Gordon had gone beyond the reach of her voice, and I said hurriedly: 'And what did she do then?'

My father tapped his pipe out on the toe of his heavy boot and said: 'She took a post as a governess—that or nursing or domestic service or the like o' that was all there was for lassies in those days. And she used to be funny about that too. In one way, you see, she was angry that she never got to the university and got made into a minister and in another way, she would say: But if things had been any different, I wouldn't be here at Reachfar now. And—' his voice became very soft '—she was always happy, all the time she was at Reachfar.'

'How did she come to Reachfar?' I asked after a moment of silence.

'She came to Poyntdale, to teach young Miss Grace and Miss Laura.'

I saw a vision of Poyntdale as it had been as late as 1918, the broad acres, the spacious house with its huge staff of servants.

'My father—your granda—was still grieve then and old Sir Turk was still alive and I was first horseman in the stables. I can mind on the first day I saw your mother. Old Sir Turk could not be kept from riding about the place on an old charger he had ever since the Boer War and he wasna safe out by himself like that so the head groom was out too, half a mile behind him. I don't know where the second groom was—out with the young masters, likely—but a message came from the Big House that the gig was to be yoked for the young leddies. My father—your granda told me I was to yoke it and take it round. When I got to the door—I was leading the pony by the head—the young leddies came out and behind them was this tall dark leddy and it was a minute before it came to me that she was the new governess I had heard about. The young leddies jumped up into the gig but she smiled at me—you mind on yon bonnie slow smile she had?—and asked me what my name was. I told her and she said: How d'you do, Mr. Sandison? and then I helped her up. The young leddies was as rough a pair o' hoydens at that time as you'd see in a day's march and they were jumping about and the whole gig was shaking on its springs and they were fighting about which o' them was going to drive. I was standing there like an eediot with the reins in my hand, not knowing what to do but getting kind of angry when your mother said: 'Be quiet, you girls! Her voice was not loud or anything but it was like the crack of a whip to these two lassies. They stopped their capers right away and then she leaned down to me and smiled again and said: Give me the reins now, Mr. Sandison, please. The pony is quite quiet? and I said yes, that it was a quiet beastie, and watched them drive away down the avenue. But I canna mind on a thing about her that day except her smile and her gloves. I noticed her gloves when I helped her up and when I gave her the reins—white gloves, they were, pure white—and on the way back to the stables, I could think of nothing for wondering if the reins were clean or whether they would spoil yon bonnie gloves.'

In the fading evening light over the garden, the roseate glow of romance was all about me. I saw my father now as a hero of legend, a Perseus rescuing an Andromeda from the place where she was imprisoned with these hoydenish girls who jumped about in the high gig.

'And what then?' I asked breathlessly.

He looked down into the empty pipe in his hand and smiled. 'I used to watch for her about the place and was for ever trying to get to take the gig or the carriage round in spite of it being the second groom's job and one day my father—your granda—gave me the devil of a swearing and said I would never be grieve o' Poyntdale if I did nothing but hang about the stable yard. Then I got the idea that if I was grieve o' Poyntdale, maybe she would —well, maybe she would take me, like. But in the end it was your mother and your granny that sorted me between them—maybe Leddy Lydia was in it too. Anyway, one night I came home to Reachfar for my supper and there was the governess leddy sitting beside the fire in yon chair where she always sat, beside the meal barrel, talking to your granny and after supper Granny said: Duncan, you must see Miss Reid home to Poyntdale. After that, she came up to Reachfar every week, sometimes oftener with a message to Granny from Leddy Lydia and it didna take long between us. She came to Poyntdale in August o' the year and we were married the following March.' He smiled out over the garden again, put his pipe in his coat pocket and drew the big silver working watch from his waistcoat. 'God sake!' he said then. 'It's half-past ten! If you are to get that Inverness train o' the morning, you'll have to get to bed.'

But after we had put our tools away and before we went into the house, he looked down at me gravely and said: 'I am not sure but what I had better come to Glasgow with you in the morning after all.'

'Och, Dad,' I said, 'it's all settled and you're just talking nonsense. I can manage fine by myself.'

Before I left Reachfar for the first time, Tom and George had impressed upon me in their oblique way that I must do all I could to be a help and that I must not in any way be a 'worry' to my father in this new life we were to have together at Cairnton and, in June of 1921, it had been borne in on me, without words being spoken, that it had gone much against the grain with my father—it had worried him—to have to ask his employer for time off to take me to Glasgow to put me on the Inverness train. It was not that there was any enmity between him and Mr. Hill, the owner of Cairnshaws. Indeed, I now think that what my father saw as a tremendous favour—the few hours off to take me to Glasgow—probably went unregarded by Mr. Hill, who was very fond of my father but my father was by birth a Reachfar Sandison and did not like to go cap in hand to any man. It was not that he was incapable of humility, for I think that this virtue was highly developed in him, but the asking of a few hours of extra free time, in the middle of the summer season, smacked to him of the breach of a bargain—a thing no Sandison ever contemplated—and a breach made in the worst way, by near-snivelling and asking for consideration of his position as a widower with a child. It did not occur to him to send Jean, our housekeeper, to Glasgow with me and this, I now think, was because he did not trust her intelligence for the small undertaking but I was glad that the idea did not occur to him for to be put in the charge of Jean was the most humiliating thing he could have done to me, so little was my regard for her. So, during the last week of June, I watched him screwing himself up to approach Mr. Hill for the second time on the matter of the forenoon off until I got him alone in the garden one evening and said: 'Dad, would you let me go from here to Inverness all on my own?'

He frowned at me. 'Eh? Change stations in Glasgow all by yourself and all?'

'Yes, Dad. Why not? Look at Tommie Hill. He goes to school in Glasgow on the train and the tramcar every day.'

'Tommie Hill is bigger than you.'

'He's a silly big lump! You said so yourself. If he can do it, so can I.'

'*How* would you do it?' he asked.

'Get out of the train at Queen Street, get a porter to carry my big case and give the man my ticket. The porter would get the cab, give him sixpence, ask the cabman to go to Buchanan Street and give him one-and-six when I get there. Then buy my ticket, Inverness, third-class, half-fare, return and get a porter to take me to the train and give him sixpence.'

I had been practising this recitation like a parrot for the last few evenings and now reeled it off glibly, hoping that there was nothing vital that I had omitted.

'Dang it,' he said, 'you seem to know it as good as myself. We-ell—'

It was not difficult to persuade him but, on the morning of my departure, we spoke very little as he carried my case the mile or so to Cairnton station. I was glad that he did not talk much for deep inside me there was a sickening little flutter of panic and when I was in the compartment of the train and he shut the door on me, I wanted to burst into tears and shout: Daddy! Daddy! as I had done when I was four years old and given to the tantrums and unreasonableress.

'Now, remember,' he said, looking up at me at the high window, 'if anything goes wrong, go to the first policeman you see. Get Tom and George to send off that wire from Inverness as soon as you get in. Now, sit down before the train moves.'

I sat down in the corner but I felt quite confident now. That moment while he had looked a little upwards at me from the platform had reminded me of his strong hands round my middle when he used to hold me at arms' length above his head in the Reachfar kitchen and as the train pulled out I smiled confidently at him through the dusty glass.

I do not remember much of the journey. I think I was so inflated with my own importance that I thought of little else and there is nothing like complacent thought of oneself for shutting out all that is interesting in the world. When the train pulled in to Inverness and I stepped down, I saw the head and shoulders of George down at the far end of the platform and, abreast with him, and the width of the platform away, the head and shoulders of Tom which was the Reachfar net spread wide that they might not miss me in the crowd.

Now that the great effort was over and I had Tom and George to do my thinking for me, I blew out my chest and began, like an old war veteran, to blow my trumpet. 'You are to send a wire to Dad from Inverness here,' I commanded them.

'We have the postcard bought and ready in Tom's pocket,' George said.

'You are to send a *wire*! I came all the way from Cairnton by myself, changed stations at Glasgow and everything!'

'Goodness gracious lord almichty me!' said Tom.

'A wire,' said George, as he stood with my suitcase at his feet. 'What will we say in it?'

'Janet arrived safe?' Tom suggested.

'How would she *not* arrive safe?' George enquired of him angrily. 'We are not going to the expense of a wire to tell him something he knows already!'

I felt that we were getting into something of a muddle some-where about something, as we frequently did when our triple logic got to work but, before I could sort it out, George picked up the case and set off purposefully in the direction of the post office. 'If it is to be a wire, we should put something real fine in it,' he said as we walked on to the pavement in front of the post office where he planted the case at his feet again. 'Wires mostly brings bad news. I'd like to think of something terrible good and right cheering for him.'

'I know a thing that Dad thinks is terribly good,' I said.

'What?'

'You wait till you see it written down,' I said and marched importantly into the post office.

They put the form in front of me, put the pencil in my hand and I wrote in large capitals: 'Sandison, Cairnshaws, Cairnton Where there is no vision the people perish Reachfar.'

'It is long for a wire,' George said, 'but it will be worth it if you are sure he will like it.'

'I am sure.'

'Certain sure?' Tom asked.

'Certain sure.'

They looked at one another over my head and then George took the form and went to the counter.

This year, my little brother, who had been a baby the year before, had turned into a little boy of two years and three months old. He was dressed in a small jersey and trousers and marched about Reachfar on sturdy bare feet, the sun catching the red-gold cock's comb of a curl which started near the nape of his neck and came right over his skull to the middle of his forehead. When I looked down at this curl and into the deep blue eyes, my first thought was that Annie Black was not bonnie at all, as a fair-haired person, compared with this brother of mine.

'What do you think of that young man?' my grandmother asked me as John and I stared at one another.

'He is terribly bonnie, Granny,' I said breathlessly. He was so unexpected and so beautiful that I felt shy of him. 'Hello, John,' I said shakily.

He gave me a fleeting smile and then turned his head away to hide it in my grandmother's apron. 'Doesn't he speak?' I asked. At that moment, George, who had been putting away the horse, came into the house and saw only the back of the red-gold head against the blue apron.

'Where's the Laird?' he said. 'Och, there you are man! Did you mind to feed the dogs like I told you?'

The head came up, the 'Laird' pushed himself free of the apron and stood erect at his full height. 'Yes,' he said, looking George firmly in the eye. 'The dogs got meat,' and then he walked sturdily out of the door, away from us all, my grandmother's eyes following the red-gold head.

It took me a little time, all of July and part of August, to discover that, for my grandmother, the whole centre of Reachfar had shifted. She no longer bothered 'to give the law' around the place to the old degree. Her commanding voice seldom rang out any more. The MY GRANDMOTHER whose name always hitherto rose in my mind in strong black capital letters on a white ground had virtually disappeared, being transmuted into a white-haired blue-eyed old lady who was 'the Laird's Granny'. She was not now, it seemed, sufficiently interested in the rest of us to order us around for our good. She was withdrawn from George, Tom, Kate and me and interested only in the Laird and in my grandfather, the two objects of her constant care. I now discovered that my grandfather was ten years older than my grandmother and that for people of their class and time they had married late in life so that, in 1922 when my father was only forty-four, my grandmother was already seventy-two and my grandfather eighty-two.

I do not mean to convey, however, that they were two old people on the verge of senility for they were to live for many years longer and did not become senile even at the end. It was simply, as I have said, that my grandmother's centre had shifted from Reachfar and its people in general to this one small red-haired scrap whom she saw as the future 'Laird of Reachfar'. It was George who had nicknamed him 'the Laird' and George, who had nicknamed many people in what my grandmother called his 'clowning' way, had never given a nickname that was not subtly apt. Neither my grandmother nor my grandfather could see any of the rest of us now for their eyes were filled with the small Laird.

My grandmother, at seventy-two, was still as active and energetic as ever, busy with something from six in the morning until ten at night but, during the last year or so, she had decided that my grandfather was 'getting frail' and there would be an occasional echo from the past on wet days when the old law-giving voice would ring out: 'Granda! Come into the house here out of the wet. Have you taken leave of your senses to be mochling about out there in the rain?' Then, at meal-times, Aunt Kate was allowed to cut the meat now and serve all of us but only after my grandmother had examined all the slices and had picked out two which she deemed fit to offer to the Laird and my grandfather, whom she always served herself, as of old. Then, in the evenings, instead of laying down the law from her chair at the fire, telling us all what we had failed to do or what we had done badly that day and what we must do without fail tomorrow, she would sit nursing the Laird in her lap until he fell asleep and looking the while with covert glances at my grandfather, half asleep over his pipe in the chair opposite to her. Then she would look into the fire over the bright head in her arms with a faraway musing smile in her wise blue eyes.

I saw all this but did not speak of it to George and Tom for I knew that they could see as much and as clearly as I could and probably a great deal more and more clearly. The time was gone when I believed that Tom and George were precisely on my own mental level, when I believed that they had to learn to tell the time just as I did. About them I had made the discovery that they chose to come to my level, that that was where they liked to be and, as I was delighted to have them there, our relationship was outwardly unchanged. Now, in our free time, we did not air our criticisms of nursery rhymes or pursue the tribulations of that poor devil Christian through *Pilgrim's Progress* but George and Tom were most interested to make an excursion with me into the French language as known to a twelve-year-old in her second year at Cairnton Academy. Indeed, anything that was relevant to Cairnton Academy was of abounding interest to them, as was anything that was relevant to my father's work at Cairnshaws.

Another discovery that I made during this summer was that my Aunt Kate who, when I was four, was part of the far-away grown-up world, was, in actual fact, only fifteen years older than myself, for she was the youngest child of the family, born in 1895 when my grandmother was forty-five so that, now, in 1922, she was only twenty-seven. I also discovered that my Aunt Kate was amazingly 'bonnie' in a way quite contrasted to the way of Annie Black, for she had jet black hair with a deep wave in it, skin like the apricots that used to grow in the glasshouses at Poyntdale and big dark brown eyes that were always ablaze either with laughter, love or fury. She had something of the quality of the Reachfar Burn, I thought, sparkling sometimes and sometimes dark and flame-lit in stormy spate but never still, always live and on the move, always lilting with laughter or rumbling with rage.

The month of July slipped past and turned into August which began to build up for me towards the day when my father would make the journey north to join us, but of course, I did not tell the other members of my family about this complex that was building up in my mind. I knew that they were all looking forward to his coming as much as I was but I felt that, now, I was nearer to him than any of them were, especially when I lingered in memory over our talk about my mother. My father belonged to me, I felt, in a special way that the other people of my family would never know. I had not discovered, at that time, that all relationships are quite peculiar and private to the two people who are involved in them and it did not occur to me that my father had a special and intimate relationship with each and all of us.

Fear of the jargon of this twentieth century gives me pause here for I feel that there is a possibility that people who know no Greek and who know perhaps less of the human personality are going to say glibly that I suffered from some form of Oedipus complex at this time of my life. And I am prepared to agree that, perhaps, I did, but, if I did, I am not prepared to agree that an Oedipus complex is the dark and deleterious experience that this phrase has come to connote. As I see it, there exists in the human being a need to worship and if that need can be fulfilled, the human being is all the more complete for that fulfilment. Sometimes to the child, and perhaps to the adult, even, God in His Heaven seems too far away for the little thirst for worship to drink from the true fountain and I cannot see that it is a matter for denigration wrapped in a pretentious phrase that this thirst should be slaked from some nearer spring. Nor do I feel it to be true to accuse the father-worshipping child of worshipping a false god. As I see it, the important matter is not the quality of the god but the quality of the worship and if the worshipper is enriched and gains satisfaction from his worship, something has been added unto him. Men have been known to worship Mammon with all apparent sincerity but is there a case on record of any man who was enriched in any spiritual sense or who gained any real satisfaction from worship of this god? But I, at this time, gained great happiness and a security of peace from my worship of my father which leads me to the belief that he was a god less false than such as Mammon and that he possessed, indeed, in a very minor way, perhaps, some of the attributes of the God of love of the Christian religion.

When the day came of his arrival home, George went with the trap to meet him at Fortavoch station and sent him alone along to the house while the horse was unyoked and stabled. My grandparents, my aunt, Tom and my little brother had all gone out to the front of the house when the trap came through the moor gate but I stayed alone, standing on the rag rug in front of the kitchen fire. When I heard that firm tramp-tramp of his feet along the yard and the clock began to strike: 'Ip-it-tee-tee-tee—' all the years of my remembered life were suddenly around me and, for a few seconds, my mother was alive again, sitting in her chair beside the meal barrel in the corner, her sewing dropped into her lap as her head turned, like my own, to see him come through the doorway, his head tilted towards his left shoulder.

No. This god of mine was not false. For me, at that time, he was all-powerful, with the might that could conquer, for a few seconds, the element of time and even death itself and when he was in the room and smiling at me, I felt that, once again, my red going-to-bed boots were kicking the white-washed rafters.

'Hello, Janet,' he said, 'how is my lass?' and then he looked down at the Laird, who was staring up at him with wonder from eyes of a blue far deeper than the deep blue of my grandmother's apron. 'Aye, man!' my father said, putting his hands in his trousers' pockets and tilting back on his heels.

John took up the same attitude at once, said: 'Aye, man!' in precisely the same way and then was overcome with shyness at his momentary boldness and hid the blue eyes and the freckled face in the nearby comforting apron.

'He is still as red as a carrot in the head,' my father said, giving his big laugh. 'Where the devil did he take that from? It must have come from Elizabeth's side.'

My grandmother put her left hand, where the ring which had been boiled in so many dumplings was worn thin, on the bright cock's comb of a curl. 'No, not from Elizabeth's side,' she said proudly. 'He took that from *my* people, from the Macdonalds. My old grandfather Rory Ruadh had a beard and hair as red as fire and eyes as blue as deep water—'

'—and the old devil is lying in Eddermory Kirkyard with three wives on either side of him,' said George, appearing in the doorway carrying my father's bag.

'Be quiet, George, with that yarn in front of the bairns!' she said with a flash of the old law-giving force. 'Come to the fire, Duncan, lad, and take a dram after that long journey.'

I had never heard of my red-haired great-great-grandfather before but I had now, since hearing of my mother's background, become very interested in my ancestors and tackled my grandmother the next day on the subject of Rory Ruadh of the six wives but I did not get very far.

73

'Granny, tell me about your grandfather, Rory Ruadh.'

'Don't be disrespeckful of the dead. His name was Roderick Macdonald,' she replied sternly.

'Tell me about him then.'

'There is nothing about him to tell. He was chust an old crofter on the hill above Eddermory.'

'Did he have six wives?'

'If all that school down south is doing for you,' she told me with disgust, 'is to soften your brains till you believe all that George says, it would be better if you left it and went to domestic service. Off you go out of here with your ask-ask-asking and fill the tattie pots for me.'

I did as I was told but I also questioned the rest of my family about Rory Ruadh. My father said he had never heard of him until the night before which I believe was the truth. Aunt Kate and Tom knew nothing and George, when questioned, boldly denied ever having mentioned six wives in a churchyard at all and said that I had dreamed it. Much water has flowed under many bridges since then but I now know that Roderick Macdonald does indeed lie in Eddermory churchyard and that on each of the gravestones on either side of him are the names of three women, followed by the words 'wife of—' but, unfortunately, all the rest of the lettering on both stones is weathered away. I do not know whether my ancestor had six wives or three wives or whether these gravestones are related to him at all. The rough stone, little more than an oblong boulder, which marks his own grave simply makes the bald announcement 'Roderick Macdonald' and not a word more.

My grandmother was a clever and wise old woman and she had something of that vision without which the people perish but, at some time later than 1922, I discovered that her type of vision has a grievous fault. My grandmother believed in looking forward only and never looking back. To her, what was past was dead and she believed that the past should bury its dead and she believed it with such force that she allowed her past to bury much that was still alive and very valuable.

I have mentioned earlier that she was the best amateur veterinarian in our countryside. She had had no specific training in this science. Her ability was born of a loving kinship with animals combined with acute observation, a nimble brain and deft hands, but this was only one of her many accomplishments. Not only could she read and write a little English but she could read and write a little Gaelic too and these were abilities very unusual in her class and time. She spoke Gaelic fluently but she would never speak it in my hearing as a child for she believed that it was worse than so much excess baggage—it was, in her eyes, actively harmful, connecting me with the 'old downtrodden people of the glens of the west'.

She also had a tremendous knowledge of herbs, flowers and fruits and their uses as medicines, dyes, lotions and food. She used to concoct a lotion from elder-flowers—or the flowers of the bore-tree, as we called it—for my mother to rub on her hands in winter time that they might stay smooth for the fine sewing that she did, but my grandmother would never show my aunt or me how this was made. 'You two have no need to know that old rubbish!' she would say angrily. 'Buy a bottle of glycerine at the chemist on Friday if your hands are hacked.' And then the lawgiving voice would soften: 'I chust make a droppie bore-tree water for Elizabeth because she has such a notion of it.'

It was the same with the dyes that she made from heather roots and the wine that she made from rowan berries—she made them only because Elizabeth had a notion of home-made dye for something or a notion of a little home-made wine. After the death of her beloved Elizabeth, no more of these things were made at Reachfar and my aunt and I had not the power over her that Elizabeth had had—Elizabeth, who could do no wrong and whose every caprice had to be satisfied. I have always regretted that I have none of that herbal knowledge of hers, that smelled

75

of the earth and sun, packed away in some remote corner of my 'minder'.

In 1922, of course, I did not see so clearly how my grand-mother looked only one way and to the future but I am now aware that her mind was, all the time, on little else but the future of her grandson, the Laird. Since my mother's death, the sleeping arrangements at Reachfar had been altered. My grand-parents had moved down into the big downstairs bedroom, the best one in the house which had been my mother's and my father, when he was at home, now slept in the room upstairs that had been theirs. The year before, when I was at home, the Laird was still sleeping in a little bed in the corner of my grandparents' room but this year, I discovered, he had been moved up to my old attic between the rooms of George and Tom and I was given the bedroom that lay immediately above the kitchen. This was a 'proper' room with straight walls and a fireplace instead of the old attic whose walls began to slope inwards about a foot above floor level and I felt very grand, superior and grown-up, going to bed in it.

A night or two after my father's arrival, I was standing in front of the empty fireplace in my nightgown, ready to go to bed, when I heard my Aunt Kate's voice come very clearly up the chimney. 'Just think of Janet coming first in her class again this year in that big school! I think it's just grand!'

I sat down on the hearth and gave all my attention to the chimney vent, for praise in my family was a scarce commodity, seldom offered to your face and hardly ever offered at all, I was finding, as I grew older. At four years old, I had been told that I was a clever lass when I learned to tell the time but at twelve years old, when I came home with my first prize, the book was admired but not myself in any way. It was good to discover that my family was pleased with me after all.

However, if I expected to hear a eulogy about myself, I was disappointed for the subject soon lapsed and they began to speak

76

of Cairnshaws and my father's work but I continued to eavesdrop largely, I think, because I had been an inquisitive eavesdropper all my life and it was a habit. The family heard with wonder that Mr. Hill had given my father still another rise in pay at the end of his second year and this was news to me. I did not know that my father had had a rise at the end of the first year. I did not know how much he was paid at all for money matters were closely-guarded secrets in our household.

'It is good that you are pleasing the man, Duncan,' I heard my grandfather say in rich praise of my father. 'And you must continue to do your best for him. A good employer is due a good servant.'

My grandfather seldom spoke but, when he did, his speech had the simple dignity and ordered balance of the English that is found in the Authorised Version of the Bible and this is not surprising, for his English had been acquired mainly from the pulpit of Achcraggan Church. The words were pronounced with a Highland intonation rather than that of an Oxford don, of course, but on the whole I think that this only made them flow more musically.

'Duncan will always do his best,' my grandmother said in a tone that indicated that my grandfather's last words had been unnecessary. 'So well Mr. Hill *might* be good to him with Duncan taking on his whole place for him when himself is too sick to do much.'

Mr. Hill had been gassed during the war, I knew, and what my grandmother said was true. He was ill in bed a great deal of the time.

'You take every penny you can get, Duncan, lad,' she went on, 'and save all you can to give the bairn a good start when he comes into Reachfar.'

'There is more than one to get a start,' I heard my father say quietly and there was a queer silence before my grandmother's voice came again: 'Janet, you mean? And this capers about the university? What good is there in that? She will only go and get married and your money will chust be thrown away.'

'Education is not thrown away on Janet,' my father said. 'Her rector tells me she is as bright a nipper as he has ever come across.'

'You give her a chance, Duncan!' came my aunt's voice. 'Never mind my mother. Give her a chance!'

'Hold your tongue, you impudent limmer!' my grandmother thundered.

'Janet will get her chance, Kate,' my father said. 'Aye, will she, Mother. Elizabeth said there was to be no difference made between them as boy and girl and I will see that no difference is made. If I have anything to leave when I go, it will be divided half-and-half between them if they are both spared until then.'

'But, Duncan! *Reachfar!*'

'Reachfar too,' my father said. 'If it is mine, it will go to both of them.'

'But your son, Duncan! Your only born son! He is the last Sandison!'

'If Reachfar is mine—'

'Reachfar is yours, Duncan,' said my grandfather. 'It has been yours since the day you were born.'

'Then after me it will go to both of them.'

'Duncan Sandison—' came the thunder of the law but it died away before the gentle voice of my grandfather.

'Duncan must do what he thinks is right with what is his own,' he said. 'We will talk about this no more.'

There was a short silence, a tense silence and then I heard my father get up and cross the kitchen floor to the door. 'Father,' he said then, 'it is a grand night. Come and take a wee look round the place before we go to bed.'

I heard the less springy feet with shorter steps also cross the floor and then the opening and closing of the kitchen door. 'Only once before in his life did Duncan defy me,' I heard my grandmother say and then she too left the kitchen and I heard her come upstairs. I shot from the hearth into the bed and pretended to be asleep for I felt that that sixth sense of hers which some people called Second Sight had told her that I was eavesdropping but she did not come into my room. She went past the door and on up the next narrower flight of stairs to the room that held the sleeping Laird.

When I awoke the next morning, the first thing to come into my mind was that speech of my grandmother's: 'Only once before in his life did Duncan defy me' and I was filled with the desire to know when and what this great occasion had been. I was not in the least interested in my father's plans for the disposal of Reachfar. Indeed, I think I was anxious to forget all that had been said on that subject for it implied the acceptance of the death of my father as a valid idea and this I could not do. It is possible that my fixation on my father's earlier act of defiance of my grandmother was even some sort of escape mechanism that filled my mind to the exclusion of the earlier talk.

It was, however, a little difficult to 'come around' the subject of my father's defiance without giving away the fact that I had been eavesdropping and, in addition, it was harvest time now and everybody was very busy but, one evening, I cornered George and Tom in the barn, where they were sharpening binder knives for the next day. George now, by the way, no longer worked at Dinchory as grieve because my grandfather and Tom could no longer work Reachfar without his help so he and Tom were even closer cronies than they had ever been.

'There is an old bag at the door there—' said Tom as I approached.

'—and wipe your feet before you come in here,' said George.

'My feet? What for?'

'Since you went to Cairnton,' said Tom, 'have you got to be so much of the city that you have not noticed that your Aunt Kate has infested the place with a flock o' geese?'

'I have always said,' said George, 'that you would be as good—'

'—with a cattle beast with the spring skitter about the place,' I said, wiping my feet on the bag, 'as a goose.'

'Where in the world did you hear the like o' that?' George asked me.

'From you. Who else?'

'When?'

'The time we read yon book with Goosey-goosey-gander in it that Lady Lydia gave me.'

'I have always been of the opeenion,' said Tom, 'that it is chust terrible the memory that is in her, George. But God knows, it is true about them geese—they are dirty clarty booggers. Chust hand me that wee file from over there on the kist, Janet.'

I handed him the file and sat down on the corn kist. 'Tom, how long have you been at Reachfar?'

'Since the year o' Waterloo,' said George. 'Why was you asking?'

'And if it is Rory Ruadh again,' said Tom, 'I have told you already that I do not know whether he had six wives or ten and I do not care either.'

'Oh, poop to Rory Raudh!' I said. 'It's my father that I wanted to ask about.'

'Your father?' Tom stopped work for a moment and looked at me. 'Well, now, that is different and sensible and reasonable. What was you needing to know?'

I had approached the matter a little rashly, I now found and could think of nothing to say for a moment until I had a flash of inspiration that made me ask the question that would come most naturally and innocently from me. 'Was he clever at school?'

'*Now*,' said Tom in a very satisfied tone, 'that is a reasonable-like thing to ask instead of all that capers about Rory Ruadh that chust puts Herself in a paddy. Yes, indeed, your father was *very* clever at the school, for myself was still at the school for a wee while after he came to it first and I mind on him fine and how he was the cleverest one that was in it. Ould Dominie Gregor thought the world of him'.

'Aye, the ould devil,' George said. 'Do ye know, Tom, that Duncan never got one walloping from old Dominie Gregor all the time he was at the school?'

'And that is more than is to be said of yourself, George, man. As I mind on it, I do not think there was one day in the nine years o' your schooling that you didna get your backside warmed.'

'I never had much liking for the school someway,' George said.

'No, nor me either forbye an' besides,' Tom agreed with him, 'but I went to it a lot more days than you did.' He turned to me. 'I don't know what way it was but temptation aye seemed to take a firmer grip on George an' it gripped him oftener than it did the rest off us. Now, an odd day here an' there, I would slip the school an' go poaching with some of the lads for rabbits round the bottom o' the Cobbler but with George it wasna chust the odd day here an' there. What with poaching an' going to sea with the fishermen or going off after gulls' eggs he was so danged busy that he never came to school unless he was fair beat. Then the Dominie would wallop him when he got hold of him and then tell Herself and *she* would wallop him at home here but none off it ever did a damn o' good.'

'I never *took* to the school, like,' George explained.

'But your father now,' Tom continued, 'that was a different thing. He was for ever at his books and never at the gulls' eggs or the poaching or any o' that and I mind when he would be about thirteen or fourteen—I was at Reachfar, working by then— he would come home o' the evening, give us a bit of a hand outside and then have his supper and then he would be into his books again.'

'And Herself would let fly at me with yon bittie stick off the rodden tree if I made a noise,' said George.

'Aye. Herself was for to make a minister or a doctor of him.'

'Of *Dad*?' I asked, amazed.

'Surely,' George told me sternly. 'They will be telling me yourself is not bad at the school. Who do ye think ye got your brains from? Tom or me?'

'Dad said I got the little I have from my mother.'

'Och, he never was one to make much of himself,' Tom said. 'I am not saying that your mother was not clever, because she was, but your father was a good scholar too. But the thing about Duncan, George, was that he never had any o' that wild ambeetion that is in Herself. When she was a young woman—maybe you will not mind on it as clear as me—she was a tartar. She hadna been that long down from Eddermory away in the west an' she hated the very stink o' the gentry.' Tom turned to me again. 'Granda wasna grieve at Poyntdale then—it wasna much of a place in those days. It was Sir Torquil an' Leddy Lydia that made a place of it. Leddy Lydia had a big fortune from the duke, her father, an' I think that helped. But in the ould days, when your father was born, it was ould Sir Turk that was at Poyntdale an' he was more a soldier than a laird. He was a Cheneral in the army, ye know, an' was away foreign a lot o' the time an' Poyntdale going wild to ruin. Then he retired from the army and him and his wife came home here. Leddy Turk was English and very high an' mighty in her ways—God sake, George, it comes to me that maybe you have never heard how Herself in the house there sorted Leddy Turk?'

'What was that?' George asked.

'Och, it was about the time when ould Queen Vick was going about reading the Bible to the crofters about Balmoral an' that an' Leddy Turk started going about here with her Bible in her oxter an' she came up here to Reachfar one day. This was before my time at Reachfar but I heard it from ould Katie Farquhar who was here when it happened. Katie was the midwife then and Duncan was only a week or two old and Katie had come up to see how he was doing, as was her way. Leddy Turk chust walked into the house with never a knock at the door or damn all an' said that she was come to read a few words o' the Bible. Katie said that Herself stood up—ye know the way she can lift that head o' hers—an' gave Leddy Turk yon glare o' her eyes and said: When I have time to read the Bible, I will read it for myself. I will thank you to take your leave. This is my house.— Ould Katie swore it was as true as she was alive and, for myself, I believe her.'

'Och, aye,' George laughed. 'It will be true right enough.'

'What happened then?' I asked, breathless.

'Well, it seems that Leddy Turk went away right enough but that night, Sir Turk himself came up to give Herself a row for being rude to his wife.' Tom now laughed. 'It was Sir Turk that got the row. Herself told him that Poyntdale was a disgrace, that he had the best land in the countryside lying idle while the folk round about was in poverty and getting the Bible read to them. She gave him a right good dressing-down and then ordered him down the hill off Reachfar too but the funny thing was he was for ever riding up here after that, coming to the door and saying: May I come in, Mrs. Reachfar? as polite as you like and then he took Himself on as grieve and started farming Poyntdale. That was when I came here, to help with the place when Reachfar himself was down the hill at Poyntdale.'

'What year would that be, Tom?' I asked.

'Och, it was a good whilie ago. I was chust out o' the school. Your father was six or seven and in the Baby Class at the time.'

'So it would be 1884 or 1885?'

'Tell me, now, Tom,' said George in a pompous voice, 'what was the date o' Waterloo?'

George and Tom did not like to be pinned down to the exactitude of precise dates, regarding this almost as an invasion of their privacy, and I recognized this question as a danger signal that meant that I was being over-scholarly, generally pompous and too big for my boots so I went off on a different tack.

'And was it true that Granny told Sir Turk, that the people were in poverty? Was there poverty at Reachfar?'

'Something very like it.'

It was George who answered me and I had never seen his face so grave since the day my mother died.

'But, Tom, if there was poverty, how could Granny be trying to make a minister or a doctor out of my father?'

'Your granny would try anything and she was fit for anything in those days. It is not *her* fault that he is not a minister or a doctor. If he had stayed at the school, she would have got the money from somewhere for the books and the university an a-all.'

'That's true,' George said. 'It was your father that left the school and she has never got over it even yet. Did you notice the other night how her mind went back to it, Tom?'

'Aye. Aye, I noticed.'

I suddenly saw that, almost by accident, I was getting to the point that I wanted to reach. 'Why did Dad leave school?' I asked.

With one accord, they both stopped working, laying aside their files and reaper knives and taking out their pipes and tobacco, they leaned against the shiny wooden side of the threshing mill.

'It was the year o' '92,' Tom said. 'That is one date I can give you, you that is so keen on dates, but there is not one living about here that was alive in that year that could not give you the date of it.'

It was beginning to grow dark in the barn, where the only light came from the open door and a dusty skylight up in the roof and it also began to feel strangely cold.

'It was a thing I have never seen happen since,' Tom said, 'and I hope that I never will see it happen again. We lost the harvest with a flood of rain that went on for a month and then we lost the tattie crop with a late September frost that didna break until January. The frost was two and a half feet in the ground in some places. Horses, cattle, pigs and sheep died. And people died too. By the start o' December here at Reachfar, there was a meal for one more week at the bottom o' the big barrel in the corner and not a hope of any more of our own until the next harvest.'

'That was the night that Duncan left the school,' George said quietly, 'the night you stole the roasted leg of mutton, Tom.'

'Aye. That was the night. But we will not speak about that mutton for, although I stole it, I have no conscience about it and it is not right to steal and have no conscience about it. I could wish that you had not mentioned it, George, but we will say no more of it.' He paused to light his pipe and then went on: 'We had had our porridge and Herself was saving the meal, ye see, so we didna have very much and your Auntie Mary that's in Canada, she was only a wee craitur, she started to cry for more. Then your Auntie Bell that's in America and Auntie Jessie that died before you was born, they were bigger but they started to cry too and say that they were hungry. It was then that I went down the hill and did that that George said I did. I brought it in and gave it to your Granny and it seems as if that gave your father the courage to speak. He was a big quiet lad, ye know, and spoke very little and never argued or was at variance with anybody, especially your Granny. He chust took it that her word was law—I don't think he knew till he was older that her word was never the law to your Granda for a lot of people have never found that out.'

I myself was among the lot of people who had never found this out. Until Tom told me that my grandmother had never been able to command my grandfather, I had thought that he obeyed her as all the rest of us did but now that I gave the matter consideration, I saw that a phrase I had learned at Cairnton, 'henpecked husband', certainly did not, somehow, fit my grandfather. But I said nothing and Tom went on: 'Anyway—dang it, if I am to make you understand right about this, I have to get back to speaking about that danged leg o' mutton!'

'I will do the speaking of the rest of it,' George said. 'I have no conscience about speaking or not speaking about that leg o' mutton. It was the best meat I ever ate.' He turned to me. 'Tom came in and hauled the leg o' mutton out from under his jacket—it had a bittie tattie bag tied round it, as I mind—and clapped it on the table in front o' your Granny. She chust looked at him but never said a word—chust took the big knife and started cutting bits off and giving them to us a-all, but your Granda started asking Tom where he got it and making a row, for he knew where Tom had got it—out o' the kitchen oven at Poyntdale. Ould Liz Robertson was the cook at Poyntdale but she was deaf and fond o' her dram into the bargain. Many a puckle scones and pots of jam I went off with out o' that kitchen when her back was turned.—It was Granda himself that had said in the house here that Sir Turk was coming up from Edinburgh with some friends o' his and that a side o' mutton an' the leg o' a bullock had been sent up before him.' George's eyes narrowed, his face sharpened. There was nothing of the genial clown about him now. 'Sir Turk might have been a good soldier to the country but he hadna much thought for the people o' the country—not even men like my father who worked for him. 'His face brightened as his grimmer thoughts were battened down again. 'Och, he wouldna be meaning to be greedy or selfish likely—it is chust that he didna think and being away so much maybe he didna know what the loss o' the harvest an' the tattie crop meant to us. It was chust a local thing in the north here—not a big thing like these famines you will be reading about in big countries like China. Anyway, your Granda was going to thrash Tom for stealing the leg o' mutton—'

'And you was squaring up to make a fight of it, George—'

'—and the lassies were frightened and started crying again and it was then that Duncan stepped in between my father an' you—' George was addressing Tom now '—and—'

'Aye,' Tom said. 'I can mind on the very words he said for I was fair flabbergasted, as they say, at Duncan coming into the row at all, much less standing up to Himself when he was in a rage. You will not hit Tom, Father, he said—'

'—for he is the only man worth a damn on Reachfar tonight,' George added. 'If you are going to tell the story, Tom, you might as well tell it right.'

'I am telling it good enough. God, I can see Himself now. He backed away from Duncan and the light from the fire shining on yon big black whisker—it is only since he got up in years a little that his whisker got white, ye know,' he informed me. 'He was as black o' the hair and whisker as the back o' the fire-grate in them days. And there was Duncan in the middle o' the floor an' his lesson books was in a bundle on the table an' he turned to your Granny an' said: You can put these books bye in the garret, Mother. I didna go to the school the-day. I went an' engaged as third ploughman at Seamuir.—God, I was frightened, George, man. Do you mind on Herself when he said that?'

'Aye. I was kind of uneasy myself,' George agreed. 'I would have said before then that Duncan was more frightened of her than any of us for I had never heard him speak back to her before —not that he spoke back to her much *then*, when I think on it. I canna mind on anything much that he *said* but I can mind on him standing there and Herself like to burst into flames but the next morning I can mind on him tramping off east by the steading there, going to work at Seamuir.'

'Did he work at Seamuir for long?' I asked.

'A year or two,' George replied. 'But by then ould Sir Turk had kind of come to his senses and was taking an interest in the estate—he had seen there was money in other things besides soldiering, I suppose and he took your father on at the winter term as fourth man—it was when he got his fourth pair o' horse. Doll an' Dandy, they were called, a grand pair o' chestnuts—I can mind on them yet. I was mad for to get taking a furrow down the Long Ley with them but your father would let nobody lay a hand on them but himself.' He turned to Tom. 'Ye know, Tom, in a way it is maybe chust as well that Duncan never got to be a doctor or a minister. He is terrible fond o' the horses an' the ground.'

'That is true, George. It is funny the way things turn out. I doubt he would not have cared for the doctoring for he'll not even put a ring in a pig's nose an' he hasna enough gab to be a minister, when you think on it. It is not that he is not clever or doesna know anything but he is not one to stand up in a pulpit an' lay off fit to split himself like the Reverend Roderick, for instance. And here, that chust reminds me, Janet. I was minding ever since we was at the kirk last Sunday to be asking you why you put the Reverend Roderick's text for his sermon in yon wire we put off to your father from Inverness. As sure as I am here, you could have knocked me down with a barley yaavin when the Reverend Roderick stood up and said—'

George, Tom and I were much given to mimicking various local personalities when those in authority were out of hearing and Tom had a complete mastery of the soft Hebridean accent of our learned minister.

'—Where there eez no veeshion, the people pereesh! Brethren, I am speaking to you this Lord's day apout the veeshion of Kod, the clorious veeshion to which our eyes, that see so much of lesser theengs, are so often plind, plind as the pat that flies in the dark off the night. Hear again these words: Where there eez no veeshion—'

'Tom!' came the voice of the law from the barn door. 'Stop that wicked blaspheming this minute! And George and Janet, fools that listen to fools are worse than fools!'

Under her stern eye, we all seized binder knives, files or oily rags and disappeared with them into the dark shadowy corner of the barn, there to stand uneasily until the presence withdrew from the doorway, so that I never had to explain to George and Tom the reason for the text of the telegram.

When I went up to bed that night, I gave my attention to the voices that came up the chimney and although I listened for a time each night until the end of the holiday, I did not hear anything more that interested me.

It is my way to follow a single thread of interest at a time and, at this time, my interest was centred entirely on my father. My little abortive excursion in search of Rory Ruadh, my red-haired great-great-grandfather of the six wives, was an offshoot, as it were, of my interest in my father and Tom, who was not in the least interested in Rory Ruadh, would talk for hours about Duncan. I recognised that on that night of the stolen leg of mutton, when my father had stood between Tom and the rage of my grandfather, my father had taken on, for Tom, the aura of a hero and a hero to Tom he still remained. Before the end of the holidays, Tom told me of many incidents in the young life of my father, George and himself but there is only one conversation that I shall record here.

I had said to Tom, concealing the fact that I was a little hurt about it, that it was 'funny' how my small brother would not speak to me at all for several days after I arrived because he was so shy and yet had said 'Aye, man!' to my father within the first few minutes and now went everywhere with him, chattering like a magpie.

'Och, but your father is special good with bairns,' Tom said, 'the best, indeed, that I have ever seen. It seems that a man is always good with things and creatures that he is terrible fond of and your father is terrible fond of bairns. You mind how I was telling you about how he went to work at Seamuir? I aye mind on the night at the end o' the six months when he came home with his first pay. He gave the money to your granny and when she counted it there was only nine pound in it and she said she thought he had bargained for ten.—So I did, he said, but I have got this—and he went out to the passage and came in with a tattie bag. Inside it was pairs o' wee boots for the three wee lassies, your aunties—not your Auntie Kate of coorse for she wasna born then—and a bag o' sweeties for them an' a wee doll for Mary. But they liked the boots better than the sweeties or the doll for they were the first boots they ever had.'

I had had no idea that there had ever been poverty of this kind at Reachfar and as I remembered my own one-two-three pairs of boots, a new thought struck me.

'But, Tom, were there bad harvests all the time? Why had they no boots? I had *three* pairs of boots when I was little.'

'Och, so you had, but Reachfar was a different place then, bigger an' better in every way.'

'Bigger?'

'Well, more of it arable. That was your father's doing too. When I first came here, there was only ten acres of arable altogether, chust the Long Park at the back o' the house. The rest of it was heather moor. The first bit that we took in was the Little Parkie out there. I can mind your father arguing with your grandfather that at one time there must have been no arable hereabouts until somebody ploughed up bits o' the moor. Your granda said the moor would never make arable but your father went on arguing in his quiet way and one spring evening he brought Doll an' Dandy up from Poyntdale an' drew the first furrow o' the Little Parkie. We had no horses up here then that would have taken a plough through yon heather. A year or two after that, we had better horses and your grandfather was for ploughing up the whole moor but your father wouldna agree to that either. He said that high as Reachfar is, we should keep the moor with the trees for winter shelter an' that is what we did an' he was right. Later on, when we got the Highland cattle an' the sheep, that sheltered moor was the life o' them an' it's the life o' them yet. An' it is from cattle an' sheep that the bairns on Reachfar gets boots.'

I tried to visualise Reachfar as it had been in those days before my birth, before the turn of the century, when there was no arable land except the field to the north of the house, at the bottom of which ran the march wall between us and the estate of Poyntdale.

'The moor came right in to the house on the east, south and west?' I asked Tom.

'Surely. And the house was low of the walls and thatched with a clay floor in the kitchen. An' we had two booggers o' goats that was for ever up on the thatch, dancing about on the roof tree. Goats is deevils to climb.'

'When was the house made as it is now?'

'When ould Kenny an' Farquhar came back from New Zealand. 1901, I think it was. You and your dates!'

It was about this time, in 1922, that comic strips were beginning to appear in the newspapers, an introduction from the United States of America. One Glasgow newspaper featured a strip entitled 'Mutt and Jeff' and another recorded the social difficulties of a newly-rich family called 'The Jiggs'. When Tom spoke in this factual way of 'ould Kenny an' Farquhar', it was as if he had casually mentioned Mutt, Jeff and Mr. and Mrs. Jiggs having paid a visit to Reachfar for, ever since 'always', Kenny and Farquhar had been, for me, the equivalent of a comic strip. They were something like Sandy of the red whiskers who lived in the deep Reachfar well, laying in wait for children who went near that dangerous place and Rory of the black whiskers who lived in the old quarry, waiting to make children fall over his precipice. By the time I was eight years old, I had forced George and Tom, the creators of Sandy and Rory, to admit that these characters were fictitious and at about the same time I made up my mind that Kenny and Farquhar were of the same ilk, but created for my amusement rather than to keep me out of danger.

'Kenny and Farquhar really existed?' I asked now.

'Existed?' Tom looked indignant as if I were making a most unjust accusation against him. 'Surely they existed! Kenny existed until he was a hundred and three an' Farquhar until he was a hundred and four. What is that academy down there doing to your brains?'

'But who *were* they?'

Tom stared at the sky. 'Who *were* they, she says! They were your granny's grand-uncles, that's who they were, an' as fine a pair of old chentlemen as you could wish to meet, if a little what they call essentric towards the end.'

'They really did run down the hill through the snow in their night-shirts when Granny tried to make them change their underwear?'

'Surely they did an' it was all George an' I could do to catch them too. They were wonderful old chentlemen for their age.'

'So they came back here from New Zealand?'

'God sake, you know that fine!' Tom said. 'How often have George an' myself told you about when they were going out there in the sailing ship an' the Irishman chumped overboard in the Indian Ocean an' was going to swim back to Ireland?'

'But, Tom, I thought it was all just a yarn.'

'You have no right,' he said virtuously, 'to make out that George an' myself is such liars as that. And it is disrespeckful to ould Kenny an' Farquhar forbye. They may have grown a little odd as they got older but when the glen of Eddermory was cleared to make way for sheep, they left for New Zealand without a penny an' the both of the two of them came back here with quite a bittie money. An' they did a lot for us here at Reachfar. They had never married an' they were glad to have a home here in the north to end their days an it was their money that made Reachfar house the fine sturdy place that it is.' He looked at me sternly. 'Chust you imachine you thinking that your great-grand —no, your great-*great*-grand-uncles—was nothing but a yarn!'

'Their names aren't on the gravestone at Achcraggan,' I defended myself.

'Why *would* they be? They were Macdonalds. When they died, we took them back to Eddermory where they belonged, the fine old chentlemen, and with some of the money they left your granny made an arrangement so that their grave will always be kept tidy an' no danged *sheep* allowed to graze on it.'

'I see,' I said.

'So well you might see, although it takes the devil of a lot of speaking to *make* you see sometimes. Where did you think we could build a house and steading like this out o' that few acres out there? Have you no sense?' He glared at me for a moment but when he spoke again, his eyes and voice softened. 'Your father was the one that planned the buildings. I can mind on him saying that where the money lay was in good well-bred stock and that you couldna raise good stock without the proper housing for them. Ould Kenny an' Farquhar put up the money but your father put up the brains that built Reachfar.'

I said no more but I was thinking that it was indeed true that where there is no vision, the people perish.

Part Three

1926-45

IN 1926, when I was sixteen, my father married as his second wife our Cairnton-born housekeeper, Jean Grey, and it seemed to me that the living god I had worshipped had had not only feet of clay but had been made throughout of some brittle shoddy substance that fell to powder at the first shock. It did not occur to me that we ourselves create the vision and the substance of the god whose presence we feel about us and that it was the thing of my creation that was brittle and shoddy and not the man who had inspired the creation. The vision of my father which I had created was romanticised, sentimentalised and grossly false, an insult to the reality that he was. I saw him as the peasant boy of fairy-tale who had married the romantic princess. I saw him as Perseus rescuing the Andromeda who had been my mother. I saw him as her bereaved lover who would go to his grave still faithful to her memory in his broken heart in the sickliest romantic tradition. I saw him as everything except what he was, simply a man and a devoted father who was doing what he thought to be the best, in his simple way, for his humble house and for his children.

There is no yardstick for measuring the human personality. Although I was still an effortless prize-winner at school and accustomed to being regarded as 'clever'—so much so that I believed it myself—I was, in reality, a slow-witted, slow-maturing, almost backward child and, into the bargain, I must have been blind as well for I lived in daily contact with my father and Jean and, yet, when he told me of his decision to marry her, the shock of something so unexpected brought me to the verge of physical collapse. I felt that my father had done this thing behind my back, that he had cheated me. I felt that he was guilty of disloyalty to the memory of my mother and of disloyalty to me because, although I had been at pains to conceal it from him so that he was unaware of it, Jean was an enemy of mine. I felt, in a snobbish way, that he was marrying 'beneath the Sandisons' and, above all, I was probably jealous, although I did not recognise it, that there was anybody in my father's life besides myself. It is impossible and it would be tedious, in any case, to make a catalogue of the feelings that raged in me and amid all that is reprehensible the only thing that I can say in my own favour is that I did not make a scene of any kind, but tried to accept the shattering development with at least a semblance of calm.

The marriage took place in the summer of 1926, my father and Jean went on a short honeymoon and then, later, they came up to join us all at Reachfar. I do not think that it is entirely my dislike of her that makes me say that Jean was not a very attractive character but it is certainly true to say that I, no matter how hard I tried to avoid it, never failed to bring out the very worst that was in her. She had a hysterical nature and a violent temper but my father had never seen a display of her temper until after the marriage took place for, before they were married, whatever I may have seen of Jean that I did not like, I concealed it from my father, as part of my policy of not being a 'worry' to him.

In my egotistic way, I have said that the marriage caused a complex of feelings in myself, but Jean also had feelings and if my father and I felt like strangers in a strange land at Cairnton, Jean felt even more of a stranger in a stranger land at Reachfar, I have no doubt. Then, the man she had married was a widower with two children and one of the children, myself, bore a strong physical resemblance to his first wife. Also, although the family at Reachfar tried hard to make her welcome, it was very close-knit in its inner relationships and Jean, not very subtle herself, made things no easier by writing Tom and George off from the start as a pair of stupid bumpkins, patronising my aunt's un-married state, shouting at my quiet grandfather as if he were stone deaf, which he was not, and laying down the law to my grandmother whom she saw as 'an auld country wifie' as con-trasted to her town-bred self. The atmosphere became more and more volcanic as the first week of the visit turned into the second and culminated in a scene between Jean and myself—a scene, I think it is true to say, that was generated through the fault of neither of us—where Jean relieved her pent-up temper by hurl-ing at me the big kitchen knife, probably the knife which once cut the stolen leg of mutton, in full view of my grandmother and Tom who happened to come into the kitchen at the crucial moment.

Until then, my grandmother had tried harder than any of us to make Jean one of the family and had accepted in a way almost unbelievable to my aunt and me her laying down of the law as an up-to-date townswoman in these backwoods but in the moment when the knife vibrated in the wood below the mantel and about six inches from my temple, Jean suddenly saw the majesty of the real law-giver of Reachfar. The next day was a Sunday but, on the Monday, the honeymoon ended in ignominy when George drove the new-wed pair away across the moor to the station at Fortavoch.

On the Sunday afternoon, however, while Jean kept to her bedroom, I went for a walk with my father and we looked at each other fully for the first time since the barrier of the mar-riage had risen between us. I remember that I felt guilty as we set off up the farmyard and through the gate into the moor and that I resented this feeling of guilt, telling myself in a self-pitying way that it was not my fault that my father was worried like this.

This guilt was the result of the Reachfar training which had laid down, from my earliest days, that 'proper persons' did not make scenes or become involved in scenes. Scenes were indulged in only by 'drunken tinker wives' and the like, and in spite of the fact that my grandmother and Tom had been witnesses of the knife-throwing episode and had spoken on my behalf, I still felt that I had been guilty of something which I had been trained to regard as low and degraded. The sense of injustice that accompanied the guilt was born of the fact that, no matter how hard I tried, Jean and I had never been able to reach any form of understanding largely because, it seemed to me at the age of sixteen, I was so completely the product of the training to which I had been subjected by my family. Everything that I had been taught, it seemed to me, was exactly what Jean deemed undesirable in a girl of sixteen. I had little personal vanity, preferred books to boys, was more interested in going to school than to the cinema—in short, I belonged to the mould of Reachfar and not to that of Cairnton. I was no nearer to having a saintly temper than I had been at four years old but, for twelve years, my mother and then my father and then Tom and George at intervals had been impressing on me that a controlled temper is a more deadly weapon than an uncontrollable one and I had proved this for myself in my relationship with Jean. At Cairnton, when my father was out at work and Jean and I came to one of our perpetual differences of opinion about something, the more hot and inarticulate she became, the more calm did I become and the more incisive my tongue grew. When I look back to those days, I find myself astonished that she had not killed me long before the day of the near-miss with the knife in the Reachfar kitchen, for I do not mean to be boastful when I say that a person of my intelligence should have behaved to someone of less intelligence in a more understanding way. But here was the training of Reachfar once more. Jean, a woman of about forty, was, to me at sixteen, part of that 'grown-up' world and although I privately thought that she was a weak-tempered fool, this was a guilty thought that was counter to all the principles of my upbringing, a main one of which was that every 'grown-up person' in the world *ipso facto* knew more than I did and was in every way entitled to my respect.

My father's face was solemn, his brows frowning a little as we went through the moor gate and, as soon as we were on the path through the heather, he said: 'Has Jean ever thrown anything at you before or tried to hurt you in any way?'

'I don't think you understand, Dad,' I said. 'She didn't really throw that knife at me or try to hurt me.'

He stopped and glared at me angrily. 'Are you trying to tell me that Granny and Tom are a pair of liars?'

I somehow understood that his rage was born of some mixture of puzzlement, disappointment and even regret, perhaps, and in that moment I discovered that I knew more about Jean than he did. It was a strange feeling, this discovery that it was possible for me to know more than my father did about anything, for even although I could speak tolerable French now and he could not speak it at all, such academic knowledge did not count for me. This knowledge which I had about Jean was what I inwardly called 'a real thing about life 'and it was strange to find that, unwittingly, I had travelled into the jungle of life on my own and had gained an inner knowledge of part of this territory called 'Jean' which was quite unknown to my father who, I had thought, controlled my whole life and all the journeys I made.

Although I seemed to discover this knowledge that I knew more of Jean than my father did in a sudden way as we walked across the moor, it had been growing in me for some time, ever, indeed, since they had returned to Cairnton from their honeymoon, when my father had first seen Jean in one of her rages. On that evening, she had not thrown anything, but had indulged in loud words and louder tears and, afterwards, my father had questioned me about the scene, just as he was questioning me now. At that time, however, the shock of the marriage was still too fresh in my mind and I was still too hurt with my father for our talk to lead anywhere. Words were difficult and we were walking on the alien soil of Cairnton. But now, on the home ground of Reachfar, from which I always seem to draw strength, when a little more time had elapsed since the marriage and my love for my father was conquering my spurious sense of injury, I felt the confidence of my knowledge of Jean and words came to me easily.

'It is no good you getting angry,' I said, which was a sort of thing—a telling him of how to behave—which I had never said to him in my life before. 'What I mean is that when Jean threw the knife yesterday, it was just chance that it was a knife. It was the nearest thing to her hand. It could have been a plate or a dish-cloth or anything.'

'So she makes a habit of throwing things?'

'Not exactly. It is that she gets in a temper and wants to *say* things but she can't find the words for what she means and she simply has to do *some*thing. I know exactly how she feels. I used to feel like that myself when I was little. I think everybody has felt like that.'

'A woman of her age should know better and control herself better,' he said, speaking the gospel of Reachfar.

'Dad,' I said, 'I don't think age has much to do with it. It is more the way people are brought up and educated. And there is another thing. Jean has never liked *me*, you know, never since we first went to Cairnton. I have never seen her get into rages like that except at me. There is just something about me that makes it that I can never please her no matter what I do.'

He walked on, looking down at the ground. 'I always thought the two of you got on fine,' he said. 'That was one of the reasons why--she always kept your clothes and everything in such splendid order when you were younger, seemed to take so much interest in how you looked and was so good about the house and all.'

'I know she looked after my clothes well, Dad, and she is a first-class housewife. But it was her pride in her job that would not have *me* looking shabby or badly looked after.'

'I never knew that the two of you did not get on,' he said in a puzzled, worried voice that I found unbearable.

'That is my fault, Dad. I always tried to hide it from you because, when we first went to Cairnton, George and Tom and everybody said I was to try not to worry you. And I thought you would be worried if you knew about the arguments between Jean and me and so—'

'It seems to me that George and Tom have made you nearly as cute and hidden as they can be themselves when it comes up their backs,' he said.

'They meant it for the best, Dad, and so did I.'

'Aye, I am sure they did and I am sure you did too. And when I married Jean, I meant that for the best too.'

We walked along the narrow 'sheep roadie' among the scattered fir trees in silence for a while, both thinking of marriage. My father's views on it were simple and straightforward, that marriage was a final and irrevocable step, that a bed made had to be lain on. I thought this too. Divorces might take place in books, newspapers and the upper classes but were as remote from the lives of people like us as were the tribal customs of Africa. But true marriage, for me, meant what had happened to my mother and father, the princess and the peasant boy who got married and came to Reachfar where they lived happily ever— But my mother had died six years ago and now my father had married Jean. It was all too difficult.

'I don't belong to the class of people that keeps servants,' he said next, 'and I have spent enough time working for other people to know that even with the best will in the world, you can't work as well for another man, or take the same interest, as when you are working with a thing that is your own. Mr. Hill has been very good to me and Cairnshaws is a good enough dairy farm but I wouldn't give one divot of this heather moor here for all the acres of it. Jean has always been good to me and has kept the house right down there and all and the time is going to come when your Aunt Kate will marry and go away from here and when Granda and Tom are going to need me here as well as George. It seemed to me a good-like thing that Jean and I should get married. A good housewife like that is worthy a place that is her own. But I didna know this about her and you.'

Love has its own strange powers. In the face of my father's worry, I felt the love for him swell and swell inside me and then it seemed to flower all over, like a tree bursting into sudden blossom, with thoughts, practical ideas that I could put into words and bring to his aid.

'But, Dad,' I said, with a nonchalant aplomb that I did not know I commanded, 'in a very few years now I'll be out in the world on my own, so there is no point in your worrying your head about *me*. And when I come south in October, I'll be at the university all day and Jean will hardly ever see me. Besides, I have more sense now and I know how to avoid making her angry. That row yesterday was mostly excitement at the young heifer calving and being in such trouble and everything. I kind of lost my head when Jean got excited and told her not to be stupid and she doesn't like to be called stupid and that was how it started.'

'So you think she is stupid?' he asked.

Every person has his or her own brand of integrity. I was prepared to go to great lengths to comfort my father in the present situation but to compliment him on having married an intelligent woman was beyond the lengths that integrity would permit.

'By my standards, for what they are worth which may not be much, she is stupid,' I said.

He walked a few steps in silence and then: 'By my standards, your standards will do,' he said. 'I know she is stupid, except for being able to do housework and cook and bake and the like. But it is for housework and the like that I wanted a wife, not for—anything else.'

When he said this, another thing that had been born in me on the evening we had talked after Jean's first fit of rage at Cairnton now seemed to be fully defined and grown and that was a queer unsympathetic pity for Jean. I did not like her any better than I ever had but I could not help feeling sorry for a woman whom a man had married because she could cook, bake, wash and clean a house and would probably cost him less as a wife than she had cost as a paid housekeeper. It is an irritating thing to feel vaguely sorry for someone whom one fundamentally dislikes and it is a disillusioning thing to feel that someone who one loves, as I loved my father, had made of marriage a sort of bargain, even if it was a bargain that pleased beyond all words the woman he had married, for there was no doubt that Jean was delighted with her new state in spite of the tribulations into which she had been led by the existence of myself. Indeed, from Jean's point of view, but for my existence, the marriage was perfect.

So, feeling sorry for Jean and disillusioned by what my father had done, in the unfair way in which my mind—and many minds are similar to mine, I think—works, I blamed all this mental discomfort not on my father whom I loved but on Jean whom I disliked. And I do not think I was the only one at Reachfar who indulged in this irrational process of thought for it seemed to me that the whole family felt and thought very much as I did. However, the situation was there, Jean was Mrs. Duncan Sandison and these facts had to be lived with and this is where George and Tom struck the note that set the tune. It is probably superfluous to mention that the note was one of laughter and the tune of 'Jean in the family' became a long joke which went on for years, nor was it many months before my father himself was one of the most melodious singers in the choir.

In the autumn of 1926, my father left Cairnton and came home, with Jean, to live in a cottage which we owned in the village of Achcraggan. This house was called Jemima Cottage and to Jean's house-proud heart it was Heaven. Very shortly after her arrival, George and Tom christened it 'Castle Chemima' in parody of Jean's attitude to it, for she did indeed regard it with more respect than many people feel for the stateliest of homes. Jean herself, they entitled 'Ta Tuchess' in parody of her attitude to herself for she made no bones of saying aloud that she was 'the mistress o' the best hoose in Achcraggan'. When George and Tom spoke of Jean, they became very, very Highland in their speech, with an accent much more pronounced than that of the Reverend Roderick Mackenzie, so that Jean became 'Ta Tuchess of Castle Chemima' and this was a parody of Jean's attitude to themselves, for she still regarded them as 'two big country lumps that has never seen naething'. Thus, as the months and then the years went past, Jean, instead of being a family disaster became, quite unknown to herself, the chief source of family amusement. She hardly ever came to Reachfar and Reachfar seldom went to Jemima Cottage but the link between the two was my father, who spent a twelve-hour day at Reachfar and a twelve-hour night at the cottage, an arrangement which Jean found perfectly satisfactory, since it gave her ample time to 'clean the hoose'.

'It is one hell of a way to live,' I said one evening when I was about twenty and was coming back up the hill with Tom and George, after we had convoyed my father on the first stage of his walk down to Achcraggan.

'It is a funny thing, the differences in people,' George's voice came thoughtfully through the evening light. 'No two people is like other. They even have their own hells and their own heavens.'

'That is the truth of it, George,' Tom corroborated. 'Duncan—your father—is chust fine, Janet. He is different from George and me and likes fine to be living down in Achcraggan. I think he got a bittie more civilised than us in the time he was at Cairnton. He is at all the whist drives and the meetings and is the chairman of the Social Commy*tee* an' all an' can make as good a speech as the minister himself. Indeed, your granny was maybe right when she wanted to make a minister of him as a boy. He is a proper man o' peace, your father. Since he went on the Social Commy*tee* there hasna been half o' the rows about things that there used to be and he can even keep Mrs. Grigor an' Teenie Findlay on speaking terms.'

'And he can even keep ould Teenie Gilchrist in tune,' said George.

'Of coorse, when it comes to keeping people in tune,' Tom commented, 'Duncan is chust a masterpiece at it for it seems that there is never a wrong word between Ta Tuchess and himself and God knows the man that can live at peace with that one has got something in him that is not in the most of us.'

This was true. In a very short time, Jean had quarrelled with everybody in Achcraggan but there was never a 'wrong word' between her and my father, nor was there ever a wrong word between my father and anybody in Achcraggan. Gradually, I arrived in my mind at an appreciation of his attitude to Jean and formed an analogy between her and the horse that drew the milk float from Seamuir Farm. This horse was a wicked-tempered beast with an ugly silver eye but it knew every door in the town of Achcraggan and how much milk should be delivered there.

The working horses were part of our community, personalities whose names everybody knew. Reachfar maintained three horses, Dulcie, the light mare who drew the trap to church on Sundays and did the less heavy work about the place, and Dick and Betsy, heavy Clydesdales, who did all the heavy work at home and the hauling of big loads, such as coal, from Achcraggan. Dulcie was well known in the little town, a sophisticated animal who was down there at least twice a week and although Dick and Betsy were less frequent town-goers, they were more dearly loved for they were impressively beautiful. Reachfar's

Dick, Betsy and Dulcie were not always the same three horses, for in my lifetime we had a succession of Dicks, Betsys and Dulcies. We simply repeated the names in a royal way in a royal line and, being all bred from the same strain, the family like-nesses were so strong that the Achcraggan people could always recognise a Betsy or a Dick Reachfar in the street, even had George or Tom not been there.

Everybody spoke to the horses and the various Betsys, in par-ticular, had charming manners. The Dicks tended to be a little shy and to develop a wildish look in their eyes when they came down from Reachfar hill to this populous bustling centre that was Achcraggan. Our Betsy of 1930 was an especial charmer, the grand-daughter of the foal who had been born on the same day as myself, for she had been more highly educated than her fore-bears. Shortly after she was born, a circus visited Inverness and George and Tom and I paid it a visit and the item that had most entranced Tom and George was the *haute école* horse with the full-habited lady rider. When they came home, it seemed a natural thing to decide that Betsy the foal should have a high-school education. She was not to be ridden, of course, for that would not be suitable to her breed, type of dignity or weight when fully grown but it was thought that she might be taught to appreciate music as well as any horse in a circus. And so, on summer evenings, the old gramophone which was a large pink horn sitting on a square oak box was taken out to the yard and set on the end of the water-trough. A record of the brass band of the Scots Guards playing a waltz called 'The Blue Danube' and another waltz called 'Chanson d'automne' was put on it and Betsy had a rope about twenty yards long attached to her little bridle. George held the end of this and Tom, in his big working boots on the cobbled yard, stood in front of Betsy and said: 'Come on now, lassie! One-two-three!' and waltzed away around the yard. In a remarkably short time, the foal was moving her front hooves in the one-two-three time of the waltz and after a few more nights, George let her dance without the controlling rope on her bridle. Very soon, all we had to do was bring the gramophone out and start the music and Betsy would waltz round and round the Little Parkie just to the east of the water trough while Betsy, her mother, looked on with pride and Dick tossed his big head and whinnied with sheer astonishment at such goings-on. Young Betsy was a real dancer, who danced not only with her feet but with her whole body, heart and soul and when she was fully grown, with her full mane and the silver-white hair long about her fetlocks, Betsy, dancing, was a wonderful sight. Her very eyes were in it and as she turned in her waltz she would arch her neck and look along her side at Tom with a glance of gay, flirtatious blandishment that had in it more than any fan ever said in the days of Franz Josef's Vienna.

Betsy's dancing was her main accomplishment but she had other minor attractions, such as pawing the ground with her big hoof for 'Thank you, and holding her right forehoof high in the air for 'How d'you do?' and this was the animal that drew one of the Reachfar carts down to Achcraggan in the early 1930's. She was by no means unique in the district. There were dozens of horses as accomplished, in a variety of different ways, as she was, like big Star from Dinchory who would stop, willy-nilly, at the door of Johnnie Leeks the greengrocer's shop and neigh until somebody came out with a carrot for him and if they did not come in what he deemed a reasonable time, he would try to go into the shop himself, cart and all. Then there was old Donald, the horse of Donald the carter, who would not pass the Plough Inn until a half-pint of beer was brought to him in a chipped enamel basin but, then, Donald the Carter seldom passed the Plough Inn either unless...

All these horses were known and spoken to by name, just as their owners were, with the exception of the Seamuir milk-float horse which was never known as anything except just that: 'the Seamuir milk-float horse', for, when it first came on the milk-round, it tried to bite the hand of the first housewife who offered it a piece of bread. It did not succeed in biting her and it did not ever succeed in biting or kicking anybody although it often tried for, after that, it was left severely alone. Everybody admitted that it was quite an intelligent beast that knew its round in every detail but this was regarded as ordinary horse-sense, merely. All the other horses knew their work too but they also contributed something extra to life in the way of some amusing personal idiosyncrasy or small social grace. The Seamuir milk-float horse did nothing of this but was merely rude and ill-natured in an ineffectual way which made it vaguely laughable rather than anything else and when you met it on the street, you noted mentally that there it was, going efficiently about its work but the sight of it did nothing to gladden your day. You merely wondered who it had tried to bite of late, then you laughed a little, inwardly, passed the time of day and had a joke on the pavement with Hamish the milkman and went on your way. Hamish was a nice fellow, the centre forward of the town football team and you had known him all your life. He was not responsible for the queer nature of the horse that had been wished on him and, after all, the brute did the job it was there for—it certainly made a good job of the milk-round.

In a way very similar to this, Achcraggan treated Jean and my father. When they first arrived at the cottage, Jean had set out to show the local housewives what was what in the way of city style as to tea parties and the social life generally and the town had made her very welcome but Jean had an extraordinarily malicious tongue which led her to criticise the quality of Mrs. Fraser's scones to Mrs. Gilchrist and Mrs. Begg while her brain did not seem capable of conceiving that Mrs. Gilchrist or Mrs. Begg might repeat what she had said to Mrs. Fraser. And, as Jean criticised everybody to everybody, in the end, naturally, the native tribe coalesced and presented a united front to the stranger. Mrs. Begg, Mrs. Gilchrist and Mrs. Fraser might all have tongues nearly—not quite, for Jean was outstanding in this —as malicious as Jean's but when the explosion took place after the first two weeks, it was a law of nature that the Begg, Gilchrist and Fraser fragments should come down together in one place and that Jean should come down, quite by herself, in another. Jean, like the Seamuir milk-float horse, was outside and, like the horse, had no name in the town but was mostly referred to as 'her at Jemima Cottage' while my father, like Hamish the milk-man, was inside and was known as 'Duncan Reachfar but he is living at Jemima Cottage now'. *Vox populi,* even in an inarticulate community which can hardly ever say exactly what it means, still has the authority and finality of *vox dei.*

And this voice of the people of Achcraggan which was an echo of the earlier voice of Reachfar had an effect on my father which made his attitude to Jean very much like that of Hamish to his horse. 'Ach, take no notice of him,' Hamish would say to people who were home on holiday and meeting the horse for the first time and 'Ach, never heed her, Johnnie!' my father would say of Jean when the coal-merchant told him that she had been complaining of the quality of the coal again. It must have been a very frustrating existence for both Jean and the horse but they seemed to be happy enough in their own ways, Jean polishing Castle Jemima and the horse going efficiently on his round and, meantime, Hamish with his local football team was a local hero and my father as a sort of unofficial provost of the township was a local institution. No umbrage was held against Hamish or my father for the antisocial creatures who were appended to them, as if the horse and Jean were accidents of life for which their harbourers were neither responsible nor culpable.

Early in 1931, having finished with school and university, I went away first to Hampshire to earn my living, then to Devon and then to Kent and a new phase in my relationship with my father developed. In 1927, when my father and Jean came to live in Jemima Cottage and I was left in lodgings with friends on

Clydeside from where I travelled daily to Glasgow University, I had made a new discovery about my father which was that he was a gifted letter-writer. I do not know why this should have astonished me, but it did. It may have been that I connected social letter-writing with my mother still for, until she died, she had always done the family letter-writing while my father, when he worked at Poyntdale and then at Cairnshaws, never seemed to write other than business letters. However, from early January of 1927 for many years, he wrote to me every Sunday in his beautiful copperplate hand and behind the paper and ink of these letters, I could hear his voice, smell the smoke of the fir wood burning in the grate, see the sunlight and feel the light wind that gilded and rippled the hay on Reachfar hill.

When in 1931, at nearly twenty-one years old, I left Reachfar for Hampshire, I went with a curious mixture of willingness and unwillingness. In one way, this was all a great adventure to which I was looking forward but, in another way, I did not want to leave Reachfar for, at some time between the day I was born in 1910 and the month of February in 1931, I had discovered in myself a desire to write—poetry, novels, I did not know what—and Reachfar seemed to be the ideal spot on the surface of the earth to pursue such a career. Such an ambition was not, however, a thing that could be disclosed lightly to a family such as mine. My grandmother and my aunt would have decided that I had taken leave of my senses, George and Tom, more politely, would have described the idea as 'outlandish', which would have been a completely true description of it, let it be remembered. I was the first member of the Sandison family ever to be academically educated and that I could write 'Master of Arts' after my name was in itself so outlandish that Tom and George commented on it with wonder for years. 'Chust think, George man, that you an' me should live to see the day when there is a Master of Arts on Reachfar hill!'

My family had heard of people of our class turning into ministers, doctors and, if female, school-teachers, but writers? No. Besides, writing was not a thing you could make a living at. It was a thing, and a fine thing, for books were splendid things to be handled carefully and read again and again, that was done by highly-gifted people who had 'private money' and who chose to benefit the world in this way in their endless leisure time. Poorer people who tried to write books came to a sad end, starving in a garret or having their morals affected, so that they took to drink or the like. It would be a disgrace to my family if I were to starve in a garret or take to drink and it would also be disgraceful in me to suggest that I 'lived off my family' at the age of twenty-one and tried to write books when I had been given the education to fend for myself and make a decent living in a less outlandish way. Lastly, if it knew of my ambition to write, the family, out of its great respect for that art, would have come to the conclusion that I had 'lost my senses and got above myself'.

On my last afternoon at Reachfar, before leaving for Hampshire, I walked down the hill towards Achcraggan with my father. It was February and already getting dark on a cold afternoon with sleety showers driving in from the north-east and we were depressed in spirit for, in addition to our own imminent parting, there had recently been a fatal accident in the district and the funeral of young Davie Smith was fresh in our minds.

'Maybe it will be warmer in the south of England whatever,' my father said. I did not reply for I felt that I preferred Reachfar in any weather to any sunlit countryside. 'It is a long way you are going,' he said next, 'and among strangers. You won't think long for home?'

'No, Dad. I don't think so. I don't think I have ever thought long in my life.'

Even if I felt that I might be homesick, I should not have said so because that would have worried him, but there was nothing noble or unselfish in my reply to his question for, although I would have preferred to stay at Reachfar, I had, even at that time, albeit unrecognised, an awareness of the fleeting nature of life and I grudged that a moment of it be spent in vain sighing and longing.

'That is true,' he agreed with me. 'Even as a bairn, when we first went to Cairnton, you never seemed to think long for Reachfar like me. I used to be fair sick—sick in my very body, even—with longing for it. It is not a good thing to think long like that. I think you must have taken the lack of longing from Tom and George. They have more sense in a lot of ways than me.—It is not much of a job that you are going to—to be nurse to this grandson o' Leddy Lydia's. It is just domestic service, after all, and I was hoping for better for you but I—well, I admire your spirit for taking the job and that's the truth.'

With a radiant warmth inside me, I raised my head into the icy wind for never before in my life had my father spoken to me such words of praise. This time that I write of was 1931 and the country was still in the grip of the great Trade Depression. There were no posts for university graduates with diplomas in secretaryship. There were no posts for anybody. Employers were reducing staffs, not increasing them.

'I know it is disappointing for you, Dad, after all the money you have spent on me and the chance you have given me but, down south nearer London, I'll have more opportunity of anything that's going. When I am up here, even if a job *was* going, no employer is going to call Janet Sandison from Reachfar for an interview. After all, I might be hump-backed and cross-eyed.'

'You are neither o' these things anyway,' he said. We were going through the gate in the east march fence at the time and as he fastened the hook again, he looked into my face. 'Be careful what you do among the men down there,' he said. 'It is easy to make a mistake when you are young and somebody pays court to you. You have plenty of time to think about getting married.'

I felt my face flush. 'Don't worry,' I said. 'I had enough of that with Victor Halloran to last me for a good long time.'

While I was at the university, I had got engaged to this young man in an inadvertent way and only the special providence that guards young fools had saved me from the disaster of marriage to him, for disaster it would undoubtedly have been.

'What in the world made you think you wanted that fellow in the first place?' my father asked me now.

'I don't think thinking came into it much, Dad. It was when I began to think that I—that I broke things off. I saw that I didn't want to get married to him or to anybody else and I told him to go to hell. I am kind of ashamed of it all. I said it in front of Aunt Alice and Uncle Jim and he looked so sort of—ach, well, anyway, there it is. But Aunt Alice sort of encouraged me to go out with him and his people were quite well-off and then he asked me to marry him and his father was a nice old boy and was kind to me—his mother *wasn't* nice to me and that came into it too. I told him I would marry him mostly to please him and all the rest but it was partly to spite his mother too. But it was all awful, just a muddle, because I didn't want to marry him at all really.'

'That is just what I mean when I tell you to be careful. There are going to be plenty of men around you. I am not telling you to be careful of the rogues and villains—you have enough sense to know one of that kind when you see him. I am not insulting you by thinking that you will come home here with an illegitimate bairn like Maggie Matheson that went to service in Edinburgh. It's not that. But getting married is a thing that should be for life, a job that you take on, a job that you like doing and that is never done, like looking after a farm or a garden, a place that gets bonnier with every day you live and work on it. It is hard to say what I mean. I don't want you to be thinking about Jean and me—that is a different thing altogether and just an arrangement for the convenience of us in our later lives, as it were. And sometimes not a all that much of a convenience, when I think on it,' he interpolated, chuckling, into his serious discourse. 'She is a devil for not getting on with people but folk are bothering about her less and less as time goes on and she is very good to young Jock and me.' My young brother was now living down at Jemima Cottage because it was more convenient for the 'bus that took him to Fortavoch Academy each day. 'She seems to be quite fond of Jock,' my father added, 'but, mercy, she has no *law* for *you*!'

I was no more brilliant or quick of wit than I had ever been but, down the years, a few gleams of intelligence had come to light my turgid brain. 'It is mostly because Jock is a boy,' I said now. 'I don't mean that Jock isn't probably a nicer person than I am—he probably is—but Jean likes male people better than female people on the whole. She feels that the male ones don't compete with her in any way, in looks or dress or the fanciness of their houses or anything.'

My father stopped on the rough cart track that led past the Smithy, down the hill to Achcraggan and looked at me. 'Who told you that?' he asked.

'Nobody told me. That is just the way I see it.'

'And I wouldn't be surprised if you are seeing by-ordinar' straight,' he said with an air of wonder. 'Maybe you will be all right down there in Hampshire after all and have outgrown that Halloran kind of nonsense.'

'You mustn't worry about me, Dad. Of course I'll be all right!'

'And even if this nursing job isn't much of a post, do your best in it. Mind on that. Never take anybody's money, even if it is only a shilling, without giving full value for it and maybe a little more, the way Granny always puts an extra bittie on a half-pound of butter. If you do that, you will never be beholden to anybody. And I hope that, before long, things will be better and you will get a job that is in your own line. You have a real notion of the secretaryship?'

116

'Yes, Dad. I like it and I feel I could do it well. But—'

'Aye?'

I stopped on the track and looked down over the snug township of Achcraggan, out to the Cobblers, the cliffs that guarded the entrance to the Firth, and beyond them to the grey of the North Sea which, in this wintry evening light, had no horizon but merged into the infinity of the grey sky.

'What I would really like to do is write,' I said.

'Write?' he repeated, not understanding me.

'Write books,' I said softly into the cold wind and then I looked at his face and, as I looked, a wondrous light dawned in his eyes and spread over his features.

'Do you think you could, Janet?' he breathed softly.

'I don't know, Dad, but I would like to try.'

'You try,' he said. 'It is a big ambition to have, but you try and keep on trying.'

He had not laughed or looked scornful. As we moved on against a new blast of sleet, all I could think of was that he had neither laughed at me nor told me that I had 'lost my senses and got above myself'.

'Don't tell anybody about this,' I said after a moment.

'No. I will not tell. It is a thing people wouldna understand right.'

In that moment, I knew that he felt as I did that some dreams are too precious for telling, too delicate of fibre for passing, by the medium of words from one mind to another, unless the minds were as closely attuned as his and mine.

When we came down to the final slope into the outskirts of Achcraggan, he stopped in the lee of the hedge.

'It is time you went back,' he said. 'You have come further than I meant on this devil of a night. It will be pitch dark before you get home.'

I laughed in the grey twilight. 'There isn't a bodach or a whigmaleerie in this district that will come near me. I have been among them for too long. All right, Dad, I will see you in the morning.'

'No,' he said. 'No. You and George will be off to the station before I get up there.'

'Oh.'

I had not thought about it but I had taken it as read that my father would drive me to Fortavoch station.

'So I'll not see you in the morning,' he went on. 'But as soon as you get to Islington Hall and get a minute to yourself, write to me and tell me about your journey. That is the one thing I am asking you to do for me now, Janet. I want you to write home every week—not to *me*, specially, but to Granny or Tom or George or Kate or any of us. I am not asking it entirely for myself, although I will be glad of your letters. I want you to do it for your own sake, so that your home is always fresh in your mind, so that you will never forget that it is there. And I want you to mind, always, on the way we live here and what we think is right and what wrong and I want you never to forget the kind of people you belong to. A lot of the young people who go away from here—and, God knows, more go away than stay in the north for there is not much of a living here for people—a lot of them are never heard of again by their families or anybody. That canna be right or good for people. You were born on Reachfar, it made you what you are and it would be a loss to you to forget it.' He paused for a moment, looking down at me. I was a good five feet eight inches tall now but I had to look up into his ruddy face and between us the rain dripped in a cold screen from the sodden brim of his tweed hat. 'You will write to us, Janet?' he asked.

Behind his downbent head, the black clouds like rags of funeral crape drove across the winter sky. 'Our Father which art in Heaven—'

'I will write, Dad, every week. I promise.'

'That's my lass.' He turned away from me and faced down the

hill towards the warm lights of Achcraggan. 'I will not say good-bye,' he said. 'I have never liked saying goodbye. Goodnight, Janet.'

'Goodnight, Dad.'

I watched him walk away from me, very tall and straight, down the steep hill towards the lights and then I turned back up the hill. The sleet drove like needles at my right cheek, the wind howled like a demon among the trees, the ragged black clouds streamed across the sky and the hot tears ran down my face while my heart ached with love for my father.

I kept my promise about the letter-writing and down the years I wrote from Hampshire, Devon, Kent and then London every week, and mostly to my father, for if at a birthday or some special occasion I wrote to Tom or George, it was always my father who replied. He wrote every Sunday. The letters usually reached me in the south of England every Tuesday morning and when I saw the envelope with the: 'Miss Janet E. Sandison' in the beautiful handwriting, I would see behind it my father— not at Jemima Cottage, for I had never seen him writing there— but at the kitchen table at Reachfar, sitting upright, the long fingers of the left hand lying alongside the margin of the paper, the flat glass ink-bottle with the metal top in front of him and the long, blue, pointed wooden penholder, with its long 'White Devil' nib, held in the classic position in the right hand, between a straight thumb and straight fore and middle fingers. There was a faint scratching sound as he wrote and I could hear the sweep of the capital letters as he ended the letter with his wishes for me which were always the same: 'Health, Happiness, Good Luck & Best Love, Your Dad, D. Sandison'.

It was while I was in Kent, in July of 1934, that I received what was, I think, the first telegram that I had ever had. It was a short message: 'Granda and Granny died Duncan Sandison'.

Long since, I had found my way from children's nursing into

secretaryship and at this time I was secretary to an old gentleman called Mr. Carter, the one-time chairman of a shipping firm who, in his retirement, was writing a history of the great port of London. Mr. Carter was an invalid who spent his days between his bed and a wheel-chair but although crippled in body, he was extremely active in mind and temper. No former secretary had stayed with him for longer than a few weeks but, at this time, I had been with him for twenty months in the course of which we had hardly spoken a civil word to one another. He was over seventy, I was twenty-four and we spent our time together in what I can describe only as an utterly agreeable state of total disagreement in a large library and on a terrace outside its french windows, in an atmosphere, mentally speaking, of loud-spoken rage and fervent activity and an atmosphere, physically speaking, of half-eaten biscuits and abysmal squalor. Although perpetually enraged, we were as happy as a pair of larks in spring for I think that we were two examples of the kind of person my father had talked of at Cairnton long ago—'thrawn-natured people who were fonder of people who can give them a good salting when they need it.'

Also in this big house with us were Mr. Carter's son, daughter-in-law, their children, old Mr. Carter's valet and a retinue of servants but we lived a detached life, physically, among our books and papers and trays of food in the library and an even more detached life, mentally, among our writings, our plans for further writings and our loud quarrels over matters like spelling without one of which no day was complete. Mr. Carter called me 'Girl' and I called him 'Sir' which illustrates the direct and undecorated nature of our relationship.

When the valet—the only person in the house permitted to enter our library—came in with the telegram on a salver, Mr. Carter looked up, frowned hideously and said: 'Get out of here with your tin plate. I am busy!'

'For the young lady, sir.'

'*What* young lady? Oh, Girl? Well, *give* her the damn' thing. Don't *stand* there!'

I took the envelope, opened it, read it and I suppose that something of what I felt showed in my face for the next thing that I remember is that the form was lying on the rug that covered Mr. Carter's knees and he was saying: 'Tell the messenger to wait and bring some Madeira in here.'

The valet went out and the old man looked at me. 'Duncan Sandison. Your father?'

'Yes, sir.'

'A man who can say what he means, anyway. Here, Girl, drink a little of this.' He glared at the valet. 'Go and ring up about trains to Inverness. There'll be one leaving London tonight.'

'But Mr. Carter—' I began. My holiday was not due until later in the year when the family were going abroad, taking Mr Carter with them.

'Hold your tongue, Girl, and drink that wine and get me a telegraph form.' I handed him the form. 'What's the address?'

'Sandison, Achcraggan, will do, sir.'

He wrote the address and the valet came into the room again. 'A train leaves King's Cross at seven, sir, reaches Inverness at nine tomorrow morning.'

'Order the car for five-thirty,' Mr. Carter said and wrote on the form: 'Girl arrives Inverness nine tomorrow morning Carter.'— 'Give that to the messenger,' he said and, as the valet went out, the old man turned to me in a menacing way: 'Now then, Girl, tell me about this granda and granny of yours and this father you have called Duncan Sandison.'

When I stepped down from the first-class sleeper coach—the first time I had ever travelled first class—at Inverness the next morning, it was the head and shoulders of my father that I saw down at the end of the platform. For a fleeting second a smile lit his face but it died away, leaving behind it a stern solemnity and the first words he said were: 'Janet, I did not mean you to ask for time off and put Mr. Carter to inconvenience. You should not—'

'I didn't ask, Dad. It was Mr. Carter who sent me—in the car to London and then first-class all the way.'

'And he sent the telegram?'

'Yes.'

'He must be a very good old gentleman, in spite of your telling me about him being so thrawn and ill-natured.' He took my suitcase from me and we made our way to the platform where the morning train to Fortavoch was waiting. 'Well, there are a lot of fine people who are a little thrawn,' he said as we sat down in the compartment. 'Granny was thrawn, right to the last, but there are not many finer people than she was.'

'What happened, dad?'

'Och, the day before yesterday, the two of them went off for their snooze after dinnertime just as usual but when Granny got up for a droppie tea at three o'clock, Granda said he thought he would just stay where he was, so she took a cup of tea ben to him and then he went off to sleep again. At supper-time, when she went ben again, he was dead. She called me ben to their room. She was quite calm. "Your father is away, Duncan" she said. That was all. Later on, she went ben and washed him and put him right. I had to go to the big box in the west garret and get a white bed-cover she wanted. I took three different ones down to her before I got the one that pleased her.'

The little train pulled out on its slow stop-at-every-station journey and he sat looking out at the summer gaiety of hills, sea and sky. 'Then we went to our beds. I stopped up at Reachfar for the night. Kate made the bed for Granny in that roomie o' yours above the kitchen. She didna come down at breakfast-time and we thought maybe she was sleeping long after the night before but about eight o'clock George said to me that we should go up. I told Kate to go up and see her but George called her back and would have it that himself and I went. I thought she was sleeping

122

at first but no. She was away.' He moved his glance from the view beyond the train windows to my face. 'I suppose it is natural that you should be crying,' he said, 'with the shock and the long journey and a-all but I don't like to see you crying, Janet. And Granda and Granny wouldna have wanted you or any of us to cry. They had the full o' their time and a good bittie more. Granny was eighty-two and Granda was ninety-two.' He looked out of the window again at the broad summer countryside. 'I suppose a lot of people would think they had hard dull lives on the top o' Reachfar hill. They were never far away from it in all their time. And people might say it wouldna matter much if they had never lived but I don't think that any o' that is right. They left Reachfar a better place than it was when they first knew it and they always did whatever came to their hand to do and did it the best way they could. And if they found things hard sometimes, they never complained about it. And they never found things dull for dullness wasn't in them. They were interested in everything right to the end. Just the day before he died, Granda was reading about some new oats that has been developed for light marginal land and told me I was to find out about it and where we could get seed.' He gave a little laugh. 'And Granny said we were always ready for any new-fangled capers, just the way she always did.'

'Reachfar will be queer without them, Dad.'

'For a little while, maybe. But for myself, they will always be about Reachfar. Even now, when I know they are both ben their room—George and I brought Granny down beside Granda —I keep expecting to see Herself come out o' the milk-house or my father come into the stable.—Well, tell me about this old gentleman, Mr. Carter, for this is a very good kindly thing he has done.'

It was indeed a good and kindly thing that Mr. Carter had done in sending me home, for the funeral of my grandparents is one of my most splendid memories. The coffins were carried down the steep cart-track from Reachfar to Poyntdale and then placed on two of the Poyntdale hay-waggons. The procession on that first stage of the journey was a small one, only the two coffins, followed by my aunt, my fourteen-year-old brother and myself. My father and Sir Torquil led this little procession at the head of my grandfather's coffin, with four other friends behind them and, next, at the head of my grandmother's coffin, came George and Tom, followed by four more friends. Then came my aunt, my brother and myself. As we came down the hill to Poyntdale farm square where the waggons were waiting, I could hardly believe what I saw for I did not know there were so many people in our district and by the time we reached Achcraggan, this crowd was further swelled by another great concourse. The little town of Achcraggan itself lay dead under the bright sun, all shops closed, all blinds drawn down and there was not a child or even a dog in sight as the big Poyntdale Clydesdales clop-clopped along the High Street on their way to the churchyard. But the one person whom I remember most distinctly throughout was my father.

He was fifty-six now and his dark hair, at the sides above the ears, had turned to a pure clear silver but from either side of the parting on the left above his high forehead, the dark hair sprang as strong and vital as ever. His skin had its old rosy ruddy glow and his head rose proud and strong from the broad shoulders under the black coat as he walked along the road by the shore at the side of the first waggon.

When we reached the gates of the churchyard and the horses stopped, he turned towards my grandfather's coffin, laid his hand on it for a moment and then he looked back at George who stood in a similar position beside the second waggon. They did not speak. They looked at one another for a moment before my father gave a strangely commanding little nod and in a second of silence the heads of the two oak coffins were simultaneously on their two left shoulders. There was no fumbling, no fussing—only an extraordinary pride and dignity and the coffins seemed to move through the air instead of on the shoulders of twelve men to the two graves that lay side by side in the sunlit church-yard where the hay wind was blowing.

I was at home for only a few days altogether for, although Mr. Carter had told me that I might stay for two weeks, my father would not allow this.

'The gentleman has been very good and kind,' he said, 'and it is wrong to take advantage of a man's generosity.'

When the funeral was over, little was said of my grandfather and grandmother that evening but, in a curious way, within the few days that I was at home, they slipped into their new dimension, that dimension where time and place are fused and which we call memory. Much of this little time I was at home was spent in the past, for I think that we all escaped into it from the sadness of the present. My father and my brother stayed at Reachfar for the few nights I was there—a thing that Jean never objected to for their absence meant that there was 'less mess' in Castle Jemima—and we were a big circle round the fire which burned white in the sunlight of the long summer evening.

My brother John, who was now fourteen, had his own re-lationship with Tom and George which was different from mine but had, of course, many points of similarity for George and Tom had, indefatigably, learned to read the time on the clock and had started to go to school again when John was five years old. John, too, could contribute his share of stories from the past.

'I have always said,' said Tom, 'and I still say it, forbye, that it is chust terrible the memories that is in Jock and Janet. I had no mind at a-all on reading that book and you saying that about a goose being as bad as a cow with the spring skitter, had you, George man?'

'Och, I think they put a lot o' things on you an' me that's chust not true, Tom,' George said.

'Oh, no, we don't!' said Jock.

'You have just got a very willing forgetter, George,' I told him, 'like the time you quite forgot ever having mentioned Rory Ruadh of the six wives.'

'Who was he?' my brother asked.

I told all I knew of Rory Ruadh which was very little and ended: 'So to use an expression which was anathema to my Professor of History at the university, our ancestry is lost in the mists of antiquity.'

'Talking of ancestors and antiquity,' my father said 'I heard a very interesting yarn when Tom and George and I were at the sales in Dingwall about a month ago. We were having a drink before we came home and Ross, the Town Clerk, came in and we had a yarn. It seems he had a letter short ago from a woman in Canada who is trying to trace her relations over here. That is common enough. Ross tells me that every Town Clerk's office in the north is infested with letters from all over the world from people trying to trace their ancestors but I was kind of taken with this yarn. This woman said her maiden name was Maciver but there had always been a story in her family that it wasn't her real name and that one of her forebears—I suppose it would be her great or great-great-grandfather for it was early in the nineteenth century—had committed some crime over here in Ross-shire and had to run away to Canada.'

'He would have stolen a sheep or something,' Jock said. 'Could she give any precise date?'

'Chust tell me, George, now,' said Tom pompously, as a comment on my brother's fourteen-year-old gravity, 'when was the Battle o' Bannockburn?'

'1314!' said George smartly and made the stock reply, for they specialised in only two historical dates, 'and can you give me the year o' Waterloo, Tom?'

126

'Here, wait a minute!' I said before Tom could give his answer. The circle of eyes round the fire stared at me while I stared back at them and then looked into the white flames. I saw a summer evening, bright like this one and a circle of eyes round the big white table that still stood behind us now. And the fire was burning sunlit white like tonight. On the window-sill there was a heap of bee-veils and gloves and, lying on top of them, my father's tweed hat. I had a feeling of being frightened and I had a feeling of shame. Yes. I was remembering that I had run away with Fly and had hidden in the moor, thus worrying my family who were all very worried already. Everybody had said good-night to me and I was on the stairs outside the closed door, lonely and uneasy in my going-to-bed boots, for my father had come home from Poyntdale too early and they were all sitting in there, round the table, talking about a thing called war that had broken out. 'It was on the fourth of August, 1914,' I said, 'the day the Great War was declared—'

'Look at her!' my aunt said sharply. 'Who said she is not like my mother? It's enough to make your flesh crawl!' and she seized the poker and broke the fire into brighter flames.

'Och, nonsense, Kate!' my father said. 'What were you minding on, Janet?'

'This woman Maciver in Canada, Dad—*we* are her people!'

'You're dotty,' said my brother.

'Oh no, I'm not. Tom, George, that day the Great War broke out, we were taking the honey off the hives. Danny Maclean was here. Dad came home early from Poyntdale—'

'Aye, that's right,' Tom said.

'And what then?' George asked.

'You all sat after supper, talking about the war. I was sent to bed but I didn't go. I was frightened. I sat on the stairs outside there where I could hear your voices and Granny said she could remember her grandfather telling of how, at the time of Water-loo, the Press Gang came round the north here.'

My father frowned in thought. 'Dang it, I do mind on something o' that now that you mention it. Can you mind on any more, Janet?'

'There were four Macdonald sons at the time, two that were old enough for the army and Great-great-granda and a younger one.'

'Aye—the younger one was Donald that died o' diptheria the year before I was born,' my father said.

'And there were three Frasers in the croft down the hill and five Macleans on the lochside,' I said, hearing my grandmother's voice. I was talking of crofts and a loch that I had never seen but I was repeating a story that could have been true of any part of the Highlands, a story that must have been born in me. 'But the Press Gang had been round dozens of times before and man after man went away to the wars and never came back and this lot had made up their minds that they weren't going to have any more of it.'

'That's it!' my father said. 'I had been telling them that Sir Torquil had said that we would have to bring in conscription if the German army was to be held—aye, I mind on that bit right enough. Go on, Janet.'

'So they all went and hid. All ten of them. The two Macdonalds hid in a cave where Prince Charlie once hid but the Press Gang found them. There was a fight and the Macdonald boys tossed two of the Gang over the cliffs and the rest of them ran for it. The two Macdonalds cleared out to Skye but they wrote back home once or twice in the name of Maciver and, that night, Granny said: "I believe the younger one, Kenneth, died in Glasgow before very long but the eldest brother, Farquhar, we heard that he had got to Canada." '

'Janet,' my aunt said sharply, 'stop staring into the fire like a witch and imitating my mother's voice like that!'

I started as if I were being suddenly awakened from sleep and my brother laughed as George said: 'Let her alone, Kate. She didna mean to imitate the Ould Leddy. It's the way her memory works.'

'And it's quite a memory,' my brother said. 'Dad, will you get the address from Dingwall and write to this woman?'

'Aye. I'll surely do that. Janet, can you mind on any more?'

'No, Dad. I think you all started to talk about the war again and I went up to bed, thinking about Prince Charlie's cave and the story of long ago. I was an escapist even then, I suppose. I didn't understand really what the word war meant and I was frightened.'

'We were all frightened that night,' he said. 'I can mind yet on the fear that was in us. It was as if the world were coming to an end.'

'The world did come to an end in a way, when you think on it,' Tom said. 'Nothing has been the same since the war, Reachfar.'

At the last word, at Tom's automatic application of the title to the new owner, my head lifted. I had been staring into the fire but now, accidentally, I was looking into the eyes of my brother and we exchanged a small, proud secret smile.

During the few days after the funeral, we had many callers, for it was the custom of our countryside to visit a bereaved household, probably in a neighbourly effort to render the gap in the family circle a little less obvious, and I remember particularly the visit of the Maclean family from Upper Dinchory. Mr. and Mrs. Maclean were contemporaries of my father but their daughter, who was some years older than myself, was married and was home on holiday from Edinburgh with her police sergeant husband and their first baby. Mr. and Mrs. Maclean were the proudest of grandparents and no wonder, I thought, for the infant girl was a beautiful child, which was not surprising for Mary Maclean, now Mrs. Dickson, was a pretty girl and her husband was a tall, golden-haired, handsome fellow. The child was about six months old and, as soon as they arrived, my father was drawn to her as if by a magnet, smiling down into the big blue eyes as she sat in her father's arms and holding out his big hands.

'What a bonnie lass! Come to me, then, till I see you,' he said and the father gave him the child.

'She will be a-all right with Reachfar,' Tom assured the grandparents.

'Och, she is a splendid bairn,' the proud granny said. 'She is not shy of anybody and she never cries the day long.'

My father went off to a chair in the corner with the baby and the bunch of keys for rattling and the silver working watch for listening to were produced and while the rest of us chatted over cups of tea round the fire, I could hear him laughing and talking to the child. When we had finished tea, he came over to us, bent down and very gently put the baby in the mother's lap and without words, he left the kitchen. The talk round the fire went on, the baby sat contentedly, looking solemnly happy behind its big blue eyes and I wondered a little sadly about my father. Had the baby reminded him too poignantly of those days before the war when my mother was alive? Was he sad that I had not married and given him a grandchild of his own by this time? But as the afternoon passed, I forgot the little incident and when he came in for supper, although he was a little late, the strange look that I had thought I had seen was gone from his eyes.

A day or two later, he and I were taken to Fortavoch in the trap by Tom and my father came to Inverness to see me on to the London train before attending some meeting in the town. We had about half-an-hour to wait for the train and as we came down the platform I saw ahead of us Mr. and Mrs. Maclean, their daughter and the son-in-law carrying the baby. The daughter was crying and the mother and father were trying to comfort her while the tall fair man walked alongside, the child in his arms, his eyes staring straight ahead.

'Come in here,' my father said suddenly and turned me into the lounge of the hotel.

'Did you see the Macleans in front of us?' I asked. 'They must have been in their compartment at Fortavoch before we got to the station.' Fortavoch was a terminus.

'Aye,' he said, frowning at my suitcase on the floor beside his chair. 'A big whisky and a little one, if you please, and some water,' he told the waiter. He looked unhappy in a way that frightened me—frowning, puzzled, angry and rebellious all at once and I could not understand it.

'Dad, is anything wrong?' I asked when the glasses with the whisky were on the table in front of us.

'It is that bairnie,' he said. 'It is not right—it is not right in its little mind.' He gave a horrible gulp that was like a sob and then swallowed a mouthful of whisky and water while I stared at him. 'I saw it the other day when they came to Reachfar. I went down to Poyntdale that afternoon and telephoned to Doctor Mackay to go to Upper Dinchory—just to call in in passing, like, as if to pass the time o' day—and take a look at the baby. He told me last night he had advised them to go back to Edinburgh to a specialist.' He looked with sad rebellious eyes round the dreary big lounge. 'I thought maybe something could be done if the doctors saw it early, but Doctor Mackay says he doesna think so. He says he has seen cases before. They grow in their bodies but in their minds they stay infants, always. They never walk or speak or—or anything.'

'Dad!'

'It is a terrible thing. Most o' the time, I think I can see justice in the ways of the Almighty. Most of the evil in the world, like the terrible wars, we make for ourselves. But when I think of the birth of a baby like that, I get lost. Why should a thing like that happen to that fine young couple and that innocent little craitur o' a bairn?' His voice shook, his eyes searched the dim corners of the room again and then he blinked and took another sip from his glass. 'Take your dram, Janet. It will help you to sleep on the journey.' He smiled a little. 'I shouldna be speaking to you like this and you just going away but it was *seeing* them there with the poor little baby.'

'But Dad, how did you notice it, that day at Reachfar? The rest of us thought she was a beautiful baby.'

He looked down at his big, highly-polished second-best boots. 'I am kind of fond of babies,' he said shyly and added more shyly still: 'and if you are very fond of anybody—*love* anybody, like—it seems that you just know about them without knowing how you know.'

I do not remember getting on board the train. My last memory of Inverness that day is the gleam of the smoky sunshine on the silver hair at my father's temple and his long-fingered hand resting on the brim of his tweed hat which lay on his knee while he looked down at the shining black boots.

In the years after 1934, until 1939, I was home for a short period once in every twelve months and among the small vicissitudes of my life which, being my own vicissitudes, seemed great to me, Reachfar was a steady rock. After old Mr. Carter died, in January of 1936, I went from one post to another around and in London and was a very gay young woman, more interested in young men, clothes and dancing than in anything else, which led to Jean, my stepmother, conceiving the interesting theory, which she expounded to my aunt and which led to some hard words between them, that I made my living as a prostitute on the London streets. This happened just before I came home for the month of July in 1938 and I was hardly in the house before my aunt came into my bedroom and told me about it.

'So I just made up my mind,' she panted indignantly, 'that I would wait till you came home and then tell your father.'

'Why?' I asked.

'Why what?'

'Why tell him?'

'Are you out of your mind?' she asked, her dark eyes alight

with red flames. 'That tongue of hers has got to be stopped!'

'Oh, rubbish, Kate. It doesn't matter a damn what she says.'

'But she may be saying it in Achcraggan!'

'What if she does? Nobody will believe her and even if they do, it doesn't matter. Anyway, you are not to worry Dad with it, Kate.—I say, what do you think of this for a hat?'

When I was at home on holiday, it was my habit to walk down to Achcraggan's outskirts with my father each evening and these walks were by way of being the annual catching-up of events between us. It was seldom now that anybody met me at Inverness, for the last stage of the journey had been much simplified by the introduction of a 'bus service between Inverness and Achcraggan and the 'bus dropped me on the county road at the entrance to Poyntdale, from where Sir Torquil's car took me as far up the hill as the weather and the condition of the Reachfar track would allow. As I usually came north in the summer, when the car could negotiate the track, my meeting with the family took place at the east end of the steading, at what was known as the granary gable, and it was here also that I would join my father to walk down to Achcraggan in the evenings.

'Kate and Jean have had a bit of a row about something,' he said to me on one of the first evenings of my holiday. 'I thought Kate had more sense than to take any notice of anything Jean says. I thought too that maybe Kate would calm down a bit when she married Hugh but devil a bit of it. She is as wild and fiery as she ever was.'

In the spring of 1937, my aunt had married Hugh Davidson, the foreman at Poyntdale Farm, but they lived at Reachfar and Hugh went down the hill to work each day as my father had done long ago.

'Kate will be fiery till the day she dies,' I said.

'Aye. There is a lot o' the Ould Leddy in Kate although she is pure Sandison in looks. You wouldna have heard what Kate and Jean fell out about?' he enquired cannily.

'Och, it was some remark Jean made. I didn't listen very carefully, to tell the truth.'

I do not know why I am always impelled to add these last four words to any statement which is a downright lie but I invariably do.

'I see,' said my father and it was borne in on me that, to him, the four words were tell-tale and that he knew I was lying. 'Och, well, maybe the less said the better if it was words spoken that caused all the bother.—And you are still liking London?'

'Yes, Dad.'

'What are they saying down there about this mannie Hitler that is making all the noise in Germany?'

'A lot of people are very worried, Dad. Sir Richard—' this was my present employer '—says that a climate of war is developing.'

'War? But, God, they *canna* let it come to that! It is not twenty years since the last slaughter ended and war, with the machines and explosives they've got now, it would be a terrible thing!'

'I know but that is what some people think.'

I did not like this conversation on the bright summer evening at the start of my holiday. I did not like talk of Hitler, Mussolini, Germany or Italy at any time for I felt that I did not know enough of the dire forces that were developing under these men in these countries and the little I did know was too frightening to contemplate.

'The Reverend Roderick had visitors lately,' my father said next, 'a Jewish gentleman that is a scientist of some kind. The Reverend Roderick has known him for a long time but he is not as old as the minister. Himself and his wife and two bairns were staying down at the manse for three months. It seems that this Hitler put them out of their home and took away most of their money, just because they were Jews. It seems he would have put them all in prison, even the bairns, if they hadna left the country. I couldna believe it, when people spoke of it to me in Achcraggan for I thought the man must have done something

134

wrong, some terrible crime, when they did that to him. But I couldna swallow the bit about the bairns—even if the father had committed the worst crime there is, nobody in their senses would want to punish the poor *bairns*, a bonnie little black-eyed laddie and lassie, they are. But one Sunday, the Reverend Roderick preached about this Hitler mannie and made the last prayer about him and after the Elders' Meeting I asked him point-blank about this friend of his and what he had done to be put out of his home and have to leave his country and the minister said it was right enough—it was just because he was a Jew.'

'I know,' I said.

'But this is a terrible thing!' My father paused on the hillside, turned and looked back up the slope of the East Moor of Reachfar where our ewes were grazing and the lambs, almost fully grown now, were having a final jumping game in the evening sunshine. Then his eyes looked wider afield, away west to the hump of Ben Wyvis at the head of the Firth and across the Firth itself to the hills of Sutherland. 'Anyone that would put a man out of his native country,' he said then, his eyes still on the distance, 'for something that is no fault of his own, is not a man but a devil.' He began to walk down the hill again, planting his ash-plant firmly on the rough path at each step. 'He must have been born with some devilish twist in his mind. Like Jean. There is something twisted in Jean's mind for that badness that gets the upper hand in her seems to be something she canna help. But then, Jean is so foolish in so many ways that her wee bitties o' badness are foolish too and canna hurt anybody except herself, for nobody listens to her. But people *listen* to this Hitler mannie and you will see pictures in the paper of hundreds of men saluting him and shouting this Heil Hitler thing that they say. It is a terrible thing.' He walked on in silence for a few yards and then: 'I mind on when the last war started and Sir Torquil got George and me reserved at home here for the farming. George was wild about it for he wanted to go to France with the Seaforths but I wasna wild. I was thankful. I don't think it is that I am what you would call a coward,' he said quietly and thoughtfully, 'but I never could see why yon war came to start at all. I couldna understand why they were fighting or what they were fighting for. It was like the Press Gang coming round here at the time o' Waterloo. I didna see why I should go and fight—me that hates fighting of any kind—when I didna know what I was doing it for or why. But this Hitler mannie is different,' he said, stopping again to look up the hill at Reachfar where the house and steading now showed as a pale rectangle lying on the green hilltop with the dark fir trees behind it, 'and I would fight him. A man that is cruel to people—even to bairns—for a thing they canna help and puts them out of their homes and their country—a man like that has got to be fought. Injustice is a thing I canna abide. I can put up with anything that is kind of half just, but not injustice.'

I wanted as, I think, most people of my age at this time did, to escape from talk and thought of the inevitable doom that seemed to hang over our brittle world. 'Dad,' I said, 'did you ever write to that woman in Canada and tell her about Granny's story about the Press Gang coming round?'

'Och surely! Did I never mention it to you in a letter? Aye. I got the address from Dingwall—it's in Montreal—and I wrote and she wrote back and we send cards at Christmas.'

'And is she related to us?'

'We canna find out for sure. All she has to go on is this bittie hearsay in her family that Maciver wasn't their right name but she has never heard the name of Macdonald mentioned. I don't think there is any connection, likely. But she seems to be a nice woman. She is well-educated too and they seem to be wealthy. The husband—he is a French-Canadian, by the way, so she is Mrs. Duchesne. Jock tells me that is how you pronounce it—D-u-c-h-e-s-n-e—the husband is high up in the Fire Brigade—she calls it the Fire Department—in Montreal and they have a son and two daughters. She always seems very pleased to get a letter from here though. It is funny how blood tells in people even after so many generations.'

'Do you write to her often?'

'Och, no. Just at the Christmas mostly although I have seen me writing to her an odd time through the year if I take the notion. Speaking o' writing, have you ever tried to do anything at it yourself as you once thought you would like to do?'

'I have tried off and on,' I said, feeling very shy and timid, 'but I don't get very far. There is my job all day and that takes my mind off it—'

'And dancing all night takes your mind off it too,' he put in.

I laughed. 'And besides, I don't really know anything about writing as a job—as a craft, you know. Sometimes, I get going and the thing looks all right and then—oh, I don't know. Something happens inside my mind and I just know that what I have written is a lot of rubbish and I tear it up and think what a fool I am to think I could ever write anything.'

On the whole, I liked talk on this subject no better than I had liked the talk of Hitler. Both subjects made me uneasy in different ways so, once more, I escaped.

'You have a very bonnie crop of calves this year, Dad. What bull was it?'

'The new Aberdeen-Angus at Poyntdale, a beautiful beast. Aye. They are a fine lot, aren't they? Have you seen the youngest one at that caper of putting his front feet on the bars o' the gate and shouting for his milk at night?'

'The one Tom and George call Hitler?' I asked. The subject seemed to be inescapable.

'Aye. I will give you that the calfie looks kind of like a politician making a speech when he looks over the gate like that but I'll have to stop them putting that name on the craitur. That calf is too well-bred to have the name o' that shit o' a mannie.'

The next time that I came home to Reachfar, Hitler, whom my father had described as quoted, was ravening across the face of Europe like a wolf, for it was August of 1939 and when I arrived at the granary gable, carrying one small suitcase, the faces that welcomed me had a deep sadness behind the smiles in their eyes. My young brother, who had turned nineteen in March, was not among them for he had joined his naval unit two days before and they knew that my time with them was short for I was already a member of the Women's Auxiliary Air Force.

'What about your baggage?' my aunt asked in the silence after the first greeting.

'It should arrive at Fortavoch later in the week,' I said and turned to Tom and George. 'It is nothing but five cases of books but they are big and heavy and you will need the three carts. And mind you handle them with care!'

'Do you mean to say you have nothing in the world but a puckle books?' my aunt asked. 'What about your clothes?'

I pointed to the small suitcase. 'In here, mostly. There are a few rags packing the books. I sold all the rest. What the hell good would clothes be to me?'

'Books!' said my aunt.

'There is nothing much better that she could have, Kate,' my father said. 'We will look after them, Janet.'

'Och, aye,' said Tom. 'George and me has a place all cleared for them in the granary, next to Jock's lot, and we will put the boxes bye where nobody can interfere with them.'

It was a strangely happy little holiday, until I was called down to London and left on the first day of September, when my father walked down through Poyntdale with me to the County Road where I caught the 'bus. The countryside was brightening towards harvest and on every side of us the corn waved in the fields in the morning sun, just as it had waved on a September morning in 1915, when I was five years old and came down

138

this way, so proudly, old enough to go to school for the first time.

As was typical of our family, we were much too early for the 'bus and we stood waiting by the roadside, the small suitcase at our feet, the sea lapping behind us, the harvest fields shining on the slope in front.

'This is a terrible business,' my father said. 'It was bad enough when Jock went and his few clothes coming home in a brown paper parcel from Portsmouth. I didna like that, that parcel coming home.' His mouth shook as he stared down into his pipe.

'Dad! There will be a parcel from me too with my clothes in it very soon now. You mustn't worry like this.'

'I canna help it. It is a terrible business. Och, yes, Jock and the young men have to go. They are all that stands between us and that—that— But the lassies like you—this is terrible. Are you sure you are right in doing this, Janet?'

'Look, Dad, in a year they will be conscripting the women. I would rather volunteer. And it's not only that—it's—Dammit, Dad, long ago you told me that you and Mother never wanted any difference to be made between Jock and me because of our sex. You *made* no difference and there is no difference now. I am as well-equipped as Jock is to do something!'

Ever since I had been at university, I had smoked cigarettes but my father did not like to see me smoke and, although he knew I did it, I never smoked in his presence. Now, however, I took my case from my handbag and clicked my lighter but the breeze from the sea blew out the flame.

'Lend me your matches, Dad.'

He handed me the box, I lit the cigarette and handed the box back.

'What were you going to say?' he asked. 'When you said: It's not only that and then started using bad language?'

I looked sullenly at the ground. 'You said once,' I told him, 'that you would fight Hitler for putting the Jews out of their homes. Well, I am fighting him for that and for another reason too.'

'Aye?'

'He works on people in a way that I cannot stomach. He not only makes them do what he wants. He forces them to *think* what he wants and no damned Hitler or anybody else is going to interfere with what *I* think and that's why I am going to this bloody war to be a cook or a dishwasher and now you know!'

I had escaped from the strain of parting into anger and I was still more angry at first when he gave a roar of laughter.

'It is a pity,' he said after a moment, 'that you canna get at Hitler face to face.' Then, as I glared at him, he became sober before smiling down at me. 'I am sorry to see you go but I admire your spirit, lass, and even if it is only dish-washing you can do for them, you make a good job of it. Yonder is the 'bus coming past Bedamnded's Corner.'

I looked east along the shore and saw the red vehicle crawling along the road. I looked up at my father. 'Don't worry, Dad. Jock and I will be all right.'

'Aye. I believe you will. I *have* to believe it, God knows.'

The 'bus was upon us and I climbed in but I did not look back. I knew I could not look back at that lonely figure on the empty road without beginning to cry.

Against all the laws of averages in our district, where the Smiths lost two sons, the Chisholms three and the Gordons five, my brother Jock and I were 'all right' and throughout the war we kept arriving at Reachfar expectedly and unexpectedly in various stages of sartorial disrepair but in excellent health and spirits. Jock, especially, was a source of endless wonder to Tom and George, for the boy of nineteen who had left them in August of 1939, arrived home in 1941 from the Northern Patrol on his twenty-first birthday, with a red beard that curled down almost to his waist. When I arrived home later in the year, Tom said: 'You have missed the most by-ordinar' sight ever seen on Reachfar—the day Rory Ruadh himself walked round the granary gable with his kitbag on his shoulder and his red whisker blowing in the wind!'

'It was a whisker of a sort that I didna know could be grown,' said George in tones of reverent awe. 'You could have put the old sow and her litter to bed in it.'

From the time when, at the age of twenty-one, I took the post as temporary nursemaid to Lady Lydia's grandson and went off to Hampshire, I lived my life by a series of accidents and when I look back upon it, these accidents have mostly a curious air of inspiration, as if some outer force that was also a unifying principle were carrying me along. I did not seem to have any ambitions, I did not seem to make any decisions. Gates opened in front of me, as it were, and I, without looking to one side or the other or back over the way I had come, walked through them and explored the country that the gates led me into. When old Mr. Carter died, I became secretary to his daughter-in-law's brother, simply because the job was there. It was an open gate and I went through. In a similar way, after about a year in Air Force operations rooms, some officer recommended me for a commission, I was called before a 'board' in London and I non-chalantly left the nervous and hopeful group of young women I had been talking to in an anteroom, had a friendly chat with this 'board' and, quite uncaring, took a train back to my unit where I had a dancing engagement with an air-gunner that evening. He was a very nice air-gunner and I was even a little annoyed with myself and my carelessness when, a week later, I was posted with commissioned rank to a secret unit in Air Intelligence and had to leave him behind.

It was thus that, in 1941, I arrived home in the kid gloves of an officer and by 1942 I had in a similar accidental way acquired a broader ring on my tunic sleeves so that, when my brother met me at Inverness in his seaman's jersey and bell-bottomed trousers, he put his fingertips to the front of his flat cap, clicked his heels and said: 'Ma'am!' This was the first occasion that he and I had contrived to converge on Reachfar on leave at the same time and this simple joke of Jock calling me 'Ma'am' was of endless amusement to the family. It was also of some embarrassment to me and I was very annoyed when I discovered that Jock had been offered a commission in the Royal Naval Volunteer Reserve and had had the initiative to refuse it because he preferred the life of the lower deck.

'Nobody asked me what I liked,' I complained to my father. 'The Wing Commander Ops. just said to me to go to London to this board and I went and this is what happened.'

'But you like your new work, don't you?'

'Yes, the work is all right and very interesting but I feel a fool with young Jock making up his own mind like that. I am ten years older than he is and it never entered my head to say that I didn't want a commission.'

'But *don't* you want it?' My father was puzzled. 'Would you rather be back at your old job?'

'No. It isn't that!' I found it difficult to explain to him what I meant and, of course, became angry in much the same way that, at the age of four, I lay on the floor and kicked because I wanted my father to be home before I went to bed. 'Dammit, it isn't fair! All you people are always saying all the time that I am the wild, thrawn-natured bloody-minded one in this family and that Jock is quiet and docile and all that. It simply isn't true. I invariably do everything that everybody tells me to do and get commissioned and everything and *Jock* is the one that goes his own way and won't do a damn' thing he is told.'

My father laughed. 'In a way, that is true but for thrawnness, there is not much to choose between the two of you. You are both inclined to go your own way but Jock goes about it quieter, that's all.'

'At his age,' I said resentfully, 'I never made up my mind about anything. I hadn't any mind to make up. And another thing. Look at him going and getting engaged! How does *he* know that he wants to marry and who he wants to marry when I don't?'

'Jock knows all right,' my father said quietly, 'and a very bonnie nice lassie she is, with a pair of beautiful soft grey eyes in her. You still haven't seen anyone to suit yourself?' he asked.

'Ach, I think I'll be a spirited old maid like Aunt Betsy,' I said. 'It is difficult to make up your mind in wartime especially where I am and we are all shut in for weeks together without leave. Sometimes you feel like marrying *all* the men, just to create a diversion, but I think it is safer not to marry any of them.'

'Maybe you are right,' he said thoughtfully. 'Nothing is normal at a time like this.'

'And then, as Monica says, you can't tell how bloody they might look when they are out of uniform. It's different with women. A woman who looks reasonable in uniform is bound to look all right in anything, God knows, but uniform makes most men look better than they really are.'

'So you and Lady Monica are still chums?'

'Oh lord, yes. If it wasn't for Monica, I sometimes think I'd go mad among all those tin huts down there. Did I tell you that that awful Muriel Thornton that I worked with at old Madame X's had got married?'

'Aye. You mentioned it in a letter.'

'If she can get married, anybody can,' I said. 'Not that she is very particular. I would as soon have married an alligator as this bloke of hers.'

'What is wrong with him?'

'I just didn't take to him. He is a French-Canadian, he says, although his name is Robertson, he says, but I wouldn't trust him as far as I could kick him.'

'Talking of French Canadians, Mrs. Duchesne's son is over in this country. He is a lieutenant in the Tank Corps. I wrote and told her he would be welcome here at any time but I don't suppose he would bother to come away up here. He is stationed in the Midlands of England somewhere.'

However, it was on the very next day that the letter arrived, having been delayed in the post, telling us that René Duchesne would arrive in Inverness at eleven o'clock the next morning.

'He must be dotty,' I said. 'Why doesn't he go to London for his leave?'

'Maybe he is a quieter more home-loving type than you are,' Jock suggested.

'René! I said. 'The only René I have ever met was a hair-dresser in a back alley in Mayfair,' whereupon I gave an imitation of Monsieur René welcoming a wealthy client to his salon. 'Crikey, if they've got René in the Tank Corps, it's a blessing we've got an Air Force.'

'Now, that's enough, Janet,' said my aunt and turned to my father. 'Since this one joined the Air Force, she is worse than ever she was. He is a very nice young fellow, likely,' she adjured me, 'for his mother writes a very nice letter.'

'And he has come a long way from home to help us with this war,' said Tom.

'Oh, I am sure he is a perfect poppet,' I said and did a little more play acting.

'Now, Janet,' my father said, 'I know you don't want strangers about Reachfar here when you are home on leave but Tom is right. We have to do what we can for the boys from abroad.' I felt my face flush and fell silent. My father knew more about me than I had thought. 'And,' he went on, 'the two of you will get up in good time tomorrow morning and meet me on the 'bus at the end of the Poyntdale road.'

'Me?' I said. 'What for?'

'Because I don't want to miss the lad at the station at Inverness. He knows that you are in the Air Force and Jock in the Navy and it is not likely that there will be another old man like me with two ugly devils like you standing on either side of him at the platform barrier.'

I looked at my brother, he looked back at me and then I said: 'Oh, all right, if that's what you want. Should Jock bring his bo'sun's whistle and pipe dear René off the train?'

My father bent a twinkling eye upon me. 'Yesterday,' he said, 'you were asking me why it was that everybody said you were more thrawn than Jock. It is a matter of wonder to me that yourself cannot see why they should think it.'

'There is not a hair of difference in thrawnness between them—' Tom began.

'It is chust that she is outspoken thrawn and Jock is chust thrawn whatever,' George ended.

'And it ill becomes either of you two,' my aunt told them severely, 'to talk of thrawnness at all,' and then she turned to my father. 'You will bring the Canadian boy up here, Duncan?' she asked anxiously.

'If you can manage with them all, Kate.'

'Och, I can manage fine.'

'It would be as well not to have our Canadian allies frightened out of the country by Jean,' George said and we all laughed for, by now, Jean was even more of a joke among us all.

The three of us went to Inverness on the following morning, speculating all the way about what René would look like and laying strategic plans that we might not miss him in the bustle of Inverness Station which, since the war, was a very different place from the quiet backwater with a few baskets of game and salmon lying about where George and Tom used to meet me on my journeys from Cairnton. It was now a milling welter of personnel of all services and all nationalities where one more khaki uniform would make no difference and, as the train came in, the three of us formed a tight group as close to the barrier as possible and my father asked the ticket collectors to direct any enquirer for Achcraggan to us. It was strangely exciting and there was a tenseness among us as the doors of the train opened and the uniforms began to pour out on to the platform and I was searching the faces for my preconceived idea of René, a small, olive-skinned slender man with a thin black moustache, when I heard my father breathe the words: 'God Almighty!' I glanced up at him, then stood on tiptoe and followed the direction of his wondering gaze. Down the platform, carrying a small suitcase, was coming the exact replica of my brother Jock, the head over-looking most of the crowd, the red hair curling up at one side of the black beret, the vivid blue eyes searching for his way in this strange place. I glanced at my brother who now looked down at me and a self-conscious flush rose over his fair skin under the sailor's cap.

'No mistake, is there?' he asked and my father walked forward to the young man who had just passed the barrier and held out his hand. 'How are you, Renny lad?' he said. 'Welcome home!'

The young man stared for a second, took the hand and said: 'Mr. Sandison? But how—'

My father stood aside and René looked at me, then at Jock and then he blinked.

Jock held out his hand. 'I would say we had a common ancestor, wouldn't you?' he said. 'I am John Sandison.'

The tension among us broke down into a burst of laughter as the two young men looked at one another as if they were looking at their own reflection in a glass and the laughter had a strange sound in the bustling station and caused a sad little group who stood near us to forget the imminent parting and smile warmly in sympathy with us.

We were a gay party at Reachfar that leave and sometimes it seemed that old Rory Ruadh had left his grave in Eddermory churchyard and was back among us, so much did we talk of him. René, in age, was my contemporary but might have been my brother's twin for men of that red-gold colouring do not change very much until they reach middle life.

I suppose it was natural that a climate of 'romance' should develop as the three of us and, later, René and I alone roamed the countryside and, certainly, he had not been at Reachfar for twenty-four hours when I became aware of this climate developing. I would intercept glances between my aunt and my father, I would feel the eyes of Tom and George move from me to René and back again and, of course, the people of Achcraggan, who had not been told how he came to be at Reachfar, had made up their minds that he was my 'young man' come to visit my people, just as Jock's 'young lady' had come about six months ago.

Feeling all this pressure about me, I did not know what I myself felt. I admired René's looks for my brother was a hand-some fellow, I liked him and I found him interesting and he complicated the issue further by making it quite obvious that he was attracted to me. I knew that, had I met him in any other circumstances, I would have already been enmeshed in flirtation or more with him, for that was my way in those days. My friend Monic-. and I were never, as she put it, out of love. But because I had met René in the way I had and because our relationship develop_d within the family at Reachfar, my normal attitude of carefree irresponsibility left me and I tried desperately hard to come to a decision.

'Renny has his eye on you,' my father said to me shyly and quietly in the hayfield where we had just taken in the last of the crop. 'He is a splendid young fellow, Janet.'

'I know, Dad.'

'What do you feel about him?'

'I don't know.'

'You like him, don't you?'

'Yes, but—'

'What, Janet?'

'Dad, I just don't know.'

'Take your time, lass. I think Renny will wait.'

At his tone, I looked at him sharply. 'He—he has said something to you?'

'Aye. He asked me if I had—if I had any objection to him courting you.'

'Oh.' I felt the pressure tightening round me.

'I said that I had none but that I couldna speak for you. But I wished him luck, Janet.'

He smiled at me as the others gathered round and we all began to walk back to the house for supper.

This was a Saturday night and I had to leave for my unit in Buckinghamshire on Monday, Jock had to go north to Scapa Flow to his ship on Tuesday and René was to take the south train on Tuesday evening but we did not speak of any of these things round the fire that night. I do not remember what the talk was about for I was busy evading René's eyes, avoiding the speaking glances of the others and tussling with my own muddled thoughts but I remember that, when we all got up to disperse, my father said: 'There is something I would like you three to do for me.'

'Yes, sir?' René said while Jock and I also looked at my father.

'I would like you to come down to church tomorrow morning.'

I knew that René, although not devout, had been brought up in the Roman Catholic religion and was about to say something of this but before I could speak, he said: 'Of course, sir.'

'Then that is chust what we will do,' Tom said. 'The whole of the five of us will come down, Reachfar—'

'—and Kate will look after the place,' said George.

'All right,' my aunt said, 'and I'll get peace to write a good long letter to Hugh,' for Hugh, her husband, was somewhere in England at this time with his regiment.

The next morning, the 'whole of the five of us' set off down the long north-east slope to Achcraggan, René and I in front, George, Tom and Jock behind and René and I walked in a self-

conscious silence so that, when we came to the outskirts of
Achcraggan, where the road began to have a metalled surface
instead of being a cart-track, at the spot where I had parted from
my father on that cold, sleet-driven February night before I went
to Hampshire, I was relieved to hear George's voice call: 'Hi,
you two! Hold on a minute!'

René and I stopped and waited till the other three came forward, whereupon Tom drew a clean duster from his coat pocket
and said: 'Put your foot on this stone for me, Janet.'

'Tom!' I protested when I saw what was in his mind.

'An army is never beat while its boots is clean,' said Tom and
began to rub the heather dust off my black shoes and one after
the other Jock and René had to submit to the same treatment.

'Do we please you now?' I asked as he hid the duster behind a
stone anent our return.

'You'll do,' said George. 'You'll do.'

At Achcraggan Church, during the war, there was often a
parade of one service or another for we had a seaplane station of
Coastal Command just across the Firth, a detachment of gunners
on each of the Cobblers and, very often, a naval unit would come
into the Firth for a few days but, on this Sunday, we three were
the only uniforms for once for there was no parade and ours was
the only family with people home on leave.

The Reverend Roderick Mackenzie, who had christened me,
must have been about seventy now for he was some years older
than my father, but he was in no way diminished in powers.
Indeed, the years of hand-to-hand struggle against mortal sin in
Achraggan had strengthened him, if anything, and although
his black hair and beard were showing streaks of grey, his dark
eyes were as full of light and as fierce as ever and his voice had
lost nothing of its expressive impressive richness. When he
entered his pulpit, he stood for a moment with his hands on the
big Bible and looked round the church, as he always did, 'making a note of defaulters' as Tom and George put it, and a gleam

of recognition and pleasure showed in his eyes as he looked along the Reachfar pew at the front of the gallery and saw, from right to left, Tom, George, Jock, René, me and my father and, such was his personality, that that glance of his directed all the other eyes in the church to the place where we stood. With hideous selfconsciousness, I felt that my brass tunic buttons were attracting all the sunlight that streamed in through the windows except for what was caught by the red-gold hair of the young man beside me whom they all wanted me to marry and I had a panic-stricken desire to thrust past my father, rush out of the pew and run away from them all. However, the moment passed. We all sat down, the Reverend Roderick bent his head in silent prayer and then the service began.

I do not remember what psalms and hymns were sung. I remember nothing until the prayer that preceded the sermon, when I was staring down into my lap and thinking of René and myself, thinking how my marrying him would please my father. Suddenly the Hebridean voice from the pulpit broke through to my consciousness: '—and a-all the members of His Machesty's forces at sea, on land and in the air.' There was a pause and then the voice went in pleading entreaty: 'This day, oh Lord, I beg the protection of Thine everlasting arms for our own young people who are with us here today.' The voice strengthened to a tone almost businesslike, as if the Reverend Roderick felt that he must make his prayer completely clear to the Almighty at this time when so many prayers of a similar kind were arriving in the receiving office of Heaven. 'They are Chon Sandison of His Majesty's Navy, René Duchesne of His Majesty's Canadian Army and Chanet Sandison of His Majesty's Air Force. If it be Thy will, oh Lord, protect them and bring them safely home. Thy will be done. Amen.'

Now that I remembered it, George and Tom had told me that the Reverend Roderick had begun to pray in this individual way for people home on leave who attended church but, thinking as I was of other things, our names coming from the pulpit seemed like another form of pressure or me to marry René. With my arms rigidly straight, my kid-gloved hands gripped the edge of the wooden seat of the pew and from the corner of my eye I saw my brother's white sailor collar tremble a little with the tension of his embarrassment. Then René's left hand covered my right, loosed its grip on the wooden seat and held it gently. As we raised our heads and the text of the sermon was announced, I drew my hand away and became very busy with the pages of my Bible but in an ineffective way, for I had not heard the announcement of chapter and verse. I felt that all ability to decide my own fate had been taken away from me and that the simple prayer from the pulpit had been some sacrament that bound me to René and from which I could never escape. I did not even know whether I wanted to escape for, in these last few days, my father had been so happy. And René was happy. They were all happy. I wished that in my mind some clear decision would form, that I could know, of myself, what I wanted to do.

'On this Lord's day,' came the voice from the pulpit, 'I take my text from the one-hundred-and-nineteenth Psalm of David, at the one-hundred-and-thirty-fourth verse.' There was a pause, a suppressed cough or two, before the Reverend Roderick's supplicating voice spoke the words of his text: 'Deliver me from the oppression of man' and continued: 'so will I keep Thy precepts' and, silently, I found myself repeating 'Deliver me from the oppression of man' and adding: 'Please God, tell me what to do about Dad and René and everything!'

At once, this little problem of mine faded into the background. I had been vouchsafed no immediate advice as to what to do but the problem faded as the Reverend Roderick, his black gown flowing about him, raised his right arm with the fist clenched in precisely the gesture with which an aircraft was flagged off the runway on an operational sortie and the voice thundered across the echoing church: 'In this world today, a man hass cried *Haffock!* and hass let slip the terrible dogs of war!'

That evening, I went for a walk across the moor with René and we talked together for a long time and when we came back to the gate above the house, I said: 'I don't know, René, I just don't know.' He smiled down at me, strangely, fleetingly reminding me of my father and yet looking so exactly like my brother. '*I* know,' he said. 'I have known since the first moment at Inverness Station.—But you will write to me?'

'I'll write, René. And next leave—well—'

'Next leave,' he said.

We came through the gate, walked down the yard and as we came towards the door of the barn, René stopped short and looked at me questioningly for it seemed that the Reverend Roderick's voice was echoing from inside: 'In this world today, a man hass cried *Haffock!* and has—'

'It's only Tom,' I explained. 'He can mimic the minister to the life.'

'Man, Jock lad,' came Tom's own voice, 'I nearly jumped out o' my shirt when he let fly yon way this morning: "—cried *Haffock!* and hass let slip the terrible dogs of wa-ar!"'

I looked at René as he stood beside me, his hair bright in the evening sun. 'That's it, René,' I said. 'I am all in a muddle and I simply can't think straight. It is a case of havoc having been cried and we are all caught up in it.'

He smiled at me again. 'Next leave,' he said, 'it will be different.'

Next leave, it was indeed different. I did not get home to Reachfar again until September of 1943 for although, in the interval, I had had short leaves from my unit, they did not give me time to make the long journey with all its wartime delays. As I climbed the hill from Poyntdale and came through the gate in the north march wall on to the ground of Reachfar, the corn was in stooks and gilded by the sunset light to the colour of René's bright hair which was now buried and lost for ever in the burning sands of North Africa. Reachfar was a sad house, that evening, for, a month ago, just after the news of René's death, had come the news that my aunt's husband, Hugh, had also been killed.

'Janet,' she said to me gently at the granary gable and, in her dark eyes as she spoke my name, I could see her thought that she and I had a great sadness in common and I hated myself because this was not so. For me, René was simply one of the many young men I had known who would never come back, like Jimmie the air-gunner, Terry the pilot and Archie the paratrooper who had danced like a gigolo. This worried me, at first, for I felt that I ought to feel something more about René than I did about the others but, although his death grieved me, the grief was part of a general desolation that I shared with everyone who had known him and in it there was nothing that was mine only. There was not in what I felt the bereaved loneliness that I knew must be in the grief felt by a lover for a dead love.

Late in the evening, after my father had gone down to Achcraggan and Tom and George had gone to bed, I was alone at the kitchen fire with my aunt and she began to talk again of René and Hugh and I felt a petty emotion rise in me that was, at first, difficult to identify. There was a general wish in me that she would stop talking about René and Hugh, because there was no point in talk-talk-talking about them like this and then, because I felt that this was callous in me, I went on listening to what she said and murmured a few sympathetic words here and there but, all the time, the wish that the subject would drop was at the back of my mind. But still Kate talked on about how handsome René had been and what a good husband Hugh had been until suddenly there was that click and flash of white light in my brain which visited me so seldom now and I knew with certainty that Kate was talking thus of Hugh because she had heard or read somewhere that this was how a widow should speak of her dead husband, that Kate's grief for Hugh was no different in kind or intensity from my own for René although, with her intelligence, she believed that her mourning was genuine and deep. While I sat listening to her talk, I began to think back over the years and it came to me that there had been a time, just before I went to Hampshire, when Kate had mourned the loss of a lover, when Malcolm Macleod had jilted her and had married his cousin. Yes. Kate had mourned then for a deeply felt loss and it was not in the conventional phrases that she was using tonight that she had mourned. There had been no gentle tears then, either. Instead, she had been a demon of frustration and rage, ready to come to blows with her own shadow, failing any other outlet for the sense of loss and desolation that was in her. Indeed, now that I remembered that time of nearly fifteen years ago, my aunt's ill-temper around the house of Reachfar had been one of the many factors that led towards my taking the Hampshire post of nurse-maid to Lady Lydia's grandson. Hugh, the husband she had lost, had been not her real love but only second-best and this grief she was displaying was, although she believed it to be real, as unreal and as much of a convention as her marriage to Hugh had been.

I rose to my feet. 'I am going to bed, Kate. I don't want to talk about René any more.'

'I know, Janet. But it is a terrible thing the little time the two of you had together.'

'Kate,' I said harshly, 'there would never have been anything real between René and me if we had had all the world and time together.'

'But I thought—' Her dark eyes stared up at me.

'You thought wrong. I am sorry he is dead, because of his mother and father more than anything, but that is all. I am going to bed. Goodnight.'

By the next evening, I had an awareness that my aunt had told my father something of what I had said and, also, in the course of the day, I had the impression that she thought I was screening my real feelings behind a shell of harshness. This was confirmed when I set out to walk down the hill with my father in the evening, for he began at once to talk of René in terms that made his loss peculiarly mine.

'Look, Dad,' I said, 'there is a false thing creeping into this business about René and me. Kate has been talking to you, hasn't she? Well, I have to be honest about this. I liked René and I am sorry he is dead but I liked him no better than dozens of others I have known and who have died.'

'Oh,' he said very quietly, 'I thought there was more in it than that. You were writing to him and all—'

'I know, Dad. I wrote to him because he asked me to and I have written and still write to lots of others as well.'

'This war is a terrible thing!' he burst out suddenly, his voice shaking. 'You have seen too much o' death in these terrible Operations Rooms as you call them—boys coming in for orders and going out into the air and never coming back! It is a terrible thing and it is all wrong. Young people shouldna see the things you have seen!'

'I am not in Ops Rooms now, Dad. And it isn't that. I am sorry René is dead but this whole relationship between him and me was an artificial thing—it was cooked up between you and Kate and everybody and foisted on to René and me. His coming here as a long-lost distant relation and meeting me had a fine romantic story-book air about it and you thought it would be fine if something developed between us. But nothing developed.'

'Renny felt for you—he spoke to me about it.'

'Maybe he thought he did but there wasn't much in it.'

'That is a hard thing to say, Janet.'

'Maybe it is, Dad, but that is the way I feel about it and the least I can do about René is to be honest. If he had lived, you might have influenced me into marrying him—it was only last night that I found out clearly what I felt about him, when Kate was talking a lot of bogus rubbish.'

'What sort of rubbish?' he asked, frowning.

'Just rubbish. But never mind about that. Dad, how did Kate come to marry Hugh?'

He looked down at me over his shoulder as we walked, a puzzled frown on his forehead. 'In much the same way that anybody comes to marry anybody,' he said. 'Hugh came to Poyntdale and he came courting her and she took him.'

'I see.'

'What do you see?'

'I don't see anything very clearly—not clearly enough to put into words anyway.'

We walked for a little way in silence before my father said on a long sigh: 'I wish to God this war was over!'

I knew what he felt. I knew that he felt that distance had come between him and me, that, this leave, communication between us had become more difficult and I knew he was disappointed in my attitude about René which seemed to him to be harsh. All this he was blaming on the war but I felt that the war was not entirely responsible for the feeling of disruption between us. The war was merely the violent outward symbol of the eternal change which is, for most of the time, imperceptible. What my father was rebelling against, in reality, was the dim perception that the child who grows up also grows away. I was thirty-three years old but until this evening, I think, he had always seen me high in his arms, kicking at the rafters with my going-to-bed boots.

And I had been very slow of development. It was only now, as we walked down the hill, that I began to see the members of my family as a number of separate individuals who could get into similar muddles and make similar mistakes to those I could make myself. This discovery was linked to my realisation of the night before that my aunt's tears for Hugh were not from her heart but from the surface of her mind. She was capable of self-delusion, the thing that had always seemed to me to be the enemy to be most closely guarded against. It was an enemy which could pounce upon you from any and every quarter. Your family, with the best intentions in the world for your welfare, could lead you into deluding yourself that you wanted to marry René. Your love for your father could lead you into deluding yourself that he was a romantic hero of legend and not an ordinary puzzled man and even books could lead you into thinking—thinking that a goose could walk up and downstairs without leaving a filthy mess behind it. There was no limit to the number of ways in which you could be led into the snare of self-delusion and until now, when I was thirty-three years old, I had been deluding myself that I, in relation to my family, was a static quantity related to a number of other static quantities and that we were all static in relation to one another. But this was not so and the true nature of our relationships was difficult to determine. Until now, all developments that I had experienced, such as my father's marriage to Jean which, when it happened, had been so difficult of acceptance, had been a question of a mental swallowing of the lump by which act my father, the god who had fallen, was reinstated in godhead but I had never seen him in relation to Jean or, indeed, in relation to anyone except myself. And it was thus with all these people at Reachfar who had been with me since 'always'. As a child, I had known with my brain that George was something called an 'uncle' to me and something else called a 'brother' to my father but, to me, he had always been just 'George', a static quantity in relation to me only and a quantity which was incapable of change.

The first feeling to emerge out of this welter of discovery that had come to me was a terrible loneliness, for all these people who had been the steady firmament of my world now appeared as a number of separate worlds, all shifting and changing as they pursued some orbit of their own and in these outer skies where they moved, I saw that all the other people I had ever known—

my brother, my friend Muriel, Jean, my friend Monica—were all separate worlds, all being moved in orbit partly by their own volition and partly by the winds of chance to trace a pattern of their own that I could never intimately and completely know. And yet, all these worlds exerted an influence on the little lonely world that was myself, an influence which could be malign, although they did not intend it so, as could have been the influence that might have pushed me into marriage with René. 'Deliver me from the oppression of man!' I could have prayed again.

'I hear from Mrs. Duchesne about every month now,' my father said. 'Did you write to her, Janet?'

'Yes, just after you asked me to. She wrote back but I didn't write again.'

'Poor woman. I think she writes because we were the last people she knew who saw Renny. He must have written a lot to her about you, Janet.'

'Yes. I think he did.'

My father sighed. 'Oh, well, he is gone, the lad. I shouldna complain. He was her only son and I have still got both of you—both spared to me.'

It was a sad leave and I was glad when it was over but there was still the wrench at the heart when I left my father on the County Road when the 'bus came along. He was sixty-five now and still ruddy-fresh of complexion and bright of eye but the head and neck no longer rose with the old resilient power out of the broad shoulders, the tread was less springy and firm and the hair that had once been brightly dark was now silvery white all over, although as strong and abundant of growth as ever.

'You will mind,' he said, looking out over the Firth as we stood by the roadside, 'that when you went off to Hampshire for the first time, I got George to see you off at the station?'

'Yes, Dad.'

'I don't do that now. Yonder is the 'bus rounding Bedamned's

Corner. The only thing a man can do as he gets a little older is to try to overcome the faults he is most ashamed of and I have tried to get a little braver and see you off myself. But I hope the war will soon be over. I never get used to seeing you go away.'

As the 'bus carried me away westwards, it seemed that, for me, the war would never be over, that war and struggle and effort were a basic condition of life, but a struggle on the perimeter of which I had contrived to stay until I was thirty-three years old. Looking back now, it seemed to me that my behaviour had been that of a high-spirited fourth-former who could get into mischief occasionally but who, basically, was deeply conventional and law-abiding. In the various jobs by which I had earned my living, I had got up to mischief in the way of teasing my employer if the job bored me, much as a fourth-former misbehaves in class when bored by the teacher or the subject and, when working in jobs that interested me, I did them efficiently enough but with little inspiration. Looking back, I found it interesting that the two posts in which I had stayed longest and which I had liked most were my posts as secretary to old Mr. Carter and as secretary to Sir Richard Ingram with whom I had been just before the war. In both of these I was working for a man who might have been my father in age and who treated me like a daughter and I was also part of a family unit, living in the homes of these employers.

In 1943, as the train carried me south from Inverness to Buckinghamshire, it became apparent to me that I had not yet walked, all by myself and unprotected, on to the stage of life. I had merely been waiting in the wings, waiting for what I did not know, unaware, even, that I was waiting and it seemed to me that I was not alone in this but that there were many people, especially women, whose lives were spent entirely in waiting from the moment they were born until the moment when they died. It was natural that Milton's phrase 'They also serve who only stand and wait' should enter my mind here and I supposed it was true that, to some degree, I had 'served'. My father was proud of the fact that ever since I had left home for Hampshire in the month before my twenty-first birthday, I had 'never sent home for a penny of help' so that, to achieve this small standard of personal independence, I must have served somebody satisfactorily in some way, I supposed. But now, in the new light in which I stood, the light that had blazed up from that first spark of self-examination about René which my aunt's attitude had induced in me, the passivity of service in the form of 'doing what I was told', the idea which had been so deeply implanted in me as a child, was no longer enough. Surely there was some means of service—there was no question in my mind that all of living was a form of service, be it to man or God or some ideal—which would be of my own choice?

As the train rattled at high speed down over the dark flats north of London and its sound made me think, as it always does, of the rushing mounting second movement of Beethoven's Ninth Symphony, I sat in a crowded compartment full of sleeping or smoking people in uniform and remembered how, long ago, thirteen years ago, I had wanted to write. I had never done it for the little immediate world had always been too much with me. There had always been my living to earn by day, someone to dance with in the evening, my hair to wash on Sunday forenoons and, then, there had been this war.

When I arrived, some thirty-six hours after I left Reachfar, at the tin hut that was the officers' mess of my unit, it was evening and my friend Monica greeted me in the anteroom. Over the drink she offered me, I said: 'Can you remember the whole text of Milton's sonnet on his blindness?'

'For Heaven's sake why?' she asked reasonably enough.

'Never mind that now,' I said.

She ran a hand through her auburn hair and wrinkled her beautiful forehead. 'It starts off: When I consider how my light is spent ere half my days in this dark world and wide—' she said, 'but I can't remember any more. If you are dead set on it, though, old Roebuck has a complete Milton in his shack. He produced it one night when we were doing a crossword.'

'No. It doesn't matter. Only, did it ever occur to you that some people have spent half their days in this dark world and wide before their light ever comes on?'

'Something of the sort has occurred to me from time to time although not in these graphic words,' she said. 'And, what is more, a lot of their lights when they do come on are unconscionably dim. You only have to look round at the faces in this so precisely named mess here to see that. Have another noggin.'

And so, not until the age of thirty-three did my light begin to come on and, in Monica's words, it was unconscionably dim, a mere flickering candle which stood away on the far horizon of my innermost mind, dipping and sputtering in every wind, so lost in distance that it was visible only to myself and fitfully so, even to me. And in 1945, at last, the war ended.

Part Four

'—that we henceforth be no more children, tossed
to and fro, and carried about with every wind of
doctrine, by the sleight of men, and the cunning
craftiness, whereby they lie in wait to deceive;
but speaking the truth in love, may grow up—'

THE EPISTLE OF PAUL THE APOSTLE
TO THE EPHESIANS iv. 14–15

YES, in 1945 the war ended and it was as if the sands in the hour-glass of time suddenly rushed from the top chamber to the bottom and as if the glass had then, with infinite speed, been reversed, whereupon the everlasting sands began to flow again but in an almost imperceptible trickle, marking a new tempo in a new world. I have thought, sometimes, that one of the reasons why mankind goes to war is its subconscious knowledge of the relief that it will experience when its wars end for, in 1945, I felt like 'that poor devil Christian' when his burden fell from his back. Like Christian too I had no idea where I was going now or what kind of world lay ahead of me but I was sure that nothing could be worse than the six years that lay behind.

I have hitherto come to regard the six years of the war as my true adolescence, the period which is commonly regarded as the most painful in life. Certainly, my years of physical adolescence, which culminated in the event of my father's second marriage, were in the main unhappy but the unhappiness, uncertainty and insecurity were of a more material kind and less painful than the unhappinesses, uncertainties and insecurities that I had felt deep in the mind during the years of the war.

Some outward change is expected in the physical adolescent, such as an outbreak of pimples in a boy or an excess of fat in a girl and is regarded as a normal thing, a passing phase and the inner change, if the mind has made its transition to a more adult state, tends to pass unnoticed behind the screen of pimples or fat. When the transition from mental adolescence is late as it was in my case, however, no outward change is visible but I, the very conscious subject of the change that was taking place in my mind was very much concerned that anyone, even my friend Monica, should 'notice anything'. I did not want it known that I was such a backward child for I felt it to be a disgrace, just as I should have felt it to be disgraceful to be unable to maintain my age standard in counting or reading when I first went to school. Also, it is with the transition from adolescence to adulthood that the sense of personal privacy develops and this, maybe because it developed late, was a very strong growth in me. I wanted to hide very carefully this new individuality, this new singularity of personality, this independent world in its separate orbit that I had discovered in myself.

Having believed for a long time that the best hiding-place is directly under the light, it seemed to me that the best way of concealing the new self of which I had become aware lay in stressing the old self that my friends and family had always known, in presenting this old self in a strident light, by way of better concealment of the new. Instead of showing any change, then, I became, consciously, even more the person I had always been in the eyes of my father and my family for the last fifteen years or so. During these fifteen years, I had been hovering on the fringes of self-knowledge merely but hovering, in their eyes, with the blithe inconsequence of a butterfly over a summer garden and now I became outwardly more blithe and inconsequent than ever in my attitude, more Micawberish than ever in my outward conviction that something would turn up for me to do and more brashly assertive than ever that all was for the best in this best possible of worlds of mine. Judging from the response of my family, which veered through many moods from irritation with me to amusement, my performance must have been fairly convincing.

It was therefore in a flippant and lightsome way that, in spite of my inner turmoil and uncertainty, I wrote home to my father and told him that I was to be demobilised in September and that

166

since even cigarettes and whisky had been rationed during the war and there had been no clothes to buy, I had a little money saved so that I thought I would spend the winter at Reachfar, 'living on my fat'. My real intention was to spend the winter on an effort to write something but I did not say this for this new cell of privacy that I had discovered inside myself had in it, a little to my own amazement, a hard core of desire to write. But, on my way home through London, for a complex or reasons, I spent a night or two with my friend Muriel Robertson and this is where the habit of a lifetime asserted itself. At Muriel's house, I was no longer in that quiet private world where the desire to write lay at the centre, I was in the public world of the push and pull of relationships and when Muriel and her husband told me of a secretarial post near Glasgow which was being offered, I decided in my old inconsequent and inadvertent way, for a complex of reasons that amounted to no real reason at all, to take the post. When I arrived home and told my father that, after all, I was going to spend only a month at Reachfar, he was part-pleased, part-disappointed and part-exasperated and I had no means of arguing myself out of the situation except those flippant means that had got me into it.

'I just don't understand your way of going about things at all,' he told me. 'Now, Jock goes about things in a sensible and reasonable way. He has always wanted to be a schoolmaster, he has stuck to it and he came out of the Navy and went straight to Aberdeen to train. But you, according to yourself, were going to spend the winter here and now you are off to Glasgow instead. You are just like a flea on a blanket, Janet. Are you never going to settle down? You are thirty-five, you know.'

'But Dad, I have always told you I liked secretaryship and this is a secretarial job and quite a good one—'

'Yes, I know and I will say that it is remarkable how you have held your own ever since you went to Hampshire and you have never sent home for a penny. I will give you credit for that, right enough. But it is your way of going *about* things that I don't understand. You never seem to have any set plans or forethought—'

'I had a forethought about spending the winter at Reachfar—' Now that I was at Reachfar, I was regretting having altered my decision about spending the winter there.

'But you are not staying at Reachfar now!' he protested.

'I know, but I still could if you want me to. I could write to Mr. Slater and say I have changed my mind about the job.'

'You will do no such thing after engaging to go to the man! That would be plain dishonest,' he told me sternly.

'But, Dad, what do you want me to do then?'

'Och, Janet, it's not that I want you to do anything in particular. It is just the way you go about things. Now, Jock—'

'Ach, poop to Jock! There is a thing that you seem to forget, Dad. I am a new experiment in this family. I am its first career woman and there is no good in expecting me to go about life in the same way as Jock. Jock is just following the normal precedent for the men of the family, only he is a university-trained professional man instead of a farmer. He has got himself engaged and will get married when he gets a job and will settle down as you call it. But I have no precedents to follow. I have to hammer out the pattern as I go along and I thought Mr. Slater's job was as good a next move as any other.'

'I suppose you are right,' he said, frowning. 'It would be a pity to refuse a good job when it falls into your lap but I am disappointed that your holiday is to be so short.'

But, deep down, under all this froth about how I 'went about things', there was, I knew, his basic desire to see me married for this was the traditional end for a daughter of our class and, pleased as he was with the outcome of the educational experiment that had been made on me—it had been pleasant to have a well-dressed, independent daughter arriving home from London each year, it had been gratifying to be the only man of his class in our district to have a daughter who was 'an officer at the war'—it was desirable now to see me 'settled' before old age came upon me. I was finding, now, that jokes about spirited spinsters fell a little flat in the Reachfar kitchen and I knew that, down in Achcraggan, Jean was referring to me in a scornful way as 'that auld maid'.

The members of my family, even George and Tom, wore a subdued air and, more often than not, my father's forehead was creased by a puzzled frown. It seemed to me, sometimes, that there was an aura of guilt about them all as if, at this stage, they had begun to wonder whether the manner of my upbringing had been, after all, a terrible mistake and this puzzlement of theirs induced a sense of guilt in myself and some self-pity too because, by my very success in becoming what they had wished me to be, I was now a disappointment to them. They had not thought the thing out to its logical conclusion, I told myself angrily for, in spite of my new awareness, I was still obtuse enough to think that logic could be applied to life. They wanted to have their cake and eat it too, I grumbled inwardly. Now that they and I had proved that a young woman could be totally independent, they wanted me to lapse back conveniently into the old familiar pattern for women of our class. In spite of my new awareness, I was still unaware that a father and a family like mine who believed in the future wanted not themselves, but their children, to have the cake and eat it too.

We were all inarticulate as well as being uncertain of what we felt and thought and there was all around us the atmosphere of after the deluge, of being between two rhythms, of our lives being like scattered debris on a beach only recently released from the tornado of the war. Tempers at Reachfar became frayed and mine, inevitably, the most frayed of all.

During the month I was at home, more and more people were demobilised and among them was young Doctor Alasdair Mackay, the son of the Achcraggan doctor, who was an exact contemporary of mine and whom I had known and had been friends with ever since I first went to school at the age of five. Alasdair and I had always gone about together if we happened to be at home from school, university, work or the war at the same time but, contrary to what the local people and, I think, both of our families thought, there never was anything remotely resembling a love affair between Alasdair and me. We had little in common except our ages, five years together at Achcraggan School and a similarity of later education in that when I went to Glasgow, Alasdair went to Edinburgh University. Although we spent a lot of time together during the holidays, this was largely because there was nobody else of our own kind in the district and most of the time we were together we quarrelled and argued out of the sheer dissimilarity of our minds and our approach to almost everything that life contained. On a very small scale, we might be said to represent the cleavage that exists between science and art, Alasdair standing for science and I for art. This is to describe the difference on a pompous level but it illustrates the nature of the difference between us.

When, one evening, just before I left for Ballydendran to take up my new post, my aunt began to quote at the supper-table Achcraggan's pronostications about Alasdair and me, I became very annoyed and, when I began to walk down the hill with my father afterwards and he made some further remark, I lost my temper completely. 'I wish to God,' I said, 'that you would all stop shoving me into bed with every man that crosses my path!'

'Janet!' he protested, shocked at this crudity, and I was at once regretful.

'Dad, I am sorry. But you have all got to stop this, you know. It is simply not fair. You have brought me up and educated me to think for myself and be independent and now you are trying to shove me at Alasdair Mackay who doesn't believe that any woman can think at all. I wouldn't live with Alasdair for a week without hitting him over the head with the nearest bottle.'

'But you have always been friends! I thought you liked Alasdair.'

'Oh, fiddlesticks! It isn't as simple as that.' I found it very difficult to explain myself and ended by not even attempting it. 'You must just leave me alone, the whole lot of you, that's all. If I see somebody I want to marry, I'll marry him but it is very unlikely that I will. And if you feel that I am an old maid and a disgrace to you all, you know what you can do about it!'

'There is no question of disgrace, Janet. But it is natural for us to want—to want—'

'—to see me settled as you call it. I know. The truth is that when you started your educational experiment and equality of the sexes stuff on me, you didn't think it through to the end and now you are all in a muddle and trying to wriggle out. Well, you can't. I know what I want in the way of a partner and if I don't find him I am not going to settle for any damned Alasdair Mackay, even if he were willing, which he isn't.'

There were no further coy hints about matrimony around Reachfar. Amicable relations were restored and, about mid-October, I departed for my new post at Ballydendran, leaving my family with the impression that they could look forward to annual or more frequent visits from a female business executive, single and self-sufficient. It was irritatingly typical of my way of living my life or of the way that life treats me that the first thing I did at Ballydendran was to fall mortally and completely in love with the Works Manager, a thickset, blue-eyed thrawn Scotsman precisely six weeks younger than myself. There was no thinking or wondering about this as there had been about René. There was no half-guilty feeling of establishing myself matrimonially as there had been with a man called Alan Stewart to whom I had been engaged in London. There was no mental muddle as there had been when I was nineteen and had got myself engaged inadvertently to Victor Halloran. This Alexander Alexander, whom I nicknamed 'Twice', was simply and unquestionably the man I wanted and I was going to marry either Alexander Alexander or nobody.

That Alexander Alexander seemed to have other ideas complicated matters a little but not fatally. He seemed to like my company, conversation and other attributes very well but, always, when I felt that I had made a little headway with my plans, he would draw back, but, in the end, I lured him to Reachfar for our summer holiday. This was in August of 1947, the culmination of an assault I had begun in October of 1945, so it was obvious that this man had a certain staying power and independence of mind. On a remote moor, in the evening light, he at last admitted that he loved me. The next morning, I informed my family that I was going to be married and then Twice and I drove back to Ballydendran. It was only then that I discovered that he was married already but had been separated from his Roman Catholic wife for sixteen years.

And thus I found myself in a situation such as I had never imagined. I had seen, in the course of my life, illicit liasions and intrigues of various kinds but I had always regarded them as spheres of life which were outside my scope for the very good reason, among others, that I knew that I had not the intelligence to follow a secretive course without being found out. And it did not occur to me, now, to follow a secretive course any more than it occurred to me to part from Twice. When my breath came back sufficiently for me to be able to speak, I suggested that if we could not be married legally, that was just too bad and we must therefore make do without the blessing of the law. It was Twice and not I who said: 'But what about your family?' and it did not occur to me to conceal the truth from my father. I thought about it a little, knowing that the step I was about to take would 'worry' him, but in spite of that my answer to Twice's question was an airy: 'Think nothing of it! I'll fix *them*!'

Twice and I went back north to Reachfar, I found my father

alone on the moor and told him what had happened while he stared away over the Firth to the north.

'A bad business,' he said when I had finished and then came the words which were the last that I expected: 'What are you going to do, Janet?' With those words, the whole tradition of Reachfar as it had been went overboard for my father showed his total acceptance of the new principle that a Sandison daughter had the right to depart from the entire family code, the entire family religion, if she chose, without being cast out of the family itself. All this was implicit in his voice as he asked that question. I told him what I intended to do and he did not remonstrate with me, but returned to the house with me where Twice was waiting with George, Tom and Kate, whereupon he told them of the situation. He told them in such a way that they accepted it without argument and gave me their tacit support.

'This is something I did not expect,' Twice told me quietly that evening, after my father had gone down to Achcraggan, 'and there is no good saying that I understand it, for I don't.'

'I don't understand it myself yet,' I agreed, 'but tomorrow is still to come.'

The next day was a Sunday. My father seldom came up to Reachfar on Sundays but he came on this day, arriving shortly after we had finished our mid-day dinner and, from the shirt and tie he was wearing, I knew that he had been to church that morning although he had changed out of his church-going suit. No formal words were spoken and no invitation was issued but, very shortly, he and Twice walked away up among the trees of the Home Moor.

I remember that, after my aunt and I had finished the washing-up, she left the scullery and I sat on the table by the window, the only window in the house that looked to the stormy north and I stared away across the Firth to the hills. I do not remember what I thought about either while I was there or, later, when I went up to my Thinking Place among the tall trees above the well. This dim green-shaded dell had been known to me as the 'Thinking Place' ever since I can remember—it was part of 'always'—but today I was not thinking. My mind was curiously still, aware that I was about to do something that was quite outside of the family tradition by which, until now, I had lived and I felt that I ought to be astonished at myself for what I was about to do but was, instead, merely vaguely astonished that I was *not* astonished.

My father found me in the Thinking Place at about four in the afternoon and as we emerged together from among the trees, I saw Twice some six hundred yards away, walking down the yard towards the house. My father sat down on one of the big boulders beside the duck-pond and took out his pipe. He took off his tweed hat and laid it on the heather beside him so that I looked down at the strong thatch of silver-white hair.

'Dad,' I said, 'I wouldn't have worried you like this for anything in the world—except Twice.'

He looked up at me where I stood above him and smiled and it was the smiling face I used to see beneath me when my going-to-bed boots kicked the rafters of the kitchen.

'I am not worried, Janet, not any more.' He looked down over the Reachfar fields, down over Poyntdale to the Firth and then to where Twice was going in through the door of the house. 'That is a good man,' he said, paused and went on: 'I was worried yesterday, at first. You see, I knew you had Twice in your eye from the minute you brought him here for the holidays. To tell you the truth, I was kind of wild at him for holding off from you the way he was doing when you first arrived.' He laughed a little. 'I didna know the lad was doing his best with the way things were. It seems to me that he has tried to do his best all the way along. He even tried to leave his job a wee while after you met at this Ballydendran place?'

'Yes, he did, now that I think of it. He did give notice but Mr. Slater persuaded him to stay on.'

'He says that maybe he should have gone and never heeded Mr. Slater but I don't see it like that. Mr. Slater needed him there at his works in Ballydendran. When you think of it, everything about the whole thing is right—right in feeling, like —except this mistake Twice made when he was young by marrying this lassie in Belfast. I couldna think of a man that I would like better to see you with than Twice, not if I had been able to pick him myself out of all the men there are. Renny was a fine fellow, Janet, but too soft and gentle for you. You would have ridden roughshod over him and then Alasdair the Doctor—he would have gone roughshod over a lot that is in yourself. I have thought a lot about Alasdair since that time you got wild at me about him just after the war. No. There is only the one thing wrong in this whole thing and that is this early mistake of a marriage and I don't think any man should have to pay for a lifetime for a mistake that he made when he was young. Mistakes are too easy to make.'

'You are being very very good about this, Dad,' I said with difficulty.

'No. It is not a question of being good in that way. If I thought you were doing wrong, I would tell you but I am danged if I can see that you are. If I had ever imagined that the like of this would happen, I think I would have imagined that I would have been angry with you or disappointed in you or something like that, but that is all just imagination. Now that this *has* happened, now that it has come to it, all I want is all I ever wanted for you—that you would find somebody you would be happy with and that you would have an easier life from a work point of view than your granny or any of the other women of our family. There is a lot of talk goes on about people being ambitious for their bairns—you will mind on how Granny used to say that I didna think a belted earl would be good enough for you but none of that is true. Not about me, anyway. The way I have always seen it is that I had to do my best to give you a future but, after that, your life is your own.' He began to fill his pipe and I watched the long strong fingers working with the tobacco. 'I think you have been unlucky, in the way of Twice being burdened with this mistake behind him but you canna complain. It is the first bit of real ill luck you have had since you were ten, when your mother died.'

'That is true, Dad.'

'And it is easy to say that if your mother hadna died, things would have been different but there is no use in saying it.' He put his tobacco away but, instead of lighting the pipe, he held it between his hands and looked down into it. 'I am not a very religious man,' he said, 'but while the war was on, I learned something. It was in the early days, when you were in the bombing down in Kent and Jock was in that minesweeper in the Western Approaches. It was a dirty October day and we were lifting the tattie crop and all at once I looked down the hill there, wishing that the postie would come and I found myself thinking: Thank God that Elizabeth is dead, for she died happy. This waiting and worrying for the post to come bringing news of the two of them would have killed her.' He paused for a moment. 'It was the first time that I was ever thankful that your mother was dead.' He now began to light his pipe and when it was going well he went on: 'I am telling you this because, after that, it came to me that there isn't anything that happens that isn't in some way for the best, but the best will never be there if you don't look for it. I am sure in my own mind that you would not be going together with Twice like this for any light reason and after speaking to Twice, I know that he will do his best by you.' Suddenly, he took the pipe from his mouth and looked straight at me. 'I am looking for the best to come out of what is between you and Twice, Janet, and it is only you and Twice that can disappoint me, mind that. I am looking for what is between you to be a better and a real-er marriage than many a one that is made in a church. You have seen plenty of shabby marriages in your time one way and

176

another so don't let yours be a shabby one. That is all I am asking for you or myself either.'

'I'll do my best, Dad,' I promised.

'I know you will. Now, we will say no more about it. You and Twice will follow the plan George made yesterday if you are wise. From the point of view of Jean and the people up here, you and Twice will have been married quietly in the south and from the point of view of them down south, you will have been married quietly up here. There is no reason in the world why anybody except us here at Reachfar should know anything o' the truth. It is none of anybody's business whatever and as Tom says: What people doesna know canna hurt them.'

The marriage between Twice and me was a success, so much of a success that we were, as my father had wished, more truly married than many couples who have been united by church and state and when, in March of 1948, I wrote home to tell my father that I was pregnant, the handwriting in the letter that he wrote in reply was larger than usual, more firm in its down-strokes but it shook a little in the last line where he wrote: 'I have not felt like this since the day you were born. Health, Happiness, Good Luck & Best Love, Your Dad, D. Sandison.'

My brother had been married in 1946 to his pretty Shona and their little daughter Elizabeth was now just a year old which explains the postcard which Twice and I received from George and Tom which said succinctly: 'This is just to tell you that Duncan Sandison is the only man in the world that ever was a grandfather twice over.' It was in the midst of all this laughter and happiness that the ill fortune which had left me unvisited for so long struck at me once again. I fell, during May, on the little bridge that led to our house at Ballydendran, I lost my baby and, from the day I fell until the following November, I lay in bed with total paralysis of my body and legs from the waist down. I had never been ill in my life before with anything more serious than a cold in the head and I did not take well to the life of the invalid, despite the kindness and luxury with which I was surrounded and my mind lapsed into a grey torpor out of which was born eventually the grisly spectre of suicide.

My father, my aunt and George all travelled south at various times to see me, but I had slipped into this grey dimension of my own in the light of which they were no longer real. Even the 'worried' look in my father's eyes failed to move me and I had no feeling either of guilt or shame at remaining unmoved. I cared for nothing and for nobody.

It was not through any courage or effort of the will of my own that I grew better again but grow better I did, although I have since thought that this was more than I deserved. The paralysis went away, gradually, but as mysteriously as it had suddenly come and by February of 1949 I was walking again and perfectly normal although, now, I would never be able to have a child.

In July of 1949, Twice and I with my friend Monica and a party of other friends went north by car to Reachfar and, the nearer we came to it, the greater did the sense of shame, which had haunted me since my health had been restored, become. Everywhere I looked, I seemed to see the worried eyes of my father as he had stood beside my bed with the sunshine on his hair and, as if on a screen behind those eyes, I would see myself lying shrouded in a grey miasma, unmoved, uncaring, making no effort to relieve the pain of those who loved me. This sense of shame was something so deeply private that I had been unable to speak of it even to Twice, to whom I could speak of most things. It was something that I kept buried within myself and tried to ignore.

As always, my father, George, Tom and my aunt were at the granary gable when we drove up to Reachfar and I, all thought of my guilt and shame well hidden for the moment even from myself, sprang out of the car to go to greet them. I did not stop to think that the last time my father had seen me I had been hobbling about on crutches, a seemingly hopeless cripple, but

178

the look of wonder on his face arrested me as I began to run towards them all. Then he said very quietly: 'Aye, Janet. You are on the move again right enough,' and he turned away for a moment so that none of us could see his face. The concealed shame inside me sprang up, a growth more rank, virulent and bitter than ever before.

There were many cross-purposes at Reachfar that holiday, the more surface of them stemming from a quarrel between me and Monica, who was much loved by my family, and in this quarrel they were all on the side of Monica. It took Twice a little time to understand this for he felt that the family should have taken my part rather than hers but, as I told him, in any quarrel of mine my family had always tended to range itself on the side opposed to me. This was a curious thing. I suppose that it was really an oblique compliment of a sort for the reason for it was my family's belief that I was a very strong thrawn quarreller and that, no matter who my enemy of the moment might be, that enemy, right or wrong, was the better of a few allies. In a similar way, when I was young, if any mischief was perpetrated in the district, I was always my family's first suspect and even if it were proved that I had not been in any way involved, nobody apologised for their wrongful suspicions. My father would merely say: 'Oh, well, if you weren't there, you were thereabout' or 'Oh, well, if you weren't mixed up in it, it was more by luck than judgment.' And this is how it was about Monica. According to my family, the responsibility for the quarrel was mine, for only anyone as thrawn as I was could possibly quarrel with Monica and even Monica herself telling them that I was not to blame did not stop them regarding me with suspicion for several weeks. I must except George from all this, however, for George sometimes draws aside from the family group and takes a second-sighted view of his own of a situation and he did this now about Monica and me, but my father was definitely ranged with Kate and Tom on Monica's side and this put distance between us.

It was not, therefore, until Monica and I had resolved our quarrel that I attained anything like my old footing with my father and when he and I, at last, found ourselves on the moor without the red-haired spectre of Monica between us, my grey miasma of shame for my behaviour during my illness made an even more impassable barrier. I wanted desperately to confess to him how I felt but I could not find the words.

'It was a bad business about your baby, Janet,' he said with obvious difficulty, startling me, on the last evening before Twice and I were to travel south to Ballydendran again. The worried look was behind his eyes and I said with an effort: 'Yes, but things are better than anybody expected. At least I can walk again. They didn't think I would for a time. I didn't think so myself either.'

'Aye. It was a bad time you had.'

'Many people have much worse. Dad, I don't think I behaved very well when I was ill and I have been ashamed of myself ever since. I didn't think about anybody except myself,' and I ended harshly, 'but I was hellish sorry for poor dear me.'

He stopped on the track through the heather and looked straight at me, his eyes very bright. 'Janet,' he said, 'you are not thinking of this accident and the loss of your baby as a judgment, in any way, on Twice and yourself?'

It was a thought that had haunted me but I had never admitted its existence even to myself and now I said nothing.

'There has been a hardness in you since that illness,' he said quietly, 'and I don't blame you for it. Hard things make hard people but I wouldna like you to be thinking that what happened was a punishment on you. It would be better not to believe in God at all than to believe in a God that gives a punishment like that. The thing was an accident, Janet, that came about through your own recklessness, running over the bridge and you the way you were. It was not God that caused it but yourself.'

'Yes. I suppose it was, Dad. But if only the baby had been saved, though—'

'Janet, leave it. After that accident of yours, it may be a mercy that the baby never lived. Janet, do you mind on yon bonnie baby that was Mrs. Maclean's grandchild?'

Over the years, I remembered him in the corner of the kitchen, dangling the keys in front of the baby. I remembered how tenderly he had given the child back to its mother and the strange look which had shown in his eyes as he went out, leaving us all.

'Yon bairnie,' he said now, 'only died last year. It was still an infant in its mind. It never walked or spoke, it never learned to sit up by itself even, and it a full-grown woman in its body.'

I swallowed. 'All right, Dad. I see what you mean.'

'And you will try to stop wishing that things were different?'

'Yes, Dad.'

It was easier now to tell him of the shame that was in my mind and I said: 'Dad, there is a thing I am ashamed of. When I was ill, I didn't care about any of you. You see, at one time I made up my mind to kill myself. I was planning to take an overdose of the sleeping pills. It seemed the best way at the time for I couldn't see how I could go on, paralysed as I was. It seemed so unfair to Twice. That is why I never bothered about any of you when you came to see me and never bothered about how worried you all were. But I am ashamed of myself now and I am very sorry.'

'You needna be ashamed, Janet, or sorry either. They say it is wrong for a person to take her own life but I wouldna like to make a judgment either way. I am seventy-one now and I am not nearly so sure about what is right and what is wrong as I was fifty years ago. It seems to me that you canna have the right without a little bit of the wrong to go along with it. I have never tried deliberately to do anything I thought was wrong so I don't know if a bittie of what was right would come out of it but I have tried time and again to do what I thought was right and I aye got a bittie wrong along with it. I think, maybe, though, that for you to have done what you say you thought of doing would have been more wrong than right. It might have been a relief to yourself to have been out of it but Twice and the rest of us would have missed you.' He walked along a little way in silence and then: 'When I have been kind of stuck and not knowing right what to do, I have found that if I think what it would mean for other folk if I did a certain thing, it works out easier and better on the whole. Yet, I don't know. That was how I looked at things when I married Jean. I was thinking that Granny was getting old, Kate would be marrying and going away likely and I wanted you to have your freedom and not feel that you had to come home and keep house at Reachfar. All that was part of the reason why I married Jean but, as things turned out, Hugh was killed and Kate is still at Reachfar and Jean would never have taken to Reachfar anyway. But in another way, things have turned out all right, for Jean, in spite of her tongue and her queer ways, has aye been good to me.'

'You have the great distinction, Dad,' I told him in a pompous voice, 'of being the only man—indeed the only human being—whom, as the novelists say, Jean has ever loved.'

He gave a chuckle of laughter. 'Maybe it is that,' he said, 'but, anyway, I meant it for the best when I married her and it has turned out not bad on the whole.' He suddenly became grave. 'Janet, if anything should happen to me, you will let Jean go on living in the cottage downbye for as long as she needs it?'

'Of course!' I said. '*I* don't want the damned cottage!' and I spoke lightly for this was a subject from which I wanted to spring lightly away, without making close contact.

'Old Aunt Betsy left the cottage to you,' he said, 'and you may be glad of it one day. A sound home is always a good thing to have behind you.'

'There is always Reachfar behind me,' I said. 'Dad, long ago, when I was a kid, I eavesdropped one night and heard you telling Granny that you wanted Reachfar to belong equally to Jock and me. Granny wasn't pleased. She thought it should go to Jock.'

He laughed a little. 'Aye. The way your granny thought about Reachfar you would think it was the old Poyntdale of before the First War that was in it or a dukedom or the like instead of a few acres of heather and rock. And maybe it is as well that Granny didna live to see this day for Jock doesna care a damn for Reachfar—he wouldna give a single one of his books for it. That is a funny thing. It is in *your* blood and bone that Reachfar is, not in Jock's. But as you say, you havena much need for either Reachfar or the cottage, with the way things are with Twice and you. Twice is going to go a long way, Janet. He is a clever man as well as a good one. When do you think you will be leaving for abroad?'

'Probably before the end of the year, Twice thinks.'

'As soon as that? Well, you must be sure and mind to—'

'Write home!' I finished for him. 'Yes, Dad, I will write home. If all the letters you and I have written to one another—a letter every week since 1931 except for holidays—were laid end to end they would make a bridge from here to this West Indian island we are going to. But never mind, I will write.'

'Long ago, you once said to me that you would like to try to write a book,' he said. 'Have you ever tried?'

'No, Dad. There have always been too many other things—my work, the war, Twice—'

'There is plenty of time yet, Janet.'

'I doubt if I could do it, Dad. I am not so brash and cheeky now as when I was young. When I was twenty-one, I thought there wasn't anything much that I would not be able to do when I was a little older but now—'

'It is a funny thing, that,' he said when I hesitated. 'The older you get, the more you know in one way but the less sure you are of the truth of what you know.'

'That is the whole point, Dad. The thing that stops me writing is the fear that I couldn't get the truth out on to the paper. The older you get, the more complex the truth gets. It gets all muddled up with all these things you think you know.'

'Aye and with every wind of doctrine, as the Reverend Roderick had it in his sermon last Sunday.'

When my father spoke the word 'wind', he pronounced it with the vowel broad and long as in the Scots dialect word 'wynd' for a narrow city lane and it seemed to me extraordinarily graphic, conjuring up a picture of truth, wandering and lost among all the wynds in the great cosmopolis of doctrine.

'I can see what you mean,' he continued, 'but in spite of all the doctrine, everybody has their own truth. It is a thing that is in you and, if you stick by it, you canna go far wrong. Here is something I will tell you now although I have never told you before, because I hadna got it thought out right. That time you came home here and told me that you were going with Twice although the two of you couldna get married, I fair lost my breath for a minute, out on the East Roadie there. I wanted to put on what you used to call my grieve's face when you were a bairn and tell you that you couldna and mustna go and do this thing. But then I said to myself: Why has she come home here and told me this at all? She needna have told me. She could be living with this man down there in the south and I would never be any the wiser. And it was then that I listened, reasonable-like, to what you had to say. I am not clever, as you know. It takes me a while to think things out and it was only later on that it came to me that you had told me just because you wanted me to know the truth about you—*your* truth. It was a good thing, that, Janet. I am pleased that you told me.—And things are right between you and Twice, aren't they?'

'As right as anything could possibly be, Dad. The legal side of it is only the doctrine, you know and the doctrine doesn't matter if, at bottom, you have got the truth.'

'Aye!' His voice was enthusiastic. 'Aye, that's it. Well, I hope you will enjoy your trip to the West Indies. Maybe when you come back you will write a book about it. That would be fine. What about that?'

'You and your books!' I said.

Puffing at his pipe, he smiled out over the Firth. 'I would like fine to see your name on the cover of a book,' he said.

'Or I could put yours on it,' I told him. 'I would need a pen-name. I would hate Twice to become known as the-husband-of-that-famous-woman-who-writes-the-books!'

With this, we both laughed uproariously and came back to the house, and the next day, Twice and I left for Ballydendran and, a few weeks later, we left Scotland for the West Indies.

At this time, we spent only a month in the island of St. Jago but, in 1950, we flew out to the island again and did not return to Scotland until early August of 1951. During this period, my father developed a new technique in the posting of his letters, having made up his mind that the time had come for him to recognise the existence of the air-mail. He regarded it as something of an extravagance, however, very much as he had always regarded the sending of telegrams and would indulge in it only once a month, air-mailing the letter that he wrote on the first Sunday of each month and sending the other three or four, as the case might be, by surface mail. The surface mail was somewhat erratic, some letters taking as little as twelve days and others taking as long as four and a half weeks to arrive and Twice and I were often in some confusion about the order of events at home, having had a letter by air on one day that told us the new foal was a bonnie filly and then another letter by sea a fortnight later which told us that it would be three weeks at least yet before Betsy would foal. This led us to develop the phrase 'Reachfar time' and remarks such as: 'By Reachfar time, that was a month ago.'

Arriving as they did, in constant progression in the orderly copperplate hand in the plain white envelopes, these letters brought, for me, an extraordinary cool sanity into the heat-crazed atmosphere of life in St. Jago. I did not acclimatise easily, either physically or mentally although, for a long period, I did not recognise my mental difficulty in accepting the life that I was expected to live in the island.

The population was roughly three per cent. white and ninety-seven per cent. negro and, in 1950, when we took up residence in a house called Guinea Corner on the sugar plantation of Paradise, this population was divided into four main categories. There were the 'island whites', who were the descendants of early settlers, British in the main but there were some French and Portuguese, there were the 'importee whites' embracing people like Twice and myself who were newly arrived in the island, there were the educated negroes in the professions and the civil service and there was the huge mass of negroes of the peasant class who lived at mere subsistence level.

In the eyes of all the negroes, all the whites were rich and, certainly, Twice and I lived at a level which we had never attained in Scotland, in what was virtually a small Georgian mansion with a staff of four servants and all the white people we knew—I think we knew all the whites resident in the island—lived on a level similar to ours or a great deal more lavish. The thing that struck me as extraordinary was that white people like ourselves, newly arrived in the island, which was developing rapidly in this post-war period, took to this life like ducks to water. The wives of technicians, such as sugar chemists, sugar agronomists and the like, many of whom had originated in the less salubrious suburbs of Glasgow or the cities of the Midlands, turned into 'great white missis-es' overnight, and apparently without effort. I could not achieve this and I could never find anyone—even any of those who had accomplished it so easily—to tell me how it was done. With my slow wits, it took me a long time to discover that they had accomplished it because it came to them easily and because they were not foolish enough, as I was, to carry their pasts about with them.

I could never forget that my own origins did not lie in the socially superior group in which I found myself in St. Jago, for even the proud island whites envied us newly arrived importees with the exclusive mark 'Made in England' or, even more exclusive 'Made in Scotland' stamped upon us, as it is stamped upon so much sugar-milling machinery and it was always in my mind that, in historic truth, I belonged to the great mass at the bottom of the social scale, the peasants who were living at subsistence level. But, as I have said, it took me a long time to work out what I felt and, in this early time in the island, I was aware of no more than a vague inner unrest and dissatisfaction that was aggravated, physically, by the heat, the dust, the tropical squalor and the ever-present mosquitoes. It is strange that the feeling of disloyalty to people of your own peasant race should be so difficult to recognise.

I think my recognition of what I felt might have been more speedy had I been able to give outward expression to my feelings of unrest and dissatisfaction, but this I could not do because I did not want Twice to feel that our new way of life did not entirely please me. His appointment by his firm to this post in the Caribbean had been a great mark of advancement and I felt that it was my duty to stand behind his shoulder, giving all the support, moral, mental and of every other kind that I could and it was not difficult to suppress these inner murmurings.

I do not want to convey the impression that I was homesick for that is not what I suffered. It was a thing much deeper than mere homesickness—a profound distrust of the entire social structure of the island which I felt to be hollow and false in conception and riddled and rotten with faults of value, just as the volcanic rock of the island itself was riddled with cavities through which the trapped waters flowed and shifted in dark and dangerous mystery. But for most of the time I was very happy and the social ground seemed to be solid enough, just as, for most of the time, the sugar cane waved free over the enormous fields, concealing the hidden waters that flowed and shifted below ground.

I was happier still, however, when, in August of 1951, Twice and I left Guinea Corner to travel home by way of New York on our first leave for, by this time, Twice had again been promoted in this Caribbean area and we were to come back at the end of some four months.

We had planned for this leave for a long time and although it could not have departed in all its aspects further from the plans we had made, it was one of the happiest periods, we agreed afterwards, in either of our lives.

In my repeated dreams of arriving at Reachfar, I had always visualised the picture that had come down the years with me, of our arriving at the top of the hill to be met by my family, surrounded by the dogs, at the granary gable but even this little detail of the plan did not carry through, for my family met us at the little house at Bedamned's Corner, where they had been attending the funeral of old senile Jamie Smith that afternoon, so we all drove up the hill together.

'It is not often,' said Tom as we sat down to supper in the Reachfar kitchen, 'that I have been able to say that I *enchoyed* a funeral, but it was a real pleasure to put that poor old booger Jamie under the ground.'

'Indeed, yes, Tom,' George agreed with him. 'A man might as well speak the truth and God knows Jamie has been no pleasure to himself or anybody else all his life.'

'Be quiet the two of you,' my father said quietly. 'If you have no good to say, say nothing,' and he covered his eyes with his hand. 'For what we are about to eat, God make us truly thankful. Amen.'

I had heard this grace or a slight variation of it three times a day, every day of my life that I had spent at home. It used to be spoken by my grandfather but, now, as I looked up the table and my father uncovered his face, I felt that it might be my grandfather who was still in that chair. My father did not wear a beard but I had never before realised that his resemblance to my grandfather was so marked, because hitherto, I think, my father's colouring had always been so striking. The colouring—the ruddy freshness of skin, the brightness of the hazel eyes and the clear silver of the moustache and abundant strong hair—was still there but now, with age, the bones had become more prominent, showing in the high forehead and in the beaky structure of the nose.

After supper, my friend Monica who had now married young Sir Torquil Daviot of Poyntdale came to call but, in spite of that, when my father rose to go down to Achcraggan, I rose too and accompanied him part of the way down the hill.

'You look very well, Dad,' I told him, 'and you are a better walker than I am. I have practically lost the use of my legs since I went to St. Jago with going everywhere by car.'

'I *am* very well,' he said, 'except for one devilish aggravating wee thing.'

'What is that?'

'It seems that I have some little weakness about my bladder—what they call the prostate gland. I am always having to get up through the night and some days I spend half my time going into the bushes instead of hoeing or whatever I am doing.'

'What does Doctor Mackay say?'

'He says it may improve but if not, there is a small operation they can do to put it right. I have no notion of hospitals and operations, as you know, but we will see how things go. It is nothing much. It is more of an aggravation than anything. Yourself has got thinner since you went to this St. Jago place.'

'Oh, not much.'

'Aye, but I notice it. Not that I want you to be fat. With your height and your Reachfar bones you would be a big coarse lump if you got fat but there is no fear of that. Fatness is not in the breed. Twice has got fatter, though.'

'I think it's with drinking so much—I don't mean booze, just water and liquid generally. It is pretty hot in these sugar factories he is always prowling around, you know.'

'It must be gey hot all over. I doubt I wouldna like it much. You don't find the heat trying yourself?'

'Well, I needn't move off my backside from morning till night unless I want to, you know.'

He laughed. 'I canna see that suiting you too well either but, mercy, Twice has fairly made his mark in that firm!'

'Yes, he has done terribly well, Dad.'

'And you are still all right the two of you? No trouble?'

'Not a trouble in the world!'

'Have you been throwing any dishes at one another lately?'

This was a reference to something that had astonished him and which had astonished myself too when it first happened. I could not remember having a tantrum that made me want to lie on the floor and kick from the time I was four years old until I met Twice but between Twice and me a situation would develop which I could resolve only by physical violence. I think this violence sprang from the same root as the tantrum on the evening that my father was late for supper. There was in me a core of feeling for Twice which I was often defeated to express in words.

My father's question referred to an evening at Reachfar, before we had gone to the West Indies, when Twice and I had one of our frequent small differences of opinion just after supper was over and I was helping my aunt to clear the table. I do not even remember the subject of the difference but a few words were exchanged and then I picked up Tom's porridge bowl from the table and hurled it down the length of the kitchen at Twice. Even as the bowl flew through the air, I was conscious of the astonished horrified faces of my family who had not, until now, seen this aspect of our relationship.

I have never been a games-player, have never had an eye for a moving object or any physical dexterity but Twice differs from me in this and he caught the bowl in mid-air and, with all his considerable force, hurled it back, neatly aimed so that it hit the wall high above my head and shattered into a thousand pieces which fell all over and about me and then he said: 'Kate, charge one porridge bowl to the Alexander account.' Then, out of the stunned silence, my family began to laugh, just as my father was laughing now, as he always did when he recalled the incident.

'I have never seen anything as quick and neat as yon was,' he said. 'And I don't know yet what made you throw the bowl in the first of it.'

'Lord, I don't know either,' I said. 'It is something in Twice that makes me do it. I think I feel like Jean felt the day she threw the knife at me long ago.' I paused suddenly, stopped walking and stood on the path, looking away over the Firth and the hills. 'We are a bit unfair to Jean,' I said then. 'That day she threw the knife, there was the most unholy fuss that she has never lived down, but I have thrown more things at Twice than Jean has ever thrown in her entire life and everybody simply laughs about it.'

My father also was looking away to the hills and, with his eyes upon them, he said: 'I am not sure that I can say what I mean about this but it seems to me that an action—an action like throwing a knife or a dish—has no meaning in itself. It is the reason why the thing is thrown that gives it its meaning and makes it a good or a bad action. Jean threw the knife out of hate but you threw the bowl at Twice out of something different and something better.' He was overcome by a sudden shyness, the shyness that always overcame him when he spoke his inner thoughts, a shyness born out of fear that such thoughts, in an 'un-clever' man like himself, might be presumptuous or pretentious.

'It is not that I want to *hit* Twice when I throw the things,' I said to put him at his ease as we walked on again. 'It is that I can't find the words for what I want to say and the next best thing is to throw something that will break and make a noise.'

'But it was *Twice* that broke the bowl and made the noise yon night,' he pointed out.

'I know. And that's another thing. I don't throw so many bowls and things now since he started that trick of catching them and breaking them himself. Just as well. It is very undignified,' I ended.

He turned his head and smiled at me. 'Aye,' he said with a perception I found uncanny in him, 'stand on your dignity, will you, rather than admit that there is something in Twice that you can't get the upper hand of?' I felt my face flush as I recognised the truth and he went on: 'You are enough like your Granny to be always in need of something to fight, something that you cannot break. I have always thought that Twice would keep you fighting ever since that morning you came into the kitchen and told us you were going to marry him, before you knew what his position was. You were just going to throw a plate at him that morning and he gave you a look out of those blue eyes of his and you thought the better of it right away. I thought then that he was the man for you. It is another bit of the reason why I encouraged you to do what you did. You see, there is Kate—' I did not grasp the transition his mind had made from myself to my aunt.

'Kate?' I asked.

'Aye, Kate is on my conscience. She was on my conscience that first time you brought Twice home here. She has been on it ever since. Kate should have been married to Malcolm Macleod from Varlich when she was a lassie. Kate had many an offer but Malcolm was the only man she—the only man she ever wanted to throw a plate at. But she let him go and stopped here to help Granny and us all. So Malcolm married his cousin from Edinburgh and Kate married poor Hugh in the end. Och, she was happy enough with Hugh and Hugh thought she was the sun and the moon, but she never threw dishes at him. She didna care enough to be bothered, you see.'

It seemed to me that my father had crystallised in words my own feeling about Twice—it was a caring, a caring for everything about him down to the lightest word that he spoke that, sometimes, I could neither express nor contain so that I had to cause some shattering explosive noise.

'You know, Dad,' I said, 'when Twice and I saw Malcolm in New York, I got the idea he was still thinking about Kate. He is a widower now. I think maybe he and Kate will start corresponding.'

He looked at me out of smiling eyes. 'D'you tell me that? Janet, I would like it fine if Kate and Malcolm was to come together after all. Goodness knows what we would do here at Reachfar without her—we would have to get a housekeeper—but Kate has given enough to all of us here. Man, Janet, I hope you are right!'

A new spring seemed to come into his step now as he walked down the sunlit hill and then he said: 'My, it is a bonnie evening! August is a bonnie month. Look at the bloom o' the heather over on the North Cobbler yonder. St. Jago canna be as bonnie as this, is it?'

'Not nearly as bonnie, Dad.'

'Mind you, I've read about these islands with their palm trees and the sea being always bright blue—they must be bonnie in their own way but I canna think on a place that could be bonnier than this.'

'You are like the old farmer that Twice tells about that farmed a place in the Borders called Maryriggs. He was on his deathbed and the minister came to see him and was telling him all about the glories of Heaven and the old man said: Aye, it'll be a fine place, Ah've no doot but Ah'd jist as sune hae anither ninety-nine years lease o' Maryriggs.—I have always thought it a fine thing to be as content with your own place as that.'

'Aye, it is a fine thing and I feel it is right when you are as content as that that you should *say* it. I don't say this is a bonnie countryside to make a boast of it—it is just that I am thankful for it. I have known it all my life and I have spent most of my life in it and I am thankful for that. I don't think I will bother to fly out to St. Jago for a holiday,' he joked before he went on: 'In spite of your letters, and they are grand letters, Janet, I canna imagine what your life can be like among all these black people and all. What are they like, the black people?' he asked.

'The trouble is that you can't get to know them, Dad. They don't trust us white people—you can't blame them, all descended from slaves as they are. What it makes me think of more than anything, the life out there, is what Tom once told me long ago about the time away back here on Reachfar, when you were a boy and everybody was so poor. Tom said that old Sir Turk had Poyntdale but he was away in the Army and hardly ever came near here. You didn't know him. He was just somebody away in the distance. Well, that is what I am like in St. Jago. As the negroes see me, I am somebody who is rich and away in the distance.'

My father could not see me in this way and he spoke of things more concrete. 'I have often heard people say that black men is awful for thieving,' he said.

'No more than anybody else. After all, Tom stole a leg of mutton once, but Tom is not a thief.'

'Aye, that is true,' he agreed, frowning.

'There is something not right about it all,' I said, 'but I can't see anything that somebody like me can do. It is all too big.'

'Aye, I know what you mean but maybe if you just do the best you can for the few that is around you? The ones in your house, like?' His voice was tentative, talking of a problem that he could barely imagine and he deliberately did not use the word 'servant' for, although proudly enough he would name himself the servant of any man whose pay he accepted, he never regarded himself or any of his as employers of servants.

'I try to do that, Dad,' I said, 'and I still have the same four people with me in the house who came when we first went to Guinea Corner but that is so very little to do.'

'But Madame, the old lady that owns Paradise, she is good to her people, isn't she?'

'Oh, yes, but it is a bit like the way Lady Turk tried to read the Bible to Granny. She doesn't try to understand them. She just bullies them for their own good.'

'I see what you are at. She has no *respect* for them. There is something terrible about that, when people forget that every man born—aye, even a good working horse—is due his share of respect. But this old Madame expects them to respect *her*?'

'Not half!' I told him.

'Aye, the ould devil!' He stopped on the track and looked away to the hills, in the way that I had so often seen him do and which, when I was a child, always brought to my mind the words of the metrical psalm we often sang in church:

'I to the hills will lift mine eyes,
From whence doth come mine aid—'

'It took me a long time to find this out,' he said after a moment, 'and maybe you have not noticed it yet either. It is that none of the big things, the things that are important to people can work just the one way. You canna respect a man that doesna respect *you* and you canna be loyal to a man that isna loyal to you— even if the man is your master and you his servant. With all the will in the world, you canna give respect and loyalty where you don't get them.'

'I hadn't thought of that before, Dad, but it is true.'

We walked on for a little way in silence before he said: 'You havena written that book for me yet and you with all these people to do your housework and cooking?'

195

'Not yet, Dad. I have tried off and on but it is a funny thing. St. Jago is a very disturbed sort of place somehow. It is difficult to concentrate on anything for long and then there is so much social life and carry-on.'

'It is myself that is thinking that the place and the way of life is not suiting you too well at all,' he said.

'No. You are wrong there, Dad.'

'But it is where Twice's work lies,' he went on as if I had not spoken, 'and you have to make the best of it. I can see how you are placed. You wouldna like to do anything that would be a disappointment or a hindrance to Twice in any way and you are right. You will not regret what you are doing, Janet. I never liked one day all the time we were in Cairnton but it got you to a good school, it got me a good wage and Mr. Hill being the fine man he was, it got me a good pension. If it wasn't for my pension, we would all have to live more sober at Reachfar. I have never regretted the few years at Cairnton, although I didn't like them at the time. You stick it, Janet. It won't be for ever. But there is one thing. Don't try to stick it if your health goes—Twice would never get over it if anything happened to your health. Now, you are *sure* you feel all right? Twice has been at me already to speak to you about this. You are very thin, you know.'

'Of course I am all right, Dad,' I said impatiently. 'You know perfectly well that except when I fall off bridges I am as strong as an ox and Twice knows it too. Now, stop cackling and listen to *me*. I am not admitting any of this stuff you are saying about not liking St. Jago and if you say one word to Twice—'

'I'll not do that, Janet. I would never interfere in that way between you. You know that. But it was Twice himself that wanted me to make sure about your health before he takes on this new appointment out there.'

'You wait till I get hold of him, going on like an old woman! His own health is more likely to crack than mine is, working like a demon day and night the way he does.'

'Aye, he is surely a devil to work,' my father agreed. 'To be honest, I see more age on Twice than I do on yourself—that will be the responsibility of his work, likely. Although you are a bittie thin, you are wearing very well for an old wifie of forty-one.'

'You are not doing so badly yourself for seventy-three.'

'I am getting on, I suppose,' he said as if this were an entirely new discovery he had made. 'But I don't feel old, Janet. Yet I have never tried to feel young. But I have had a good life on the whole and I think there is an awful lot in taking things just the way they are. Now, Jean is for ever hiding her age and trying to look young and she has aged more than any of us. Kate is the one that has stood up best to the years.'

'She has, but that floors your argument completely. Kate has never been content with anything the way it is and has had a fight against something nearly every day of her life,' I said and he laughed. 'George and Tom are the ones,' I went on. 'I wouldn't be surprised if they are rip-roaring around here when we are all under the sod.'

'Aye, that's true. You wait till Shona and Jock come up with wee Elizabeth. She is just an *awful* bonnie little nipper, Janet, and more like yourself than either Jock or Shona. And she is very clever too. She is beginning to have a notion of the reading and George and Tom—'

'Heavens, don't tell me those two are learning to read all over *again*!'

'What then?' He smiled at me. 'They are at all their old capers with her that they had with you and her being so like you at that age I am hard put to it sometimes not to believe that the clock has gone back about forty years.'

'Dad,' I said, hoping to find out something that I had long wanted to know, 'I know George's age, but how old is Tom?'

'The one that finds that out,' he said, 'will be cleverer than you or me is as yet. All I can tell you is that Tom is older than me but it may be a lot or just a year. You know how it is when you are young. There is yourself and then there is all the ones that are a lot older, grown-up, like. When I was a boy at school, Tom was working at Reachfar here, grown-up. Then I went to work too and then Tom seemed to be the same age as myself. But he is older than me—och aye, he is older than me. But with wee Elizabeth, he is just four years old again.'

It was not until late November, shortly before Twice and I left for London on our way back to the West Indies, that we saw little Elizabeth at Reachfar although we had spent a few days earlier in our leave with Jock and Shona at their home. Elizabeth was not a dream-pretty child but she had the beauty that is inherent in all young and healthy creatures. She looked upon the world about her from a pair of beautiful wide grey eyes and she stumped about that world with a firm sturdy independence. We all gathered at the granary gable as Jock's car came up the hill and, as soon as it stopped, Jock opened the back door and, a book under one arm and her eyes on her grandfather, Elizabeth stepped down straight into a mess left behind by one of Kate's ducks. She looked down at the small soiled shoe, the grey eyes moved from the face of my father to the faces of George and Tom, a wicked light dawned in them and: 'Oh, poop!' she said.

'Elizabeth!' Shona's voice said sternly from the car and at once George and Tom moved forward, between car and child, as one man, and began to engage Jock and Shona in a burst of conversation while my father picked Elizabeth up so that the small shoes waved and kicked high above his head. It was a strange thing to stand there, looking at what might have been myself of forty years ago and I felt again an uprush of the security that came from the allies, George and Tom who might teach one 'swear words' like 'poop' but who also screened one's peccadilloes from the scolding world and the comfort that came from the big hands that held one round the middle while the eyes smiled up with such perfect love.

My father set the child down and we all moved along the yard to the door of the house where she paused, sniffed, wrinkled her small nose and said: 'Reachfar smell!'

'Elizabeth!' Shona protested again.

'Nice,' Elizabeth reassured her mother and stumped on into the kitchen.

I knew precisely what the child meant, for this smell had always been, for me, the final certainty that I was home. When I was away, in Cairnton, London, Buckinghamshire or the West Indies, I knew the smell existed but I could not experience it in other places, as I could experience, for instance, the view over the Firth by the simple act of closing my eyes and remembering. The smell was elusive, not to be called up at will. It was a compound of the smell of scones baking, fir-wood burning, the farmyard outside, the heather of the moor, the honeysuckle of the garden hedge, white household soap and the strong black tobacco smoked by George and Tom. It probably had other components but the smell of any one of these ingredients was enough to remind me, anywhere, that the Reachfar smell existed and to set me vainly trying to capture it in its entirety.

The table was laid for the afternoon cup of tea and having looked at the scones and the pancakes, Elizabeth then looked at the glass jam dish and said: 'Granda, dancing jam!'

'Damson, Elizabeth,' my brother said. '*Dam*-son.'

'Granda,' said Elizabeth with terrible smugness, 'scold Daddy for saying bad words.'

'You bad boy, John Sandison,' my father said at once and sternly, 'don't you dare to say bad things like that about the jam!'

'You can't win,' my brother said sadly to Twice.

I no longer saw Elizabeth as myself at her age in relation to my father. When I was a child, he had been capable of scolding me, of putting on what I used to call his 'grieve's face', the stern mask which he wore when discipline became necessary but, with this child, he was incapable of any resistance. In relation to her, he had abdicated from authority, leaving all the discipline to be carried out by Jock and Shona in his own absence and, while the child was with him, he was her total ally, a child like herself and also her grandfather who could protect her by being still the authoritative father of Jock, Shona, Twice and myself.

Damson jam as made at Reachfar still contained the whole fruit, pips and all and when tea was over and another part of my childhood came back when Elizabeth came round all our plates, counting the pips. 'A laird, a lord, a lily, a leaf, a rich man, a poor man, a beggar, a thief.' Long before I could count the chimes of the clock, I could count damson pips to this old rhyme of my father's and it was interesting to note that now, as always, Tom and George, who were the last to be counted, were a beggar and a thief respectively, to the delight of the child.

'Man, Tom,' George said, 'I have never met a puckle o' these danged dancings in all my born days but they gave me a bad name.'

'No, nor me either, George,' said Tom sadly while Elizabeth danced with glee, secure in her world of 'always', where the damson pips invariably labelled Tom and George beggar and thief, making them look ludicrously rueful.

When Elizabeth's bedtime came, she, George and Tom retired to the bathroom, a new amenity at Reachfar since my childhood, and when she emerged in her pyjamas and slippers, she fetched her book from the little table in the corner where she had put it safely when she arrived and climbed on to my father's knee where he sat in the grandfather's chair beside the fire.

'This is the big moment,' my brother whispered to me.

'Can she read?'

'Yes. I thought it was all memory for a bit but it isn't.'

'This is my new book I got in Inverness today, Granda,' Elizabeth said and then from the cover she read: 'N-n- Nursery R- huh- Rhymes.'

'Dang it, Tom, man,' said George, 'I'll bet you my Sunday boots yon dang foolish yarn about that goose is in that book!'

'Indeed an' it is myself that wouldna be surprised, George.'

'What goose?' Elizabeth asked.

'Chust you take a look,' said Tom. 'There is near certain to be that goose in it somewhere.'

In no time at all, Goosey-goosey-gander was found, a mid-century instead of early-century Goosey-goosey-gander so that it had no sun-bonnet and flowing ribbons but carried a large umbrella tucked under one wing, rightly prepared for the worst of weather. Elizabeth began to read but, as I and my brother had done before her, she got no further than the end of the first stanza '—and in my lady's chamber' before the commentary began.

'Dang it, that goose is still at it, George, walking up and down the stair!'

'That book has no sense,' said George. 'You would be as good with a cow with the spring skitter in the house as a goose, the clarty brute!'

'George!' my aunt protested.

'Well, it's the God's truth,' Tom defended his ally.

But everybody was reckoning without Elizabeth who could think more clearly, it seemed, than either her father or I could do at her age and who could also put into words what she thought with more coherence than Jock or I had been able to command.

'You two,' she said to George and Tom commandingly, 'don't be so silly!'

'Elizabeth, don't dare to—' Shona began.

'Let the bairn be,' said my father.

'This goose in my book is a pretending goose,' the child explained from her perch on her grandfather's knee, 'and pretending gooses don't make messes.'

'Pretending gooses?' George questioned, dying hard. 'Real ones is bad enough without making books about pretending ones.'

'Pretending ones are not bad or messy and they are *fun*,' said Elizabeth firmly. 'People have to have *fun*, don't we?'

With one accord, George and Tom raised their right hands and rubbed the backs of their necks, their seldom-used gesture which indicated that they were at a loss for further words.

'Maybe that is so,' George said after a moment.

'You'd better read us the next bittie,' said Tom, 'till we see is it funny after all.'

Having given them a stern glance, Elizabeth read the second stanza: '—and caught him by the left leg and threw him down the stairs,' whereupon George and Tom startled her and all of us by slapping their knees and bursting into uproarious laughter. And then, as suddenly as they had laughed, they became solemn.

'Why was you laughing, George?' Tom asked.

George gave a loud hiccup. 'Because it was the *left* leg,' he said, beginning to laugh again. 'It wouldna be funny at all if it had been the right—if it had been the—'

'—The right leg!' Tom shouted and began to laugh again. 'That goose must have been what the mannie in the wireless boxie calls a southpaw!'

Everybody was laughing now, most of us at the defeat of George and Tom more than at the rhyme and we went on laughing until Elizabeth said: 'This next one I am going to read is sad, but only pretending sad,' whereupon she read Jack and Jill and was gratified by George's and Tom's head-shakings and lugubrious faces. Very soon, she came to the last page of the book, read out: 'The end,' closed it and added: 'It's all done, Granda, and I am only here at Reachfar today.'

'Och, but we will find you another book for tomorrow night,' he told her.

'George,' said Tom, 'is the book about yon poor devil Christian in your room? It is a whilie since I saw it.'

'Aye. It's in the wee press under the window.'

'Who is yon poor devil Christian?' Elizabeth asked.

'A mannie in a book o' ours,' said George, 'that got into that much bother one way and another that a body is fair heart-sorry for him and no danged pretending about it.'

'Aye, and him trying to do his best, the poor devil,' said Tom 'And yet he is quite a bit of fun to read about. Av coorse, I would always rather read about a man than a goose if you was to give me my choice.'

'Read about him now?' Elizabeth asked.

'No. Tomorrow,' my brother said firmly.

'Poor Christian will be in just the same bother tomorrow as he has been in for hundreds o' years, Elizabeth,' my father said and when Shona had taken the child upstairs, he added: 'I have sometimes thought that Christian would have got on better if he had thought a little less about his own soul and a little more about his wife and bairns.'

Too soon, the last night that Twice and I could spend at Reach-far came along and when my father rose to go down to Ach-craggan, I suddenly seemed to see him look much older, as if the youth he had regained from Elizabeth in the course of the last few days had fallen away in the few hours since she had gone to bed.

'I'll drive you down, Dad,' my brother said.

'My car is still outside, Jock,' said Twice.

'No, lads. No, thanks. It is fine bright moonlight and Janet will see me down a bit of the way.' He picked up his tweed hat and took his ash-plant from the corner by the kitchen door. 'I am not saying goodbye to you, Twice, lad. I am just going to start looking forward to seeing you home again. Goodnight, all.'

It was a clear, frosty, moonlit November night, an infinite night of whites, silvers, blacks and greys that spread from the sparkling heather about our feet down over the silver fields, across the black waters of the Firth on to the grey hills beyond and then away to the vast sky where the white moon sailed cold, detached, pure and beyond all communication.

'Elizabeth is a darling of a bairn,' I said to my father.

'Aye. And poor Shona has a job with her. Of course, it will be easier when the new one is born. Shona must get gey tired by the end of the day, pregnant the way she is and with no help about the house or anything and that mischevious wee devil getting into everything.'

'Shona will get a rest here at Reachfar anyway, with you and George and Tom as nursemaids.'

'Aye. We are great hands at the nursing, the three of us. We are getting a bittie too old for much else.—Janet, I have been wanting to thank you for what you did for Kate.' In the course of our leave, Malcolm Macleod had come home from New York on holiday and now he and my aunt were to be married. 'She was telling me that it was through you that she started writing to Malcolm again,' he went on, 'and how grateful she was to you. And I am grateful too. I told you Kate has been on my conscience.'

'But I didn't do anything, really, Dad and you have no need to feel grateful. I think that seeing me reminded Malcolm a bit of Kate—I am not nearly as bonnie as she is but there is a kind of family resemblance—and that started him thinking and then she wrote to him and that helped. But *I* didn't do anything.'

'Maybe you didn't but you were there or thereabout. It is a good thing that maybe we do a bittie good for people sometimes without knowing we are doing it. It is funny to think of Kate going off to New York at her age.'

'Kate is not all that old if you think of it,' I said. 'And she looks a lot younger since Malcolm came back.'

'Aye, so she does. Well, it has given the neighbours something to speak about anyway and a better thing to speak about than when Malcolm went off and left her. I am pleased about that for Kate too. Her pride got a sore hurt yon time Malcolm went away. There is pride and pride. Some kinds of it are the better for a fall but when it is the right kind o' pride that canna fall but can get sore wounded, it is a cruel thing.—Och, well, your holiday is nearly over but you should be back again in two years or so, Twice tells me.'

'Yes, Dad.'

'It's not too long. And there will be the letters. You make a grand job o' the letters, Janet. Ye know, it seems to me that you have a real gift for the pen. I was just thinking, back there in the house tonight, you havena nearly as much to say in the way of gab and chat as Kate or Shona or most women but put a pen in your hand it's a different thing altogether. Shona is a fine lassie and grand company sitting at the fire but although she has as good an education if not better than yours, she canna write a letter that speaks, the way you can. You will try and have a real go at a book, Janet?'

'I have tried already, off and on, Dad, but—' I stopped because there were so many reasons why I felt I could not write that I did not know where to begin.

'You know,' my father surprised me by producing one of the reasons, 'People like us here on Reachfar have aye had the idea that books don't get written by people like us. At least, I had aye that idea anyway, for a long time. But lately, I've begun to think there is not all that much difference in people, at bottom. A thing like writing is a kind of gift, something extra that is given to some people, like Betsy the old mare had an extra gift for music, for a horse. Then look at the ould Reverend Roderick—if ever a man had a gift for preaching, he has and yet he was born the son o' a poor fisherman in the Lewis. Now, I have always thought it is about the most hurtful thing you can do if somebody gives you a present and you don't show them you value it. I mind Mrs. Hill gave me a tie one Christmas at Cairnton and, lord, I didna like it! It was devilish bright and gaudy but I felt I had to wear that tie till it was fair in ribbons—and so I did—so that her feelings wouldna be hurt about it. It seems to me that if you have been given a gift for writing, it is terrible bad manners—a kind of sin, indeed—not to use it.'

'I *have* tried, Dad and I'll try again but—'

'Aye?'

'The writing part is all right,' I said. 'I—I *have* written bits now and then that, sometimes, I have thought were not too bad but I can't bear the thought of sending them to a publisher or anybody. Think if they sent the thing back and wrote and said it was no good? You'd feel—you'd feel like a woman that had had a baby and it turned out not to be like Elizabeth but like that baby that Mrs. Maclean's daughter had.'

'Och, Janet!'

'It is true, Dad! That is how I would feel—as if I had produced an idiot child. You see, you just can't judge a bit of writing you are doing, any more than the mother can see how her baby is developing inside her. At least, *I* can't. I can make judgments on other peoples' writing but not on my own.'

'I see,' he said quietly. 'I see what you mean but I didna know till now the thing was so deep. But, Janet, it seems to me the older I get that everything that is worth doing at all needs courage and the more worthwhile the thing is, the more courage it needs. Now, you have never been frightened of anything in all the time I have known you.'

'Well, I am frightened of this thing.'

'I read a book out o' the library lately,' he said, 'by a young airman that was killed in the war, poor fellow. It was called *The Last Enemy*. I suppose everybody has a last enemy, a last thing that they are frightened of. Well, it is up to yourself but as I have aye said, I would like to see your name on the cover of a book.' After a short silence, he said: 'How long will you have in London before you sail?'

'About a fortnight, Dad. Twice suggested that I should stay here at Reachfar but I said I wouldn't. He would hate to be alone in London, really.'

'Aye, you are quite right, Janet. It was good o' Twice to suggest it but you go with him. That is your place and it is right you should go. The people in St. Jago must think a lot o' Twice to trust him with so much o' their business over here.' We went another few yards in the cold frosty silence before he said in his shy voice: 'You know, I was a happy man leaving the house the-night—happy in a silly childish kind o' way.'

'Oh? Why?'

'I never thought to see the day when two big cars would be sitting at Reachfar and both owned by sons o' mine. It's not the cars in themselves that are anything—I am not as foolish as that—it is that I am thankful that I have lived to see the day when there is more in life for my bairns and people of my kind than an everlasting struggle against hunger and cold.'

'But for the struggle that you and George and Tom and Twice's father made,' I said, 'the cars would not be there.'

'But that is just the thing about it. The cars and what goes with them have made the whole thing worth while. It is good to feel that the poor bit of a shape you made at things was worth while after all. And I am lucky too. I have lived to see it. Twice's father didn't. Aye, Janet. I am a lucky man and the least I can do is to show that I know it.'

I looked out over the still stark beauty of the hills and the Firth and, like a cold keen spear, the knowledge entered my mind that, if the sound roofs, warm fires and well-furnished cupboards of Reachfar and Jemima Cottage did not lie behind and before us, this silver, grey and black panorama would hold more of terror than of beauty. My father suddenly halted and looked from the frozen snow of Ben Wyvis in the west along the white northern hills and out to the silver sea beyond the

Cobblers. 'It is as bonnie a night as I have seen for a long time,' he said.

He had known, I remembered as we stood side by side, the everlasting struggle against hunger and cold. He had known the harshness of life in this uncompromising countryside but he had forgiven it all and had come, through his own struggle, to gratitude for what he had achieved and to a deep love for the harsh rock which had given him birth.

'It is bonnie enough,' I said, 'if you have a good roof and a good fire to go home to. As Reachfar was about sixty years ago, a hard night like this would have looked a little different, I think.'

He turned his head slowly and looked down at me over his shoulder. 'That is true, Janet,' he said, 'and I am glad that you have the wits to see it. Sometimes, when you were young, when you were at school, I used to worry in case I was keeping you too short of pocket-money and the clothes that the other lassies had but I always had the thought of the expense of the university for you and Jock at the back of my mind. I did not want to send you to university so that you would get famous and bring glory to Reachfar hill.' He laughed a little at his own joke. 'I wanted you both to be able to earn a living in a way that would leave you time and the money to look about you and see that places like Reachfar hill were bonnie places. I never knew it was bonnie until your mother pointed it out to me. Before that, I was always too busy or too tired to see it.' He gave a last glance at the hills to the north and began to walk on. 'I have often thought of that lost and wasted time—nearly thirty years that I did not have time to look and see how bonnie this hill was.'

'The work that made you too tired to see the beauty of Reachfar wasn't entirely wasted, Dad,' I comforted him. 'It has culminated in the two cars outside the house tonight and in a lot of other things.'

'I know and I am not complaining. I have had a lot that has

made me happy this last while that you have all been at home here and it is funny that one of the things that pleased me most was a thing that wee Elizabeth said the night she came. Out of the mouths of babes and sucklings, as it says in the Bible.'

He went into his shy silence and I said: 'What was that, Dad?'

'You remember when she was reading about the goose to Tom and George and she said: People have to have fun, don't we?' He walked on silently for another few steps. 'I am happy to see the day when a little one of our family can stand up and claim her right to have fun.'

'But, Dad, when I was little, I had fun all the time!' I protested. 'George and Tom and I had nothing *but* fun!'

'Aye, out in the barn or in the stackyard or up in Tom's bed on Sundays,' he agreed, 'but it was not a thing you had openly and as a right. And all your fun was based on what your granny called downright badness, imitating Lady Ishbel and the Miss Boyds and the minister and the like. But your fun was based on badness because there wasn't any other kind of fun to .be had. And Granny kind of thought that fun was bad whatever because it wasted precious time. Maybe I am not explaining myself very well but what makes me happy is that you and Jock had a better start and more fun that Tom and George and I had and wee Elizabeth is having a better start and more fun than any of us.'

The lights of Achcraggan now lay below us like a cluster of gems in a cavity lined with black velvet and he stopped near the spot where we had stopped on that sleety night before I went to Hampshire twenty years before.

'You must go back,' he said and then, as a joke: 'Twice will be thinking you are lost on the Reachfar moor!'

I tried to smile at him. It was difficult. He took off his hat for a moment and the moonlight sparkled on the strong silver hair. 'Well, I am going to start looking forward to your next leave,' he said. 'My blessing on you till then and don't forget to write, Janet. I am not going to bid you goodbye. Goodnight, lass.'

'Goodnight, Dad.'

He put his hat on, turned abruptly away and I watched the broad shoulders go down the hill towards the jewelled lights.

Part Five

'Children's children are the crown of old men;
and the glory of children are their fathers.'

PROVERBS xvii. 6

TWICE and I arrived back in St. Jago about the middle of December and all went well with us for about eighteen months. In December 1951, I had made my third landfall in St. Jago and I had a vague idea, born probably of the wish that it might be so, that this time after four months at home and arriving in the island for the third time, I might at last come to terms with it, but this was not so. I continued to feel that this place was the domain of dark and mysterious gods whom, so far, I had failed to propitiate.

In retrospect, this feeling of mine has about it the characteristics of the old problem: Which came first, the chicken or the egg? I do not know if the dark, mysterious unpropitiated gods were really in St. Jago and my awareness of them was a result of their presence or whether it was I, by generating the idea in my mind, who thereby peopled the island with dark, mysterious unpropitiated gods but this does not matter for the things that happened happened.

At the first opportunity, I did what I could to break through the social barriers of the island and was, to some degree, successful for I made friends with a family of negro farmers and, through them, came to be accepted in the homes of many more of the island people and I did this without coming to be regarded as a renegade by my own kind. In a small way, Twice and I, at Guinea Corner, formed a social bridgehead between white and negro but I was happier still in the situation that prevailed in our house itself, between Twice and me and our 'people' as my father had called our servants.

When we had gone on leave, I had been warned by various white friends that, although we had provided for our people while we were away, we need never expect to see them again. Negro memories were short, they said, and when they had squandered their four months' money in the first week, they would find other jobs and when Twice and I returned we would have to find and train new staff. In the face of this, it was very pleasant to be welcomed home by all four of our people, with broad smiles on their black faces and hands only too willing to take the baggage into the house. They were Cookie, a middle-aged woman, Minna the laundress who was old and had white wool instead of black under her red bandana headcloth, Clorinda, the housemaid, a young, pert and pretty little chit with a flirtatious wag about her hips and Caleb, the yard boy who was about sixteen but a fully-grown, very handsome, coal-black full-blooded negro. The three women flapped and fluttered round Twice or 'the Massa' as they had always done but Caleb stood at my elbow and said in a quiet voice: 'Me take dat fe you, Missis,' as he had always done, for this was the way that the allegiances of our house had ever been divided.

If Caleb liked me more than the women did, I liked Caleb more than I liked the women for I felt that I had more in common with him than with them. The garden was Caleb's domain and I would always choose to work in a garden rather than do any form of housework other than cooking, so Caleb and I spent a lot of time together in the garden and invaded the kitchen together on Cookie's days off.

Caleb was one of the many grandchildren of an old woman known as 'Missy Rosie', a skinny, toothless old negress, the whites of whose eyes had turned yellow and whose hair was like grey sheep's wool and who wore the old-fashioned head-cloth as did the laundress, Minna. I think that most people visualise tropical scenes and tropical crowds as being very vivid and gaily coloured and it is true that the oranges and reds of the tropics are more orange and red than these colours seem to be in more temperate zones and the tropical sun is brighter than other suns and the tropical seas more blue. But pictures I have seen of, for instance, West Indian vegetable markets do not convey the truth of such places as seen by my eyes, for all these red and blue and yellow and purple dresses of the women and shirts of the men simply are not, in fact, so. Garments are of these bright colours when they are new from the shops but they are made of cheap cotton, poorly dyed, and the colours do not last beyond the first careless laundering and drying in the pitiless sun. The scene in a vegetable market is drab in colour in the main for the heaps of oranges and pimentos, for all their brilliant colour, cannot overcome the brown of the dust, the dull grey of the baskets and sacks and the drab, washed-out sun-faded clothing of ninety-nine of the people among whom the hundredth may be wearing a flame-coloured shirt, newly bought that day. Also, I have seen pictures in which the skin of the negroes has a satiny sheen but this is not real of negro people who are living at mere subsistence level. It is only when the negro is well-fed and free from disease that this high-lit satiny sheen comes upon him and the skins of the people congregated in a vegetable market are, in the main, not even true black or brown. They look as if the dark colour is not more than a thin wash over-lying a sickly grey-green.

Old Missy Rosie had skin of this faded bleached colour that had once been black and it was dry and creased into thousands of wrinkles. Her arms and legs were skinny and, at the ends of them, her hands and feet seemed to be enormous and misshapen with years of work and of walking bare-footed on rutted hard-baked ground. She was the mistress of a patch of earth of about two acres, down in the river bottom at the edge of the Paradise Plantation, a patch of alluvial soil of fantastic fecundity which produced more food for human consumption in a year than did all of Reachfar. It was like a fruit-bearing jungle with orange, grapefruit, banana, coconut, bread-fruit, mango and avocado pear trees all growing through and over one another while, under them, yams, sweet potatoes and all the ground crops rioted, and in and out ran goats, pigs, ducks and hens, squealing and grunting and cackling. In the middle of this 'cultivation' as it was called stood a rickety shack, its walls made from odds and ends of old packing-cases and petrol tins, its roof made of rusty, second-hand corrugated iron and under this roof lived Missy Rosie and old Timothy, then about a dozen men and women a generation younger and then about three dozen boys and girls and babies who were a generation younger again. I do not know whether Missy Rosie and old Timothy were wife and husband, brother and sister or merely the best of friends. I do not know if any of the second generation were the children of both of them for, in the cases of the one or two I happened to enquire about, Missy Rosie said: 'Simon, ma'am? Simon mine, ma'am, but not Timoffy's' or 'Frankie, ma'am? Timoffy de fadder.'

This second generation which contained Simon and Frankie was a floating one which worked by roving commission from Missy Rosie's, the men of it appearing at Paradise at crop time to cut sugar cane or going to the hotels in the tourist season in various capacities and the women of it operating in a similar way but never did I go to Missy Rosie's without there being at home at least one woman of this second generation in a heavily pregnant condition. It was not only the soil down there in the river bottom that burgeoned all the year round with fruit. It was not only the pigs and goats that bred constantly. Missy Rosie was never without a naked infant or two playing around in the sunlit dust at her door and was never but expecting a new baby to arrive any minute.

When Twice and I first came to Guinea Corner, Cookie and Clorinda were already installed in the house, having been hired for us by Marion Maclean, the estate manager's wife, and several labourers were working in the garden, which was very overgrown, for the house had been lying empty for some years. It soon became obvious, Twice being the active sort of engineer that he was, that somebody was required to deal with the rising tide of clothing soaked in sweat, oil and molasses and, after a conference with Cookie and Clorinda, Minna joined the staff. Then the labourers went away, having felled a few dangerous trees, mended the garden wall, dug up a few beds and burned a heap of debris and I was left with a garden to make.

'Get a boy,' said Twice, looking at what might have been the site of a hard-fought battle, 'or maybe three,' and went off back to the sugar factory.

I went to the kitchen and had speech with Cookie, Clorinda and Minna on the subject of a boy and with one voice they said: 'Must send fe Missy Rosie, Missis,' so that is what I did or, rather, I indicated my willingness that this should be done and by some process of grapevine telegraph, Missy Rosie appeared on the veranda early the next morning. When I told her of my position, she said: 'Me sure have jus' de boy fe you, Ma'am,' and took thought for a moment, concentrating very hard and counting off on her left hand with the gnarled fingers of her right, murmuring a sort of incantation the while. To me, she looked like an old witch in washed-out clothes and it did not occur to me that she was merely examining her inventory of the grandsons she had in stock at the moment.

'Caleb!' she said in a pleased way after a moment. 'Caleb. Him is de one. Him a good boy, ma'am.'

'How old is he?' I asked.

She studied me with her yellowed eyes and it suddenly came to me that she was prepared to make Caleb the age I liked best, give or take a year or two.

'Sebbenteen, ma'am.'

Missy Rosie had made a bad shot. 'Far too old,' I told her. 'I can only pay ten shillings a week. I want a young boy, a boy who needs good food and quarters more than money.'

She gave an eldritch cackle of laughter. 'Me make foolish

mistake, ma'am! Caleb? *Him* not sebbenteen! Me t'inking of Winston. Caleb only twelve, ma'am.'

It was too difficult for me. 'All right, send him to see me,' I said.

I have never known whether the boy who came the next day had been christened Caleb at birth or only the day before but although he might have been more than twelve, he certainly was not seventeen. However, he claimed that he was twelve, that his name was Caleb and, yes, he had always lived at Missy Rosie's and his mother, Miss Lucille who was a shop-lady in St. Jago Bay, she lived at Missy Rosie's too when she was not being a shop-lady but he was not sure if Missy Rosie was his grand-mother. She was, he said, Missy Rosie.

Caleb himself was, at this time, a skinny boy in clean but faded and worn khaki shirt and shorts, with fine teeth and beautiful eyes which looked too big for his face which seemed to be mainly dull greenish-black skin stretched over strong negroid skull bones. I took him out to the back of the house where the block that contained the kitchen, the laundry and servants' rooms lay, connected by a covered walkway to the house itself and there I showed him what would be his room. It was small, big enough to hold only the single bed, a chair and a small chest of drawers. On one wall was a row of hooks and a small looking-glass. It reminded me of the room I had occupied for five years as an intelligence officer during the war. Caleb stood staring at the bed in silence, at the white cotton sheets and pillow case for, without telling any of my white acquaintances what I had done, I had bought a bolt of cheap calico and had made four sheets and two pillowcases for each of these rooms.

'Now, Caleb,' I said, 'you must keep your room clean.'
'Yes, missis.'
'And your sheets and pillow case must be washed every week.'
'Yes, missis.'
'Can you wash clothes, Caleb?'

'Missy Rosie will wash, missis.'

'I see. All right.'

My white friends had told me that sheets and pillow cases, if provided, would simply disappear, that they would be taken to some shack 'over the hill' and never seen again but I was risking this. I am not much of a gambler. The bolt of calico had cost only fifteen shillings.

'In this drawer, Caleb, are two clean sheets, a pillow case and two towels.'

'Yes, missis.'

'Now, let's go out to the garden.'

In no time at all it was obvious that, although Caleb had never seen a bed with white sheets on it that was all for himself before, he was a born 'cultivator', as the St. Jagoan peasants called themselves, and there was a steady flow of seeds, plants and cuttings to Guinea Corner from Missy Rosie's fecund den in the river bottom, brought back by Caleb each Sunday evening along with his clean sheets, pillow case and towel.

'Dis is yellah yam, missis,' he would say on Monday morning, showing me some brown lumps on a sheet of newspaper. 'Dem good eatin', ma'am, or 'dese is white coco, ma'am. Good eatin', missis.'

Eating was very important to Caleb and the quantity he could eat was astonishing but it had a most gratifying result. He seemed to grow taller and broader every day and the green undertint disappeared from his skin and in its place came a high satiny gloss from which the sun struck highlights as we worked together in the garden. At first, Caleb had little patience with the flower beds and, if I retired into the house and out of the sun for a little, he would disappear and would be found round at the back, doing something in his vegetable garden which had none of the neat orderliness of a British garden but which, under Caleb's hands, was growing more and more like the riotous fecund jungle at the river bottom. Later on, however, when three meals a day were no longer some dream that might vanish, he informed me one day that he knew where he could get some 'pretty roses' for my bed at the front of the house.

'Roses, Caleb? I doubt if we would have enough water.'

'Dis roses not wattah roses, missis.'

'Oh, very well, Caleb. You bring them and we'll try.'

The plants he produced were gerberas. It was only then that I discovered that, to Caleb, all flowers were roses and not really a great deal of use at that and when I named his plants as gerberas, he looked upon me with great respect, pointed to some begonias and said: 'Dese roses got a next name too, ma'am?'

We thereupon agreed that if Caleb was an expert on the cultivation of 'good eatin'', I was something of an expert on 'roses' and thereafter we worked along on a fine basis of mutual respect, for that is what it was, the thing between us.

So Cookie, Clorinda, Minna and Caleb who had come to us in 1950, when we first went to Guinea Corner, welcomed us back there in 1951 and were still with us in 1955. I do not mean to convey that these four years in our household were one grand sweet song or that Twice and Janet Alexander, the moment they set up house in St. Jago, settled the colour-white-master-servant problem in one miraculous stroke. No. We had our ups and downs and vicissitudes of all kinds. Quite early on, Minna developed appendicitis and, in her fatalistic negro way, took to her bed and prepared herself for death and there was a prolonged argument between her and me before she would go into hospital. She said that to 'have her belly cut', she was sure would kill her, whereupon I said that as she had decided to die anyway, she might as well do it quickly, with which Minna gave a heart-rending wail, rolled her old head over on her pillow to look at Twice and the doctor in the doorway of her room and said: 'Oh, Massa, sah, de missis don' have no heart!'

'No heart at all, Minna,' Twice agreed, shaking his head sadly. 'You had better get into the car and come with me to the hospital,' and, weeping, Minna staggered out to the car and went.

The 'cutting of the belly' was a great success but it took Minna about three months after she came home to Guinea Corner to convince herself that she was going to live or, rather, to fail to convince the rest of us that she was going to die and, meantime, Cookie, Clorinda and Caleb did the laundry between them, muttering imprecations of: 'Dat Minna! Pity her *don'* jus' die. De missis have too much heart.' My heart or the lack of it came in for a deal of criticism from them all and it was all very exasperating.

Shortly after Minna had decided to live, cut belly and all, I discovered that Clorinda was pregnant and when I enquired about the status, marital and financial, of the father of the child with a view to making provision of some sort for it, Clorinda gathered her white apron into a bundle between her hands, gave me a coy and pleased look from her pretty eyes and said: 'Me not ezzackly sure who de fadder, ma'am.'

'Come, come now, Clorinda!' I said sternly because I could not think quickly of anything else to say.

'Well, ma'am,' said Clorinda in a hurt tone, 'it was de night of de Cropovah an' all dem tractor men was in—dem *strangers*, ma'am!'

So that was that. Clorinda had what Twice insisted on refer-ring to as 'the Little Stranger' and we disregarded the Paradise law of 'No children in the quarters' and had him rolling about in the sun in the back garden. He was named Alexander, after Twice, and was a beautiful child who had a bloom on his skin like a dark grape right from the start.

It was about the time that the Little Stranger came that Cookie got religion, a virulent dose of a new brand that had come down from the United States and took a serious hold on her home village. I do not know the name of this religion but its chief symptom was 'de spirit comin'' and for about three months, the

221

spirit kept coming into Cookie. It came at all times of the day or night with a fine disregard for human convenience so that, when I would be writing letters of a forenoon, Clorinda would arrive in the drawing room and say: 'Please ma'am to come an' look at de beef. De spirit done come into Cookie an' her outside, prayin'' and I would have to go and cook the lunch. Then, at about three of a moonlit morning, I would wake with a vague sense of disquiet to hear Twice's voice say: 'That damn' spirit's in Cookie again,' and he would get up and shout from the window: 'Cookie! Take yourself and that spirit round to the other side of the house!' and across the lawn the praying would die away. In the end, we had to send Cookie home for a fortnight until the spirit came out of her for good.

For a long time, I was very uppish with Twice in the way of pointing out how little trouble 'my' Caleb was compared to 'his' women, for Caleb became more and more useful and showed not the slightest desire, as he grew older, to go away and become a waiter or a taxi-driver in St. Jago Bay and acquire large tips from tourists as most of the boys did. As he became more useful, we kept raising his pay but, as I said to Twice, this did not really represent an increase in the cost of keeping Caleb for, now that he had filled out, he ate less. Each additional five shillings a week was more than counter-balanced by the drop in the amount of food that Caleb consumed and, these days, Caleb was more interested in clothes than in food. Caleb had turned into a negro dandy and although some of his pay went home to Missy Rosie each Sunday, the pegs in his room became more and more full of fancy shirts and narrow-bottomed trousers and the top of his chest of drawers was a closely packed array of highly-perfumed shaving lotions, talcum powders and hair oils.

Caleb was very proud of his room and after a few months he began to decorate it, the first item being a calendar that a Chinese grocer had sent me at Christmas and which I had put in the wastepaper basket. It had a picture of two kittens in a pink basket with blue ribbons round their necks, a type of picture which I do not happen to like but it appealed to Caleb who asked if he might have it and, later, I was invited out to his room to see it in position. Thereafter, I was frequently invited to his room to see some new piece of decoration and it was thus that I was in a position to observe the growing array of clothes and toiletries.

'Caleb has got a new bottle of stuff,' I told Twice one evening. 'It is called Kiss of Conquest.' I was giggling, of course, and Twice regarded me more in sorrow than in anger.

'No good can come of it,' he said. 'No good can possibly come from anybody as big and black and buckish as Caleb plastering himself with something called Kiss of Conquest.'

'Oh, rot,' I said. 'Caleb isn't buckish at all. He never even looks at Clorinda or any of the other young women around the Compound.'

It was on the following Easter Sunday forenoon that Caleb, who had gone home the night before as usual, arrived carrying proudly a very pretty, very black little baby girl dressed in pink organdie.

'Dis me dahtah, ma'am,' he said, beaming. 'She name' Rosie.'

With the Little Stranger already tumbling about out at the back, I began to feel that things were getting out of hand and that I would be in trouble with the estate management for our goings-on at Guinea Corner, so I had a serious speech with Caleb on the subject of Rosie, while the baby sat on my lap and looked solemnly at me out of her enormous eyes under the pink frilly bonnet. All I elicited was that the child's mother was called Adeline, that she worked in a drapery store in St. Jago Bay and that she had absolutely no intention of marrying Caleb. He was allowed to have the baby occasionally to show to his friends, but that was all.

'Please tell Adeline that I wish to see her, Caleb,' I said in my sternest voice.

It may seem odd, at first glance, that someone in my own

matrimonial position should have worked so hard on the side of law and order but I am truly on the side of law and order 'when reasonable', as Tom would say, when there is no unsurmountable legal or religious impediment and between Caleb and Adeline there was none. Adeline was a pretty townified slip of a thing with straightened hair and high-heeled shoes and when I suggested that she and Caleb should marry and set up house together, she was horrified.

'*Me*, Miz Alexander? Marry *Caleb*? But him a *yard* boy!'

There was no question of it. The social cleavage was much too great. Adeline's mother was charmed to look after the baby, Adeline was back behind her shop counter, Caleb occasionally bought some pretty thing and presented it to the child and that was that. And Caleb, of course, the buck who could interest the sophisticated 'shop ladies' of St. Jago Bay, would not lower himself to have affairs with Clorinda or any of the other domestics on Paradise.

'It is all too mysterious,' I said to Twice.

'I told you that Kiss of Conquest was bound to lead to something,' he replied. 'It is only you who could have a starry-eyed belief that a young buck like Caleb could be stinking himself up with Kiss of Conquest and wearing a yellow zoot suit and yet still be a black-faced angel child. He is seventeen if he is a day and whoring round half the island.'

Nevertheless, Kiss of Conquest, zoot suit and whoring around all taken into account, Caleb and I remained friends and got along together very well and when Twice and I decided to spend the month of August in 1953 at a mountain cottage that had been lent to us by a friend, Caleb was the only member of our staff who elected to come with us. When the idea was first presented to them, the women all said that they would come but, as the first of August drew nearer, the thought of 'way up in de bush' appalled them more and more and, in the end, Twice and I left Paradise for High Hope with only Caleb and our dog Dram.

By this time, we had decided that in spite of Twice's lucrative appointment our future did not lie in the Caribbean and that when, in 1954, our present tour came to an end and we went back to Britain, Twice would relinquish his appointment for a less lucrative one, if necessary, that would keep us in the British Isles.

In a contrary way, as soon as I knew that my time in the island was limited, I began to like it much better. The vague sense of uneasiness that had always haunted it for me seemed to disappear and I felt that, by our decision to go back to our own country, we had propitiated its dark mysterious gods. I no longer felt, as I had felt before, that the island was lying in wait for me, to wreak vengeance upon me as a representative of the white race for all the past sins of slavery and cruelty that white men had committed there and I went to High Hope in a mood more truly carefree than I had ever known since I had lived in St. Jago.

High Hope itself was a tropical version of Reachfar for, from the front of the house you could see the whole north coast of the island from Hurricane Point in the east to St. Jago Bay in the west, just as, from Reachfar, you could see from Achcraggan in the east along the sweep of the Firth to Ben Wyvis in the west, and it was with a clear bright happiness that I sat in the sun in front of the cottage—cool and pleasant at this elevation—writing to my father a long description of this place where we were spending a short holiday.

It was out of this blue sunlit sky, out of the crystal clear air of High Hope that misfortune struck. Unknown to us, Twice had had heart disease for years and the elevation of this place had suddenly brought it to light but, before a doctor could come and make this diagnosis, I had spent a long, stark moonlit night, watching over him while he panted for breath and with Caleb the only living being within miles. Twice was ill for a long time. He nearly died on the day he was hospitalised and when he became better we were told that he would never, now, be able to work as he had done formerly but must have a sedentary position and that we would be wise not to risk the rigours of the British climate. In many ways, we were fortunate. Twice was given a good sedentary post at Paradise, we could continue to live at Guinea Corner. We merely had to settle down to a new way of life with a future that did not contain a home in Britain.

The women servants did not see Twice from the August day when we left for High Hope until the day near the end of October when we came home from the hospital but Caleb had been in daily contact with us as well as having been at High Hope at the time of the stunning crisis itself. And it was Caleb who was with me when I was overcome by the next crisis on the day that we came home from the hospital for it was on that day that the letters came from my family to tell me of the sale of Reachfar. When I opened the first letter and read what had happened, my mind broke down momentarily into a black whirling chaos and it was the voice of Caleb that recalled me, the soft negro voice asking, with deep concern: 'Somet'ing not right fe you, ma'am?'

Something, indeed, was very much not right for me. Reachfar was the land of 'always' and, now, in a single stroke, 'always' had been swept utterly away, for this is how I saw it, at first. It seemed as if I had been stripped of everything I had ever known, as if, now, twelve and a dozen were no longer what they had been, as if, never again, would I be able to look at the clock and tell the time of day, just as, here in St. Jago, I had no need of going-to-bed boots for it was always warm enough to go bare-footed. That is how it was. I had suddenly been turned into a person who knew nothing of twelves and dozens, who could not tell the time and had no need of going-to-bed boots. I was an exile from everything I knew for ever, an exile from life itself, for life.

But life will not let one be like this. You cannot be exiled from it or exile yourself from it for its duration if you have a dearly loved invalid husband who must not be upset or worried in any way and, in time, I came to accept the fact that my home had been sold and two of the main factors in this acceptance were Caleb and my father.

Quite soon, I told Caleb of what had happened because I could see that he was worrying about me from the time when I opened the first letter and, because he could never completely understand what Reachfar meant to me, it was easier to talk about it to him than to anybody else. As far as Twice was concerned, I merely made a light announcement that the family 'had sold Reachfar at last' and left it at that for many months because I was afraid I could not discuss it with Twice without breaking down and causing an emotional upset. With Caleb, it was different. Caleb was a 'cultivator', a peasant at heart like myself, and the thing that the St. Jagoan negro values more than any other thing is what he calls a 'lickle piece o' lan''. Given this, in that climate, he can live, merely at subsistence level, it is true, but he can live and although Caleb could not see the value to a rich white missis like me of a lickle piece o' lan' in Scotland, he was sympathetic in principle about its loss. I think that, in the first instance, I must have used the phrase 'I have lost Reachfar' when I told him what had happened for Caleb never broke free of the idea that Reachfar had been taken from my family for failure to pay a mortgage or claimed in payment of a gambling debt, for these were the only ways Caleb knew of 'losin' a piece o' lan''. At all events, there it was, and while we worked in the garden, I would tell Caleb of Reachfar and of how 'Irish' potatoes grew in long rows in the fields and of how the corn that made 'oats porridge' waved white-gold in September and of how, in winter, the snow lay deep all round and the cattle were all indoors and had to be fed and looked after like invalids in bed.

Caleb had been to school before he came to us but only for short periods, I think, and he could write little more than his own name, and that only with great difficulty, but one of his jobs was to fetch the letters from the factory office at times when Twice was away or forgot to bring them home with him at lunch-time. Very early in his time with us, Caleb handed me a letter from my father one day and said: 'Please, ma'am, dat very pretty writin'.'

'Yes, Caleb, isn't it? That is my father's handwriting,' I said and, after that, he would bring the letters and say with a smile: 'One come today from yo' fadder, missis.'

A little later, I discovered that Caleb was taking the discarded envelopes from the waste basket and copying my father's writing on to the kitchen slate which I used to note the groceries and, as time went on, Caleb achieved a proficiency that could have amounted, almost, to forgery. It is in these curious ways that the bonds between people grow strong.

The sale of Reachfar was something that I should have foreseen as the logical outcome of socio-economic trends, quite apart from our family situation, whereby my brother moved in academic circles, Twice and I were four thousand miles away, my father, Tom and George were growing old and, since my aunt married Malcolm Macleod and went to New York, they had been plagued with a succession of dissatisfied housekeepers who did not like to live in a place so remote. But I did not foresee any of this, any more than I had foreseen at four years old that there must be some evenings when my father did not come home in time for supper. Reachfar, for me, had been 'always', a thing that was ever there and never changed and this was the thing of which my father, in his letters, showed such a complete understanding, right from the start, in that first letter that was waiting when I brought Twice home from the hospital.

'My dear Janet, I do not like to write this to you after all the trouble you have come through in the last months for I know that it is going to be harder for you than for any of us, but I have to write it. We have sold Reachfar.

'When you were home in 1951, I had decided that we would have to sell and I thought of telling you but I did not do it. As you know, I am sometimes a bit of a coward about saying things

228

that are hard to say but it was not like that about this. I was not cowardly. It was just that I made up my mind that I would leave you happy for as long as I could.

'You would not know that we have been dropping a little money on it every year since just after the war. This is because it is both too big and too small. It is too big for the market gardening or poultry that the smaller people go in for now and it is too small for mechanised farming with tractors and things. And George, Tom and I have no notion of tractors and engines anyway.

'Since Kate got married and went to New York, it has been a pouring of money down the well. As you know, Reachfar is a croft and not a farm and in crofting the women of the family are as important as the men if not more so. It is the pennies, as you always called them, the pennies for the eggs and butter that make the difference between a profit and a loss and no paid housekeeper is going to take the right sort of interest and you cannot blame them. The place is not their own and they do not take a pride in it. We sold to the limited company that farms Dinchory and the other places to the west and we got such a high price that it is on my conscience. It was Tom and George that drove the final bargain in the lawyer's office. I was there, of course but when it came to naming our figure, George and Tom had it fixed between them beforehand and came out with it before I could speak. I thought the lawyer would throw us out into Dingwall High Street but he only hummed and hawed a bit and Tom said Take it or leave it but you won't get it for less and then he said he would take it but we had named the limit that he was allowed to go to. I felt ashamed in a way and went for Tom and George about it in the Royal bar after we left the lawyer but Tom just said that he had not looked after the trees on the Home Moor all these years to let the high winter shelter go for a song and then they both laughed at me. I suppose it is all right taking the high price for if the Dinchory people did not want Reachfar

229

and think it was worth it, they would not pay it, as George says.

'I know that none of this is going to be any comfort to you but it means that if you and Twice are short of money after this terrible illness you know that we have a little to spare now and you have only to let us know. Things have gone very hard with you both this last wee while but it is very fine of the Paradise people to have found the right job for Twice. As for the doctors saying that he cannot come home to Scotland, there is no telling what a little time may do and I for one am looking forward to the day when we will welcome you home on leave again.

'Meantime, take care of your own health and look after Twice and mind to write for we are all wondering about you every day. As George and Tom have told you, they are coming to the cottage as *paying guests*. Jean is very pleased and feels that she is about to make her fortune as a landlady and I am very pleased too for George and Tom will be fine company for me, now that I have completely retired. Write soon. Health, Happiness, Good Luck and Best Love, Your Dad, D. Sandison.'

'Now that I have completely retired'. These were the only words he used in connection with his own sense of loss at the sale of Reachfar, a loss that must have been far deeper than mine for Reachfar, the 'always' that I had grown up with, had been largely the creation of his own brain and hands.

The letters continued to come in, one each month by airmail, the remainder by surface, but, for about eighteen months, the phrase 'Reachfar time' dropped out of Twice's and my intimate vocabulary. We simply did not mention Reachfar at all for a long, long time although during all of this time I spoke of it almost daily to Caleb but, in the end, the phrase came back into use for I had come to the understanding that, as long as my father, Tom, George and I were alive, Reachfar and its time would remain with us.

Towards the end of 1955, Twice and I were still at Guinea Corner, never having been home to Scotland since 1951, and

Cookie, Minna, Clorinda and Caleb were still with us through further vicissitudes. By this time, I had come to some sort of compromise with the island. I felt that now it had done its worst to me, I was no longer afraid of it and I bore it no grudge. Twice's health was still very delicate and uncertain but better than the doctors had ever expected it to be and we were surrounded with friends and very happy.

Among our more educated coloured friends, the talk these days was all of the formation of the Federation of the West Indies, a political idea which had been in the air ever since we first came to St. Jago in 1949 and I used to become very bored with all this talk because I am not politically minded and, apart from that, I failed to see how people could talk blithely of 'federation' when Barbadians hated Jamaicans and St. Jagoans hated Trinidadians and everybody hated everybody, or so it seemed to me. All the talk seemed very pointless and I much preferred to converse with the women servants or Caleb about the smaller, more immediately human problems with which they were constantly beset.

One day, I found old Minna in tears in the laundry and when I asked her what was the matter, she told me that her little niece was ill and that the doctor said she had measles.

'But, Minna, most children get measles. Little Dorcille will be all right.'

'No, ma'am. She goin' die. De lickle boy in de nex' yard, him get measles an' him die.'

Two days later, little Dorcille died and two days after that there were big black headlines in the local newspaper *The Island Sun*: 'Measles epidemic Raging. Health Authority Worried' and a long list of instructions about precautions. The epidemic was confined to St. Jago Bay, the crowded island capital, and it was thought that the infection had been brought in by a holidaymaker from abroad, for this was late November and the beginning of the winter tourist season. However the infection arrived in the island, the disease when it took a hold among the negroes took a virulent form and, within a fortnight, the death-roll in St. Jago Bay had risen into hundreds.

'Damn it,' I said to Twice, 'we whites are nothing but a corruption to this island in every way. No whites are getting measles. I just don't understand it.'

'Darling, we have immunities that the negroes haven't got and another factor is this damned fatalistic temperament of theirs. They are making up their minds to die as soon as it hits them now.'

But while Twice and I discussed the epidemic in the drawing-room, Cookie, Minna, Clorinda and Caleb sang songs in the kitchen. Negro memories are short, they had already finished crying for little Dorcille, and St. Jago Bay and its epidemic were all of thirteen miles away from Paradise.

As a rule, I paid scant attention to the *Island Sun* for it was a badly composed, badly printed and sensational daily document that was far from reliable and my father sent us the weekly edition of a national newspaper from home but now, daily, I read the reports of the measles epidemic. I do not know why the horror of the thing took such a hold on me but it seemed to be one more manifestation of the distortion here in the island of things as I knew them, that a childish disease so common and comparatively harmless in Britain should be decimating these simple people. And, of course, since it was in the forefront of my mind, I wrote to my father of the epidemic, telling him of the death-roll that was mounting daily and how, to Caleb and our own negro people, the horror did not seem to be real because it was a few miles away, although Minna had lost her little niece through it. 'They do not seem to care about the people who are dying,' I wrote. 'It is terribly hard to understand the negro temperament. They just sing in the sun all the time, go to bed when it rains and prepare to die when they get ill. They never question things or fight things as we do.' And, all the time, while

I was thinking about the epidemic, writing to my father about it and trying to understand why some unknown and unknowing white visitor should have brought this scourge upon the island people, Cookie, Clorinda and Minna and Caleb sang gaily about their work and even the *Island Sun*, tiring of the epidemic, was reporting only the new total of deaths in a few terse lines while three columns were taken up in the description of 'Federation Shirts', a new importation to the island. Some enterprising cotton manufacturer in Lancashire or perhaps Japan or Hong Kong had hit upon the idea of printing cotton in garish colours with a map of the Caribbean and on the sea between the islands. Federation of the West Indies' was printed on flowing banners. According to the *Island Sun*, no well-dressed man in St. Jago could afford to be without a Federation Shirt and no young lady could do better than present one to her young gentleman for Christmas.

On a Sunday early in December Caleb, dressed in his 'sharpest' clothes, went off home to Missy Rosie's and probably elsewhere, came back on Monday morning, and went to work in the garden as usual but when I went out in the afternoon to sow some seeds in the bed he had prepared—December was the sowing month in St. Jago for British vegetables such as carrots and beetroot—I noticed that he was sweating very profusely. This was unusual for a healthy negro like Caleb could work in the hottest sun without breaking into sweat.

Malaria ran in the bloodstream of most St. Jagoans and although it did not manifest itself in an acute form as a rule, Caleb and the three women servants had all had attacks in the past so when I said: 'You are not feeling well, Caleb?' he merely replied: 'Got a lickle fevah, missis. A shower catch me yestiddy.' To be caught in a light shower of rain was enough to bring down any St. Jagoan with what they called 'a chill an' a fevah' so I told Caleb to stop working, go to bed and I would bring him some aspirin.

Before I went to bed that night, I went out to his room to see him and found that his temperature had risen but this was the normal course of 'a chill an' a fevah' and, even now, in spite of all my concern about the epidemic, I did not think of measles. I gave the boy a drink of orange juice, more aspirin and went to bed.

Since Twice's heart weakness had been discovered, I had turned his little downstairs study into a single bedroom and he slept there and used the downstairs bathroom so that he could avoid climbing the stairs but I still occupied our large bedroom on the first floor. It was just dawn in the morning when I was awakened by a tearing retching sound and I fled downstairs to Twice's room, to stop short outside the closed door of wire mosquito mesh for, through it, I could see Twice sleeping soundly. It was only then that I thought of Caleb and ran out through the kitchen and round to the quarters, bare-footed and in pyjamas as I was. When I went into the little room, the boy was hanging over the edge of his bed above his enamel wash-basin, retching violently, while the sweat poured from his head and face and trickled over his bare shoulders. The first thing that I noticed was that Caleb no longer had the bloom of a black grape. His skin had been invaded in the course of a few hours by the greenish hue of the sick negro.

I did what I could for him, then woke Clorinda and sent her to the clinic for the estate doctor and yet, still, I did not think of measles. People have—or, rather, I have—strange rigidities of mind. When I was four years old and first heard of measles, either Tom or George told me that 'measles was red spotties' and there were no red spots on Caleb. It did not occur to me that red spots would not show on a coal black skin. When Doctor Gurbat Singh arrived, I was sitting beside the boy's bed, still bare-footed and in pyjamas, for I had been sponging the sweat off Caleb and changing his wet sheets. The doctor did not even examine him, beyond lowering the sheet and looking at the skin of his body.

'Please to come out of doors, Mrs. Alexander,' he said and when we were in the vegetable garden he went on: 'Have you ever had measles?'

'Me? No. I've never had anything in my life. Doctor, has Caleb got measles?'

'Yes, Mrs. Alexander. How much contact have you had with him?'

'Well, I have been sponging him and changing—Oh, fiddlesticks! I see what you mean. But I will be all right. I won't get it.'

'And Mr. Alexander?'

'Oh.—Oh, but Twice has *had* measles!' It was strange to feel this joyous relief that Twice had once suffered from measles. 'I *know* he has! Besides, I haven't been near Twice this morning.'

The doctor began to cast about for ways and means of removing Caleb to be nursed elsewhere but all the hospitals were full and it would have been madness, as I pointed out, to send him home to the crowded river-bottom at Missy Rosie's.

'Look,' I said to the doctor and Twice, the doctor and I standing in the garden, Twice behind the mesh of his bedroom window, 'I have gone and done it now anyway. If I am going to get it, I will get it so the best thing I can do is to stay out of the house. We will move Clorinda's bed into the laundry and put the camp bed for me into her room and the rest of you can just keep away from Caleb and me, that's all.'

These arrangements were made and Caleb's little room was turned into a small isolation unit with disinfectant-soaked curtains hung over window and door and I wore long white coats which the doctor lent me; but none of this was easy, for Cookie, Minna and Clorinda, who had been singing the day before, were now in a mood that was a compound of panic fear, anger with Caleb for 'bringin' dem measles about de place', resentment at me for my ferocious driving of them to help me in my fight against the illness for 'Caleb gwine die anyway' and a general sulkiness at their routine being upset and the fact that I would not allow them to visit their homes in their villages.

In the meantime, behind the disinfected curtain, Caleb was growing more and more ill, more and more weak and more and more prepared to die and hourly I became more angry and, the angrier I grew, the more relentlessly and ferociously did I drive Cookie, Minna and Clorinda.

'Cookie, more orange juice and see that it is really cold!'

'Minna, fill that washtub again for these sheets!'

'Clorinda, spray this curtain with disinfectant again. It's nearly dry! Are you blind?'

And the more sullen their faces became, the more resentfully their big eyes looked at me, the more terrible became my energy and will to fight, for I hate illness, because I fear it so much and I have to battle against it as against a deadly enemy. It was my own fear as much as the illness that I was fighting, the fear which I concealed under my fierce energy and rage.

That day and the next and the next, I remember in little detail except for my own angry voice shouting at the three women outside in the merciless sun and speaking in soft whispers to the sick boy inside the dim disinfectant-smelling room while he became more and more ill and more and more weak. On the third evening, when Twice came home from the factory, he brought with him a letter from my father which he pushed under the curtain of the door. 'How is Caleb?' he whispered.

'Sleeping a little. Just holding his own and no more. Twice, please go into the house. Keep away from here, darling.'

'Are you all right?'

'Of course! Didn't Gurbat Singh examine me again this morning? Please stop worrying, Twice.'

'Oh, all right.'

I wanted to weep with exasperation at myself and my temper that made me short even with Twice and as his footsteps went

236

away along the path I opened my father's letter with shaking hands.

'My dear Janet, I am sending this by airmail so that by the time you get it my operation will be over and you will not have to be worrying. Maybe you remember that when you were home I told you that my water-works were being a nuisance. It seemed to grow better for a time but this last year it has got worse than ever and I have made up my mind to have the little operation done. I am going to the hospital in Inverness tomorrow and young Doctor Alasdair says I should be home in about ten days, in plenty of time for the New Year. I will post this letter in Inverness.' I now looked at the postmark on the envelope and it had indeed been franked in Inverness five days before.

'This is a dreadful thing that you tell me about the measles among the nègro people. I remember when I was about twenty, two Finlayson brothers who were at school with me went off to Glasgow and joined the police. They got measles and they both died within the same week and the old doctor said it was with them going from the clean air of the north here into all the dirt and germs of Glasgow. They had no resistance.

'It is terrible what you say about feeling that many of the deaths are because their people are too afraid to nurse them or go near them but you must not be so hard on the island people for their fear. I can understand simple country people feeling like that. I am more than a little like the negroes myself. Young Alasdair has explained to me all about this operation. He has made it sound simple and reasonable but I am still in need of all my courage to go to the hospital. I just do not like the idea of illness and I am afraid of it but I think it is natural to be afraid of something one has never known and I can understand how the people of the island are afraid of measles. But I can understand too your feeling that you would like to go down to the town and nurse some of the sick children yourself but it would be little you could do in an epidemic like you tell of and you have Twice and your own people to look after.

'No more now or this will cost too much in stamps but write to me soon. I will write again as soon as I can. Health, Happiness, Good Luck and Best Love, Your Dad, D. Sandison.'

'Wattah!' said the weak voice of Caleb.

I put the letter aside. As it said, I had my own people to look after and I took up the spoon and the glass and dripped weak orange juice between Caleb's thick cracked lips and I went on doing that at short intervals all that day and all through the long dark night that followed, trying to shut from my mind the picture of my father in a white hospital bed.

The next morning, Caleb was more ill than ever, weaker than ever and my rage increased beyond all bounds, driving the three women until I could think of nothing more for them or myself to do and had to stand, frustrated, outside the disinfected curtain. Caleb was dying and what of my father?

'Clorinda, go up to the office for the letters.'

'It nearly lunch, ma'am. De Massa bring dem.'

'Do as I say at once, please! Fetch the letters!'

Sulkily, Clorinda went on her way and, feeling ashamed of myself, I watched her go, seeing the fatalistic acceptance of the worst in her languid movement under the pitiless sun.

'Wattah!' came the whisper from behind the curtain.

Clorinda came back in the car with Twice who had picked her up before she had reached the office but they brought with them an airmail letter from my father, written in pencil on a sixpenny form. The handwriting was a little less firm than usual but it was his and the sight of it was of more comfort than anything any of the other members of my family could write.

'My dear Janet, This is just to let you know that I have had my operation and I am sitting up in bed here like a lord and eating like a horse. I think I am eating so much because there is nothing else to do but read and my eyes get tired now if I read all the

238

time. It was good of Twice to write to me for I know that the letters are your job but your hands must be full, nursing the sick boy. How is he, I wonder? But there may be another note from Twice tomorrow. Twice said that Caleb was very ill indeed and I am thinking of what you said about how they make up their minds to die. I am sure that you will do all you can for him and that is right and mind to do all you can to encourage him to live. Ask him what he would like for Christmas or something childish like that—something that is in the future. The hospital here is a wonderful place and the nurse lassies are just splendid. I do not know how bonnie young lassies like them choose to take a hard dirty job like looking after sick people. They must have a real calling for it. They are very good to me and it seems ungrateful that in spite of all their kindness I am looking forward to going home. There is no more room on this paper. I hope the boy Caleb is better. Health, Happiness, Good Luck and Best Love, Your Dad, D. Sandison.'

'Wattah,' came the husky whisper from the bed.

Caleb was now a livid greenish colour and emaciated beyond belief in the short time of his illness so that the skin seemed to be stretched over the big bones of the skull, shoulders and chest and, as the heat of the day mounted towards its peak and then dropped back towards the cool of the evening, Caleb's closed eyes sank deeper and deeper into their sockets. The whispering husky voice no longer came for by night-time he had sunk into a coma. When Doctor Gurbat Singh came, he merely looked down at the bed, shook his head and went away. I sat down on the chair and while I waited for the deep night to come on, I thought of how I would soon have to write to my father and confess to him that death had won the battle for this boy. It seemed that in so many things that my father would have valued I had been a failure.

Suddenly, shortly after midnight, when the household had gone to bed and only myself seemed to be alive in the dead, black muffled darkness of the moonless tropic night, Caleb started up to a sitting position, opened glittering eyes and, with a terrible travesty of a pleased smile on his wasted face, he said: 'Dem *sharp*, sah!'

Terror clutched at me for I knew that I had not the physical strength to control this wild energy of delirium. I sprang to the bed and sat on the boy's legs.

'All right, Caleb. Lie back now.'

'Me gwine get one!' he babbled fiercely, not looking at me but through me, as if he saw something splendid on the wall at my back.

'Lie back now, Caleb.'

'Yes, *sah*! Me gwine get one. Dem *sharp*, see? Me gwine get Femmerashum shirt!'

As suddenly as the dreadful energy had come to him, it went away and he fell back senseless against the pillows. Shaking, I took the glass and the spoon and dripped a little watery orange juice between the parted lips. Then I slipped my hand under his on the sheet and sat staring at the wall.

I do not remember any more of the silent night until, just as dawn was breaking, I drew the curtain of the window aside in my thankfulness for the coming light that caused the little oil lamp to burn pale. With an effort I looked, then, at Caleb's face on the pillow. For a fearsome moment I thought that he was dead for an extraordinary change had come over him. He did not look any more like the sick boy with whom I had spent all of these last days. It was with an upsurge of sheer wonder that I realised that he was asleep, sleeping serenely and peacefully, as he had never slept through all these endless days and nights. I slipped my fingers under the wasted wrist and on to the pulse and there it was, beating faintly but regularly and the skin had a glad dewy coolness. With tears in my eyes, I tiptoed out to the garden and, as the quick sun sprang over the horizon to the east, I thought of my father whose hospital room would still be in darkness as yet, at six o'clock on a Highland December morning. My hand closed about his letter in the pocket of my white coat and then I was running, knocking at the laundry door.

'Clorinda! Clorinda! Get up! I need you!' and when she appeared dressed in the doorway: 'Take Caleb's bicycle and go up to the store at the factory. Wake up Mr. Chen and tell him I want the sharpest Federation shirt he's got!'

'A Femmerashum shirt, ma'am?' The girl gaped at me.

'Yes. And a real *sharp* one, mind. Tell him to put it on the account.'

'But what size, ma'am?' She sounded as if she were humouring me and as if she thought I had become delirious. She looked frightened.

'Size? To fit *Caleb*, you idiot! Hurry now!'

Caleb was still asleep when she came back with the package and I took out the shirt, took one of Caleb's many coat-hangers, hung the shirt on it and suspended it from the edge of the shelf on the wall at the foot of the bed It was an atrocity of a garment —a brilliant turquoise blue with the map of the islands in purples and yellows and the lettering 'Federation of the West Indies' in magenta on black banners. The buttons down the front were of glass backed with tin foil so that they glittered in the early morning light.

When Caleb awoke, he looked up at me without recognition for a moment and then his eyes focused as if memory were dawning in them, as if I were someone he remembered from another life long long ago. And then, very faintly, he smiled.

'Hello, Caleb,' I said.

'Me sick, missis?'

'Yes, Caleb. You have been sick.'

'Me gettin' bettah, yes, missis?'

'Yes, Caleb. You are getting better.'

I poured cold orange juice from the thermos, took up the spoon. 'Come, Caleb,' I said, putting a hand behind his head to raise it but he was staring with eyes that glowed with life at the shirt that hung on the wall.

'Jee-*suss*!' he said. 'A Femmerashum shirt!'

'Yes, Caleb. It is for you.'

'Jee-*suss*! T'anks, missis. My, it *sharp*, no?'

From that moment, Caleb grew steadily stronger. It may be that he would have got well in any case but I think that the Federation shirt, presented to him more by my father than by me, was an important factor for he was so anxious to wear it that it hastened his recovery. To wear it in his room, as I suggested, would not do. It would merely have got all 'crushed up' and, besides, there was no glory in the privacy of his room. No. Caleb wished to appear in public, to parade before the envious men and the admiring women in his Federation shirt and, meantime, he lay in bed, growing stronger by the minute, feasting his eyes upon it.

On that first morning, when the doctor called, he agreed with me that Caleb had improved but he was non-committal until the following morning when he said: 'This, three days ago, Mrs. Alexander, I would not have believed. You can take a rest now. The boy will be all right' and it was only then that I began to feel tired. When the doctor had gone, I sat down on an upturned box in the arbour that supported Caleb's cho-cho vine where the green, pear-shaped and almost tasteless fruits swung on their long stringy stems in the early morning wind and it was here that Clorinda handed me the envelope. I opened it and read the typewritten message on the cable form: 'Father died in his sleep last night. Reachfar.'

EPILOGUE

ABOUT a fortnight after my family's cable reached me, Twice brought down from the factory office a familiar white envelope, addressed in the copperplate hand with the blue penholder and the White Devil nib. My father's agreement with me, when I left for the West Indies, had been that he would write by air-mail on the first Sunday of each month and by sea-mail on the other Sundays. The air-mail letter telling me that he was going to hospital had been an extra or emergency dispatch as, also, had been the air-letter from the hospital itself. This was the normal Sunday letter, written on the same day as the first airmail letter and posted, along with it, in Inverness.

'My dear Janet, By the time you get this, I will most likely be home again and it will be nearly Christmas. I am sure the hospital will be a fine place but, as you know, I have never been sick much and am not much good at lying in bed so I am not looking forward to it and will be pleased when it is behind me.

'We have had some fine dry frosty weather lately and yesterday Monica came and took George, Tom and me for a drive up to Reachfar to see the improvements and alterations they are making. The countryside was very bonnie in the bright sun. Reachfar is to be turned into their main store for winter feeding and the like and even the house building will be used for this for they cannot get workers to stay in a house that is so far from

243

the main road, the 'bus and the school. I am quite pleased about this. I would as soon not see other people living there although this may be selfish in a way.

'We came back along the Top Road and called at the Smiddy to see Big John the Smith for a while. Like the rest of us, he is not getting any younger and feels the cold a lot but his health is good and we all had a dram round the fire. And he is as full of nonsense as ever and was talking about the day you let your ferret loose in Miss Tulloch's shop among all the women. Then we looked in at the churchyard as we were passing because I had the people from Dingwall down to regild the lettering on the stones and they just finished the work on Friday. They have made a good job. Earlier in the year, there was the biggest crop of berries I have seen for a long time on the tree at the head of the plot so it looks as if we are in for a hard winter. Indeed, there are all the signs of it for the third coat of snow is on Ben Wyvis already although this is only December and that means that we will get it down here any day now.

'I am glad to hear that Twice is holding his own so well. Take good care of him and with God's will we may see the two of you home here on leave next summer. I am always looking forward to that in spite of what the doctors say. They cannot see into the future any more than the rest of us and it is always better to have hope than not.

'Jean is in great form with her *paying guests* and saving the pennies like mad but there is no harm if a few pounds in the Post Office makes her happy.

'We had a letter from Jock yesterday and he tells us that wee Duncan is starting to read now so Tom and George have got the old *Pilgrim's Progress* out and dusted and we will be having that poor devil Christian with us for the Christmas holidays, no doubt. It seems to me that poor Christian has been-struggling in the Slough of Despond for a very long time now, ever since you were a little bairn. I like it grand when the bairns come though and Shona is very good at keeping things tidy and not getting Jean out of tune because the house is in a mess. Elizabeth is a clever little nipper and doing very well at school and she has long plaits of hair like you had. Some time ago you asked me if there was anything special I would like for Christmas or whether you and Twice would order a book for me as usual. I should have answered about this before but time goes past. There is nothing special. I have everything in the world that I need or want and would rather have the book than anything except one thing. I would like the book better if it had your name (or pen-name) on the cover. I have written you a letter by airmail today telling you about going to the hospital. I did not want you to be worrying so I have not mentioned the hospital before. As soon as I am well enough I will write to you from there.

'God bless you both and write soon. Health, Happiness, Good Luck and Best Love. Your Dad, D. Sandison.'

I dropped the sheets of paper into my lap and looked away across the garden, across the bright green fields of sugar cane to the far north-east where Reachfar lay, probably under a heavy coat of December snow. My mind travelled back from this letter, which was the last I would ever receive from my father, to that first letter from him that lay on the steel fender on a Christmas morning so long ago. That feeling of his godlike quality came back to my mind, that feeling that he was my familiar father and, yet, that he was also Santa Claus, God and all the great mysterious visions that were yet invisible and now I recognised that this blinding light about him in my mind, a light that made his image come and go, change outline and size, be now the image of a man and then the image of a god was the white radiance of his love for me. It was a love that dazzled the eyes of my mind, a love that passed all my understanding.

I then remembered our conversation in the garden at Cairnton when he had said: 'I have often thought to myself that when a man has to die, that is the way to do it—just do it quietly in your sleep and not be a nuisance to yourself or anybody else' and I remembered. too, how we had talked of Granda Gordon's Heaven. If Heaven was as we had tried to comprehend it that evening, my father, too, had a Heaven. My father which art in Heaven. . . .

The sky to the north-east was a hard pale blue and on it I seemed to see, in my father's handwriting, one phrase from the letter in my lap: 'but time goes past'. With the stabbing pang of the too-late, the agony of the never-more, I faced the careless selfishness in myself by which I had let time go past and had never made the effort to write his book with my name on the cover.

From time to time, I had tried to write a book for him but I had never tried hard enough and all that I had achieved had been a great heap of discarded manuscript which I stored in the linen cupboard. A few days after the cable which told me of his death had reached me, I made a violent gesture towards evading the truth of my careless selfishness and the finality of the too-late and never-more by carrying all this discarded manuscript downstairs and making a bonfire of it in the back yard, telling myself that I would never, now, try to write a book. But, today, looking down at this last letter from him, I knew that he would want me to face the truth of myself as far as I could see it and that he would want me to go on beyond the too-late and the never-more and, looking to the far sky above Reachfar, I hoped that, one day, I would write a book with my name (or pen-name) on the cover, a book of the kind he would enjoy and which would be dedicated to the memory of My Friend My Father.